Journey of

D0455761

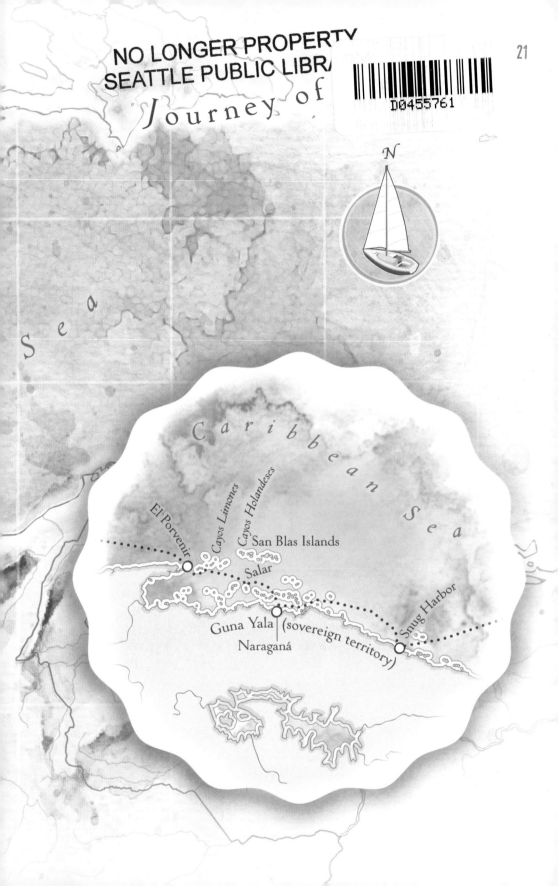

Sea

Sea

Caribbean

Sea

El Porvenir

Cayos Limones

Cayos Holandeses

San Blas Islands

Salar

Snug Harbor

Guna Yala (sovereign territory)

Naraganá

ALSO BY AMITY GAIGE

Schroder
The Folded World
O My Darling

Sea Wife

Sea Wife

AMITY GAIGE

ALFRED A. KNOPF
New York
2020

THIS IS A BORZOI BOOK
PUBLISHED BY ALFRED A. KNOPF

Copyright © 2020 by Amity Gaige

All rights reserved. Published in the United States by Alfred A. Knopf,
a division of Penguin Random House LLC, New York, and distributed
in Canada by Penguin Random House Canada Limited, Toronto.

www.aaknopf.com

Knopf, Borzoi Books, and the colophon are registered trademarks
of Penguin Random House LLC.

Grateful acknowledgment is made to the following for permission
to reprint previously published material:

New Directions Publishing Corp.: Excerpt from "You May All Go Home Now"
from *Collected Poems of Kenneth Patchen* by Kenneth Patchen,
copyright © 1939 by New Directions Publishing Corp.
Reprinted by permission of New Directions Publishing Corp.

SLL/Sterling Lord Literistic, Inc.: Excerpt from "Man and Wife" from
Live or Die by Anne Sexton, copyright © 1966 by Anne Sexton, copyright
renewed 1994 by Linda Gray Sexton. Excerpt from "The Double Image" from
To Bedlam and Part Way Back by Anne Sexton, copyright © 1960 by Anne Sexton,
copyright renewed 1988 by Linda Gray Sexton.
Reprinted by permission of SLL/Sterling Lord Literistic, Inc.

Library of Congress Cataloging-in-Publication Data
Names: Gaige, Amity, [date], author.
Title: Sea wife / Amity Gaige.
Description: First Edition. | New York : Alfred A. Knopf, 2020.
Identifiers: LCCN 2019010984 (print) | LCCN 2019012979 (ebook) |
ISBN 9780525656500 (ebook) | ISBN 9780525656494 (hardcover) |
ISBN 9781524711832 (open market)
Classification: LCC PS3557.A3518 (ebook) |
LCC PS3557.A3518 S43 2020 (print) | DDC 813/.54—dc23
LC record available at https://lccn.loc.gov/2019010984

This is a work of fiction. Names, characters, places, and incidents
either are the product of the author's imagination or are used
fictitiously. Any resemblance to actual persons, living or dead,
events, or locales is entirely coincidental.

Jacket photograph by Bryan Vallazza/500px/Getty Images
Jacket design by Janet Hansen

Manufactured in the United States of America
First Edition

to Tim

and to my mother, Austra

Sea Wife

I

⋙

Where does a mistake begin? Lately I've found this simple question difficult. Impossible, actually. A mistake has roots in both time and space—a person's reasoning and her whereabouts. Somewhere in the intersection of those two dimensions is the precisely bounded mistake—in nautical terms, its coordinates.

Did my mistake begin with the boat? Or my marriage itself? I don't think so. I now suspect that my mistake took root in an innocent experience I forgot to decipher, the mystery of which has quietly ruled me. For example, I remember standing beside a blindingly blue Howard Johnson's motel pool at twelve years old, watching a couple undress one another through a half-drawn curtain, while my estranged father disputed the bill in the lobby. Should I have looked away? Did the miscalculation occur even earlier, as I sat on a rope rug in clean kindergarten sunlight, and I leaned toward the boy beside me and accepted his insistent whisper? I still feel his dew in my ear.

And now I am sitting in a closet.

Michael's closet.

I should explain.

I moved in a couple of days ago. I came in here looking for something of his, and discovered that the carpet is very plush. The slatted bifold doors filter the sunlight beautifully. I feel calm in here.

Hiding in closets is the habit of children, I know. I used to hide in my mother's closet when I was a kid. Her closet contained some dressy silks and wools she never wore. I loved holding these fabrics against my body, or stepping into her high heels, as if onto a dais, rehearsing my future. I never felt ashamed.

Surely there is some connection between seeking refuge in my mother's closet long ago and hiding in Michael's now, but that insight does not help me.

Sometimes life just writes you tiny, awful poems.

I am uncertain whether or not I can survive this day.

I mean, if I want to.

To go out, to go *outside,* requires preparation and composure. If I were to go out, to start walking around and seeing people again and going to the grocery store and getting on with it, invariably what someone would ask me is, Do you wish you'd never gone? They will expect me to say, Yes, our journey was a mistake.

Maybe that's what they hope I will say.

But saying yes to the boat was my clearest act of loyalty toward my husband.

I can't afford to regret it.

If I did, I would only be left with my many disloyalties.

January 17. 10:15 a.m. LOG OF YACHT 'JULIET.' From Porvenir. Toward Cayos Limones. 09° 33.5′N 078° 56.98′W. NW wind 10 knots. Seas 2–4 feet. NOTES AND REMARKS: We are 102 nautical miles ENE of Panama City, catching prevailing winds into the sovereign territory of San Blas. The shape of the coast is still visible behind us, but ahead is just water. Nothing but water. That's when I realize there's only one ocean. One big mother ocean. Yes, there are bays & seas & straits. But those are just words. Artificial divisions. Once you're out here, you see there's just one unbroken country of water.

You would never feel this way on land.

(Not in our country.)

What a feeling. Generations of sailors have failed to describe it, so what are <u>my</u> chances? Me, Michael Partlow.

Michael Partlow, who can't tell you the title of a single poem. Just ask my wife, her head is full of them.

When I first met him, I thought, *I'd never marry a guy like that.* Too persnickety. Too conventional. No sense of humor! But I was wrong. Marriage and kids and the grind made Michael morbidly funny. He got funnier and funnier, while I, who *had* been funny, got less funny.

There was this muscle shirt to which he was superstitiously attached when we were living aboard the boat. The memory of this shirt makes me laugh out loud. While sailing in hot climates, you start wearing as little as possible. And cruising kids, they dress like mental patients—grass skirts and flamenco dresses with muck boots and welding visors and shell necklaces—mementos of places they've been. I have no idea where Michael got the muscle shirt. Panama City? It was white, with huge armholes. Standing ashore, beaming, with his boyish face and unwashed hair, he looked like a prep-school kid who'd gotten lost on a hike about twenty years ago.

The crew of our vessel is fit and in good spirits. Bosun Sybil Partlow (age 7) is sitting in First Mate Juliet Partlow's lap in the cockpit. Deckhand George "Doodle" Partlow (age 2½) is doing his best to stand upright in the small swell. He's pantless, waiting for First Mate to let him whiz off of the side of the boat. His slightly delayed vocabulary is strictly maritime. Boat go, fish go. We were just visited by a very large sea turtle! Surfacing portside with a head like a periscope. Sybil says it's a spy. Whenever Sybil says anything cute, she tells me to write it down. That turtle's a spy, write that down in your book, Daddy.

Pardon me? I say. Are you speaking to <u>me</u>? What do you call me underway, Bosun?

She laughs. Fine, write that down in your book, Captain.

The muscle shirt was so funny because he's normally such a neat-nik, a dandy, and a rearranger. He needs almost no sleep. His mother said he'd always been that way. Here at the house, he used to work late into the night, sending emails and finishing reports, but mostly, man-tinkering. Learning about electrical wiring by gutting another appliance or making little toys for the kids. Some-times he'd even go across the brook, where he'd built a fire pit, and we'd sleep to the rustic scent of wood smoke.

In the morning, he'd leave for work as shiny as an apple. He wouldn't let the children eat in his commuting car. Goldfish, Triscuits—verboten. But the family car, *my* car? Lawless. A layer of organic material composted under the seats. Mysterious objects thumped against the wheel wells whenever I made a sharp turn.

I understand it now, sitting here. I understand how nice it must have been for him to have a little fiefdom—a closet, where shoes are paired, and the world is shut out, and you get to make all your own choices.

My closet, just there on the other side of our bedroom, is hap-hazard. I gave up trying to neaten it when Sybil was a toddler. After months of hanging them up, I just left all the blouses on the floor, where they'd fallen after she'd pulled them off the hangers. She'd shuffle out of the closet in my shoes, unsteady as a drunk, and leave them where I'd never find them.

But I am a mother. Gradually, I just gave them all away, all my spaces, one by one, down to the very last closet.

> January 17. 6 p.m. LOG OF YACHT 'JULIET.' Cayos Limones. 09° 32.7′N 078° 54.0′W. NOTES AND REMARKS: Made it here to Cayos Limones no problem & are anchored off small island with a good holding. Sybil is jumping off the transom while her mom is wrestling Doodle out of his swimmy shirt.

Smile! they used to say to sad-sack little girls like me. Then femi-nism came along and said fuck smiling—you'd never force a boy to smile. But as it turns out—recent studies show—that the physical act of smiling *does* increase one's feeling of well-being.

So sometimes I practice.

I sit here in my closet and grimace.

January 18. 2 a.m. LOG OF YACHT 'JULIET.' Cayos Limones. NOTES AND REMARKS: We are inching toward middle of nowhere. Limones is an untouched archipelago of many sheltered islands w/ fringing reefs & clear waters. Not one single man-made structure. Only the sound of the surf crashing against the windward reef. It's the middle of the night & I can't sleep. Just cleaned all the corroded connections on the battery. More company here than I would like, due to proximity to the mainland. Folks from all over the world. At least our kids have other kids to play w/ & Juliet has other women to commiserate w/ over warm white wine.

I know it appears that what we are doing is radical. But the truth is, there are <u>so many people</u> out here. Sprinkled all around the hydrosphere. Sailboats, sloops, catamarans, re-creations of famous schooners, wealthy paranoids, retirees, people traveling with cats, people traveling w/ lizards, people sick of giving one quarter of their income to the government, free spirits, charlatans, and yes, children. There are <u>thousands</u> of children sailing this world as we speak, some who've never lived on land.

We say we want kids to be joyful/unmaterialistic/resilient. That's what sailing kids are like. They climb masts & can correctly identify obscure plant life. They don't care what somebody looks like when they meet them, they sometimes don't even speak the same language, but they work it out. They don't sit around ranking one kind of life against another. 71% of the earth is ocean. These kids literally cannot believe they are the center of the world. Because where would that <u>be</u>, exactly? They measure their days against a candid & endless horizon.

Let me begin by saying that buying a boat was the most absurd idea I'd ever heard. I'd never boarded anything but a ferry in my life, and Michael hadn't sailed since he was in college.

You've got to be kidding me, I said to him. You want *me*, and our two little kids, to live on a boat with you in the middle of the sea?

Just for a year, he said.

I don't even know how to sail, Michael!

You don't *need* to know how to sail, he said. All you need to know is which way to point the boat. I can teach you the rest as we go.

You're insane, I said.

But even Juliet was hard to convince. How do you sell your wife on the benefits of assuming risk? After all, if your wife is like mine, she probably married you for your stability.

In order to convince Juliet to buy the boat, I had to channel that great salesman—Artist of Spit and Staples, Prankster, Tightwad—my dad, Glenn Partlow. Nothing made Dad happier than sailing on Lake Erie in his old Westsail 32. He'd bought her on a lark from some guy at work who was trying to get rid of her quick. Those days, apparently even a supervising technician at the GM plant could afford a boat. He kept her at a marina on Lake Erie about a half hour's drive from our house. My sister Therese joined us for the first several outings, but she got seasick. After that, it was just me & Dad on a boat neither of us deserved to sail.

The boat was named 'Odille.' Probably somebody's old flame. My mom didn't want anything to do w/ the boat. She was completely absorbed by raising us, which is not to say this was good for her or for us. It was just what moms like her in Ashtabula, Ohio, did at the time. She'd drive us around, handing us our trumpet case or our paper-bag lunch. When Dad & I went sailing on 'Odille,' she didn't complain. At least not to me.

We couldn't have taken more than 2 dozen voyages on that boat, but they clog my memory. I remember the sea-glass green surface of that windy lake, the short fetch of the waves. If I wanted to see my 13th year of life, I had to learn <u>fast</u>. Which sheet to pull, which one to tie off, how to ready the lines for Dad, when to ask questions, when to shut up. I didn't want to bother him. He looked so important at the helm.

When I was in 10th grade, GM offered dad a transfer from Parma, Ohio, to Pittsburgh. For reasons I never inquired about, he took the deal & sold the Westsail.

He set us up in a modest brick house on a hillside in the City of Bridges, the steep streets of which had no traction in the ice.

This last detail, of course, rearranged my life.

Of *course* I said no. My first reaction was shock. I thought he'd lost his mind. Me and the kids living on a boat? Michael might as well have said, Let's live upside down and walk on the ceiling.

More than once, Juliet pointed out that my father died when he was just a little older than I am now. So maybe I was feeling something breathing down my neck—i.e. eternal quietus? And she could understand how spooky that might feel but maybe could this particular psychodrama be solved w/ something less extreme, like a triathalon?

I don't disagree! She was right. Every marriage needs one skeptic to keep it safe. But a marriage of two skeptics will fail to thrive.

Michael and I both recognized we had problems, we just couldn't agree on the solution. I think what was happening was, I wasn't just talking about the implausible plan to walk away from our house and the kids' schools and Michael's job, no matter how assured we would be of getting these things back. *I was wondering, whether we were to go or to stay, what would we do—about us?*

You think this will solve all our problems. It's magical thinking, Michael. It's the way a child thinks.

She kept avoiding the other thing. I wasn't really allowed to talk about it directly, so I dropped hints. Did she know, I ventured to ask, that the ancient Romans believed that sea voyages could cure depression?

She put down her book and glared at me.

Yeah, she said. They also advised eating the brains of baby rams.

She started reading her book again.

I figured, what did I have to lose? I gently lowered her book with my finger.

Juliet, I said. Don't you see? You're stuck. It's been years since I've seen you happy. You want to stay here in Connecticut and be depressed and <u>not</u> finish your dissertation? That's your <u>endgame</u>? Maybe this would be good for <u>you</u>.

I'm not "depressed," she said. Besides, I hate that word.

OK, what should we call it?

She fluffed the pillow behind her back, indignant.

I'm very faithful to my problems.

Listen—I did not want to go. Not because I was happy where I was. Not because I thought sailing was unsafe or unwise. Not even because I thought it would stress our marriage, because, well—too late.

I did not want to go because I was already struggling with a deficit of—I also dislike the word "self-esteem." It had been a rough couple of years after both children were born. There's a lot more to say about that. I'd also recently deserted my dissertation.

The truth was, I was worried I'd be a terrible sailor. An embarrassment.

January 23. 10:15 a.m. LOG OF YACHT 'JULIET.' Cayos Limones. A.M. rain followed by clear skies. NOTES AND REMARKS: You know how folks out here define sailing? Sailing is repairing a boat in exotic places. First time I heard that one, I laughed. Not so funny anymore! This morning I opened up the electrical panel because a couple of the lamps were blinking & saw that half the wires were jiggled loose. Shocked that we have any lights. I've got my Twelve Bolt Bible here & my heat-shrink tubing & while seabirds cross the cloudless sky, I'm giving myself a tutorial on crimp fitting.

Doodle is sitting here next to me looking thoughtful.

Crimper, I say.

He passes me a Lego.

Tubing, I say.

He passes me a crayon.

But just when you're starting to hate on your boat, something oppositely beautiful happens. The water beside us ripples as a pod of stingrays wash their wings in our lee.

I *do* know a lot of poems—from all those hours in my carrel at Boston College, trying to write my dissertation, before we moved out to the Land of Steady Habits.

Ironically, one reason I gave up on studying poetry is that it seemed brutally impractical compared to the urgencies of two children. But these days, inside my closet, poetry is as real to me as an ax. I need it more than food.

Lines come and go in my mind. I don't even remember who wrote them.

Battles are lost in the same spirit in which they are won.

I eat very little, mostly just dinner with the kids, and I lap from the bathroom tap when I'm thirsty. During the day, when I have to leave the closet, I push open the bifold doors and cross our car-peted bedroom in my socks. The body creaks. The bladder longs. I avoid the bathroom mirror. When I return to our bedroom, sometimes I linger by the front windows, where birds mob our blighted apple tree. I spy on them, just as the occasional curious neighbor spies on me. Our plain white house is now a point of interest. It's been on the news. I see the way people walking past our house slow down, and how, if in pairs in the evening, they exchange a somber look.

> *Vivas to those who have fail'd!*
> *And to those whose war-vessels sank in the sea!*
> *And to those themselves who sank in the sea!*

It's true—history is written by the victors. That's why we need poets.

To sing of the defeats.

January 25. 11 p.m. LOG OF YACHT 'JULIET.' Cayos Limones. Brisk NE winds. Clear weather. NOTES AND REMARKS: Will sail east in 2 days. Maybe finally get off the beaten path. Sky tonight amazing. A bowl of stars. I love it on deck at night. Sometimes after Juliet falls asleep, I come up here & crawl into the sail cover. You don't even need a head-lamp to write by, the moon is so bright. Like a spotlight. Like the sun of a black & white world. You can see every frond of every palm on the island, thrashing in the trade winds. The sand bright as snow. The surf rolling up & down the beach.

If I had it my way we'd be circumnavigating the globe. If I was by myself I'd be halfway to the Marquesas. 3 weeks out of sight of land. Then I'd have me a real night watch!! Instead, in order to reassure Juliet, we've plotted a course that clings to the coast of Central & South America. Panama City, Cartagena, Caracas. From there I am hoping she will sign off on a crossing. We could go anywhere across this huge sea.

Monserrat? Punta Cana? Havana?

But for now, it's just me, my Captain's log & a couple curassows I can see when their roosting tree blows a certain way. Somebody forgot to secure their halyard the next boat over. I have half a mind to swim over there & fix it. Funny how the more alone you get out here, the aloner you want to be. You want to find an anchorage with nobody in it at all. Just you and the stars, stars, stars. Stars get you thinking.

We're just a hyphen between our parents and our kids. That's what you learn in middle age. Mostly this is something a mature person can live with. But every once in a while you just want to send up a flare. I too am here! Everybody is sympathetic until you try and make your minuscule life interesting and then they're like, What's wrong with you? You think you're special?

You learn a lot about people when you tell them you're going to sea w/ your kids. About 10% of them will say, Hey, that's amazing, Godspeed, and the other 90% won't hesitate to tell you why it's impossible. Then they want you to spend a couple hours walking them back, explaining how you are going to get food, or take a shower, or keep up with the news.

Whenever we told people that we were going to sail as a family, they'd fixate on different things. Some folks worried about whether it'd be good for me & Juliet's marriage. Wouldn't it be tough to live 24/7 in a 44-foot floating capsule?

(A fair question, one that I'm still mulling over.)

Everyone was worried about the kids. How could you do this w/ kids? they asked. Aren't you worried about their safety? What if they fall overboard? What if they miss home? Why not wait until they're 18? Why not wait until you're retired?

First of all (I wanted to say to these people but didn't), some of you won't even let your kid climb a tree w/out first taking a tree-climbing class & wearing a harness. So I'm just not going to listen to you.

Secondly, I think there's something wrong with the line of thought that it's reasonable to defer your modest dream for several <u>decades</u>. What are we, characters in a Greek myth? Waiting for the eagle who comes to eat our liver every day because in a Greek myth, that's normal?

I knew my mom and my sister would miss us while we were gone. I get that. It's a lot to ask. But there were other people who hardly knew us, strangers who wouldn't miss us at all, who seemed offended by our decision to try out life at sea. It's like they were thinking, What's wrong w/ highways & parking lots & elbow pads & Christmas caroling? What's wrong w/ <u>us</u>?

On Michael's side of the bed: a framed photo of Sybil. Age three, crooked pigtails, ambrosial. Even in my dark days, during my worst blues, I loved studying my daughter's face. Even now, I never tire of staring. Look at that *nose,* I often think—so damned cute, so *wee.* Sybil's face is heart-shaped, wide at the temples, with a small, emphatic chin. The truth is, it's her father's face. Distantly Finnish, midwestern, wide open and friendly. You can almost sense the ball fields and the Coca-Cola and the square dances that it took to produce that kind of a face.

Me, I'm the dun-eyed child of upstate New York, a plain split-level house and a messy divorce, as well as a couple other things I'd rather not talk about. My father's people—a tribe of hard-bitten Irish depressives—culled their numbers with committed lifelong cigarette smoking. My mother's mother was a tyrannical lady from San Juan by whom I was awed the few times I saw her. My mother used to say that she was treated like a human clothes-pin as a child: *Stand there, hold that.*

In short, when Sybil was born, I was relieved that she took after Michael's side of the family. I was relieved that she didn't look like me.

It's sad, though, I realize, to be relieved that your kid doesn't look like you.

Listen, sometimes I don't know whether something is "sad" or not.

I mean, sad poems or songs make me *feel* better. I think—yes, that is pre*cise*ly how I feel. Then I feel better.

But others seem dispirited by the news sad poems deliver.

I used to have to check with Michael.

Was that a "sad" movie? I would ask him, leaving the theater. Is this a "sad" song? I mean, according to you.

Yes! he'd say, laughing. According to *anybody*.

If ever there was a method for squaring dreams w/ reality, it's buying a boat. Especially a boat you've never seen. But what a boat! She's a 1988 CSY 44 Walkover. Center cockpit. Two berths & a saloon. Larger-than-king-size bed in the aft master cabin. Perfect split berth for the kids forward. Huge fridge, three-burner stove. Very roomy. Fiberglass, mostly. No wood laminate, just wood for the bulkheads and the interior furniture. A horizon-pointing bowsprit for me, wood carvings in the bulkheads for my poet wife. We had to buy her w/out seeing her. Of course we would have preferred to buy something nearby. But the fact that she was in Panama made her 20 grand cheaper. I had already scoured the marinas from Westport to Larchmont. We don't have that kind of $$. I paid for her outright. 60 grand. The payout from Dad's life insurance. Our nest egg. (Talk about poetry.) OK, technically I didn't have the full amount. But I solved that, w/ just a little creativity.

We got down here in September, but after 2 weeks in Bocas del Toro, she still wasn't even in the water. Her hull needed a scraping, followed by 3 new coats of paint. Juliet spent days hanging out with the kids outside of the supermini eating fried yucca, waiting to practice her Spanish w/ someone. Eventually she got sick of this & took the kids to sit at the marina bar & let them inhale bowlfuls of ice cream.

I could see them from the boatyard. I had the pleasure of watching a whole U.N. of sailors flirting w/ my wife—Jamaicans, Australians, Panamanians—leaning on the bar drinking cold Stags. They didn't seem to mind the toddler in her lap, & neither did she. Juliet has a very distinct laugh, you could hear it clear across the boatyard.

The thing about depressed people is, once they feel a little better, they are prone to large, generous gestures they can't really live up to.

For months, throughout an entire winter, we argued about Michael's proposal endlessly. It's amazing how many good reasons I had for not taking the children to live on a sailboat, and also how none of those reasons were my real reason. I simply could not afford another failure. I had already let down "my crew," as it were. I already knew what that felt like.

One night in early spring, we were sitting in bed. It was late. We'd made a habit out of arguing at night. I had a bowl of popcorn in my lap. Popcorn was a good mid-argument snack. Also easy to see in the dark. In the time-outs, we were friends. I fed him little handfuls.

He was speaking about, among other things, how he felt he was being "called" by the sea. He wanted to learn from the sea. He wanted to have "confidence in the face of risk." He believed that was part of his American heritage. Bravery built our nation, he said. I nodded, half listening.

I want this so badly I can feel it in my loins, he said.

Where *are* the "loins," anyway? I asked idly, licking salt off my fingers. I mean, are they a real body part? I've always wondered.

Michael sighed and rolled onto his back. Hand over his eyes. Getting ready for another Juliet-style wild-goose chase.

Suddenly, I felt very bad for him.

I loved him. Long ago, and then, I'm sure now.

I don't know what loins are, Juliet, he said, finally.

I stared out the window, into the dark night sky, etched with branches.

Well, whatever they are, I said, they sound delicious. If we come across any cannibals at sea, I bet they'll eat our loins first.

Michael took his hands from his eyes and looked at me. A husband's eyes look so shiny and plaintive in the darkness.

He threw off the covers and ran around to my side of the bed.

He knelt down and clasped my hand.

Juliet, he said. Is that a *yes?*

Who was I to complain?
This whole damned thing was my idea.

We arrived in Panama right in the middle of rainy season. I'd never seen rain like that. Every hour or so, the air would go quiet, the streets would empty, and then, with absolutely no further warning, the sky would just tantrum. Rain drilled the corrugated roof of our little apartment above the boatyard so loudly that one had to shout to be heard. On the street, the rain pocked the dirt with hail-size divots, turning the streets to estuaries; as it drove into puddles, it bubbled and geysered, giving the impression that the rain was coming not only from above but from below. We were so clueless that we often left our laundry on the line, until we realized *no one* attempted to dry laundry outside during rainy season.

The rain was only matched in passion by my own dumb tears. Those first couple of weeks in Bocas del Toro, I cried every night—I mean, hours of muffled, dehydrating bouts of crying, Michael sometimes rubbing my back, sometimes snoring into my neck.

Then one day I said to myself, *Stop your damned crying, Juliet. There's too much water here already.*

The kitchen in our apartment in Bocas was just big enough to turn around in, tiled with big mislaid chunks and old grout, a printed curtain hanging from the countertop, one of those ancient two-burner stoves that needed to be lit with a match. The kids didn't mind. The kids thought the whole thing was a party. Someone had given George a little FIFA skill ball and that's about all he needed. He carried it around like a pet. At the super-mini across the street they had these ice pops, called *duros*—thick, fresh-squeezed juice frozen in a plastic cup—and we'd sit there licking them like deer at salt. Sybil loved the cartoonish toot of the public bus, and she loved to sit outside the supermini licking her *duro*. Whenever a bus arrived, a whole new wave of people would fawn over her and tousle her hair, like it was her birthday on the hour.

Funny thing was, after living in Bocas for a month, it wasn't too hard to get used to living aboard the boat. I found the small space of the boat immediately comforting, like being straitjacketed. No oversize Ethan Allen sectionals, no ottomans, no flat-screen TVs, no free weights, no full-length mirrors, no garment steamers, ironing boards, or vacuum cleaners, no talking, life-size Minnie Mouses or Barbie playhouses with elevators, no plastic Exersaucers or bouncers or strollers, no cake stands, casserole dishes, waffle makers, decanters, no heirlooms, antiques, or gewgaws, no framed certificates, no eight-by-ten photos, no coffee-table books, no takeout menus, or paperwork from the previous millennium, no glass, no vases, no valuables, no art, nothing that could break, shatter, or make you cry if you lost it, which gradually, of course, changed the relationship I had to *things,* basically dissolving it.

Once we got her in the water, we discovered a laundry list of other necessary fixes, small & large. After an idle rainy season in the tropics, she smelled like a gym towel. The upholstery was a joke, as were the moldy life jackets. Her batteries were dead. The head pump didn't work. I went back & forth on buying a new mainsail. After a shakedown cruise by myself in October, watching her heel, all sails set & drawing, I shelled out for a new mainsail. The engine worked perfectly. The dinghy was a tough little inflatable w/ an 8-horsepower outboard. Sybil named it 'Oily Residue.' The kids and I knocked around in 'Oily Residue' whenever Juliet needed some alone time. We circled the marina at Bocas, waving at all of Juliet's boyfriends. I even taught Sybil how to steer the dinghy, and all the guys back on shore would pat her head and tell her what a fine sailor she was.

3 weeks turned to 4. 4 weeks turned to 5.

By the time you realize how over-budget you are, you've already fallen in love. I remember when I first saw her, sitting on stilts in the boatyard, her dirty keel exposed, while they blasted away at her with hoses. Took me a couple hours to believe she was real, & that we had done it, after so much doubt & back & forth & finally just the letting go.

The next day they got down to it and painted the boat with two coats of brick-red antifouling. I felt jealous pangs watching the men at the boatyard stroke her hull w/ paint. It seemed kind of intimate. OK, I'd be lying if I denied having vaguely romantic feelings for the boat, a kind of chaste but thirsty love, not unlike the attraction I felt for Juliet when she was in her third trimester, w/ big, jaunty breasts, awesomely wide-beamed.

(Please God, do not let Juliet ever find this log.)

The double Juliets, that was my idea.

Before the guys in the boatyard put her in the water, the last thing we did was scrape off the words on the transom and rename her.

The lettering was on the schmaltzy side, a loopy, romantic script.

Eventually there was my boat, just as I had imagined her: 'Juliet.'

As soon as we moved onto the boat, the differences in our skill level became clear. Michael was always doing something. Whenever we were at anchor, or if seas were calm, or the children were asleep, he could be found with a knife or shredding rope, or glaring at a broken shackle.

Back in Connecticut, I'd never once seen him smooth a tablecloth or fluff a pillow. The home, the children, had been my sphere. Whether or not I had particular gifts in that area had not mattered. We divided everything up unconsciously along gender lines I'd thought had been consigned to the cultural ash heap. For a poet, I had a lamentable lack of imagination around my daily life—losing myself in laundry and small fascinations. And Michael was the kind of dad who, when left in charge, would send urgent texts asking questions I'd answered when he was not listening the day before, so that I'd spend half of my time away conducting remote assistance, like a NASCAR crew chief.

Who says smiling isn't important for men? He asked all his favors with remorseless good nature. He was confident in his actions, whether or not they were the right ones. Sybil would be hopping from foot to foot needing a toilet, but instead Michael would take forty-five minutes to lash a freshly cut Christmas tree to the car rack, as if we were going to drive home via the landing strip at Bradley airport.

But aboard the boat, our spheres overlapped, ungendering us. Because the boat was not just a boat, it was our home. So he understood what it meant to take care of it. On deck, he coiled the lines in perfect chignons. He liked to buff the chain plates and grease the winches. I had to learn how to slop fish guts overboard and start a flooded outboard motor; it was patently ridiculous to wait for someone else to do these things.

At first, my fears were confirmed—I was a barely competent crewmember. I bumped my head on the same things every day— the companionway, the shelving over the children's berths. There was no learning. I was a cack-handed first mate, a housewife-on-the-run, a poet who'd run out of verse. I had my Ph. but not the D. Someday, due to my inattention, I was sure I'd be hit with the boom and thrown overboard, and the best thing about drowning would be that I wouldn't have to pump the damned head anymore. The piston stuck. You had to grease it with olive oil every couple of days.

Everything at sea was an effort. Especially in the tropics, where equipment dried stiff or rusty or tacky after a downpour, and every crevice was clogged with salt . . .

I did not know that I was becoming a sailor.

I did not know what the sea would ask of me.

Naysayers? Turns out they're everywhere.

One of the guys back in the Bocas boatyard, he used to get under my skin.

You rename the boat? this man asked me.

He wasn't even the foreman, just some dude the other guys seemed to look up to, the one who considered himself big man. He had a gut, w/ skinny legs, and he wore American-style work boots, which no one else wore. Even I went around in supermini flip-flops. When the men worked, this guy would talk & talk. Literally nonstop, no one else ever taking a turn or interrupting him. It was like he was hypnotizing them w/ this endless monologue, which was only broken up by loud machinery.

Bad luck to change the name, this guy had said to me, shaking his head.

You think so? I said, trying to be friendly. I've heard that said.

We looked up at 'Juliet' in her cradle, her hull red like the breast of a robin.

Bad luck, he said again, still shaking his head.

Well you know, I said, people rename their boats all the time.

And you ever know what happen to those boats, my friend?

He tapped me on the arm, even though I was right there.

You study what happen to those boats?

Anger twisted in my chest.

Thanks for your concern, man, I said.

No problem, he said.

I really feel your love, thank you.

No problem, he said coldly.

I left him standing there, looking at me. Then he started up again with the talking.

Walking up the path I heard a chorus of laughter at my back.

Hombre muerto, someone muttered.

We worked so hard to prepare her, to provision, to plot course, that we lost track of days. We even forgot Thanksgiving. Other cruisers in Bocas had told us we would know when we were ready.

And suddenly, we were.

One day, there was a palpable feeling of preparedness.

The ocean waiting like so much road.

We'd take our first overnight sail immediately. Two days across the Golfo de los Mosquitos to the colonial town of Porto-belo. Michael didn't relinquish the helm once. We arrived with a buoyant and slightly manic captain. We decided to stay in Porto-belo and have an honest Christmas.

Days slipped by. Petals falling on water.

It wasn't until January that we made our first push into San Blas, stopping first at Cayos Limones.

San Blas is the Spanish word.

Guna Yala is its real name.

Nearly four hundred tiny islands: the semiautonomous home-land of the Guna.

The Guna permitted no commerce, no buying and selling. The farther you got into the territory, the fewer traces of mankind there were. The casual tourist stayed away. Because there was only the sea. The sea and small atolls of sand and palm. You won-dered if you kept sailing, would you yourself disappear; the idea was not unpleasant.

I have a very clear memory: We were en route from Limones. Eastward into the heart of Guna Yala. Halfway across the May-flower Channel. I was sitting with my back to the mast. Day-dreaming.

The horizon had that effect on me. The undeviating line of sea and sky emptied my mind. Scarves of thought pulled pain-lessly from the magic hat. You must understand, we were never fully out of sight of land—not until that final crossing. So fear, if one felt it, could be soothed by finding the shoreline, which was always there.

Let's face it, I was a terrible watchman. The changes in per-spective entranced me. The different kinds of wind entranced me, and I kept trying to *name* them: *questioning* wind, *tender* wind, *triumphant* wind. On watch, I was only dimly aware of what was happening in the near distance, or on the boat itself.

Suddenly Sybil was screaming.

Mommy! Daddy! Captain Daddy! Sailboat starboard, Daddy!

My heart dropped. She was right—a sailboat was crossing our starboard quarter at a mysteriously close distance. Where had it come from? From behind the large island to starboard, obviously. I was stunned to realize that Michael was below, while also remembering that he'd told me he was leaving the helm moments earlier. Uselessly, I beheld the boat, not much longer than us, but filling the horizon. Her almond-shaped hull was blond wood, and piles of complicated sails gave her the look of origami.

By the time I had scrambled across the cabin top to the cockpit, Michael was already at the helm, face flushed with purpose.

All right, crew, he said. Are we the stand-on vessel?

Yes? I cried. *No?* Do you want me to look it up, Michael?

He laughed. No, Juliet, honey. I was hoping you'd know. We've got to give way. Let's see you do it.

Is this the best time for a teaching moment, Michael?

But he had already stepped away from the helm, and I had to lunge forward to keep the wheel from spinning.

We are on a port tack, I said. We have to go behind.

I turned the wheel hard, and *Juliet* fell off. Like a spurned woman, giving the passing ship her shoulder.

The origami ship glided past like something from a myth. We were close enough to see the objects in the cockpit, the very cleats on the deck.

One old man stood at the helm steering with his arm looped through the wheel. Despite the dangerous nearness of our boats, he seemed unfazed. I could have heard him if he'd spoken.

He looked at us with a kind of ancient patience, gave us a perfunctory wave, and then was gone.

Am I doing the right thing? Hell, I don't know. That's a completely different subject.

Already, I revise the past. I make it sound like the boat was our first real point of contention. Back in Connecticut, we didn't just argue about the boat. Michael and I had much bigger problems. We weren't in a great place. As a couple, I mean. We didn't see the world the same way. We fundamentally disagreed. We weren't—how do I put this? How do I put this *now*?

Never told Juliet this so maybe not such a great idea to write it down. I wouldn't put it past her snooping. (HEY, JULIET. If you are taking the time to read this, you must be A] really, really bored, or B] confined to a hospital bed.) When I was still working at Omni, I used to sneak down to this freshwater marina near the Long Island Sound in the middle of the workday. Just to look at the boats. In my corporate uniform. Nobody ever said to me, What are you doing here? Nobody ever asked me a single personal question. Like it was the most natural thing for a guy in business wear to walk around the docks in the middle of the day asking the cruisers where they'd come from or where they were going. Then I'd go back to work w/ some B.S. about where I'd been.

There was a boat of Canadians, a mother, father & two kids, sailing the most beautiful gaff-rigged sailboat. I'd watch them for long stretches, the kids playing w/ buckets & kayaks & mom and dad working on the boat, or just sitting on deck . . .

One day an older gentleman came up to me.

Some boat, he said.

I know, I said.

They live on that boat, he told me. Already been around the world once.

Me & the old guy stood there looking at the boat in silence. I don't think I've ever wanted anything so badly. I mean, until then, I'd never really envied somebody else's life.

People think they're running from their problems, the man said. But those people are not running from problems.

They just want different problems. They don't want the problems of paperwork and traffic and political correctness. They want the problems of wind and weather. The problem of which way to go.

I looked over at the guy. He had a full head of gray hair that sprouted out the sides of his MAGA baseball cap.

Harry Borawski, he said, extending his hand. You'd be surprised how affordable a boat like that is.

After Georgie, something had changed in our marriage, and there was nowhere solid to put the blame. We were almost forty, and simultaneously our marriage had—I don't know—thickened, agglutinated, become oatmeal-like. Differences between us that had once provided sparks now seemed inefficient. Was there love? Yes, yes—but at the margins. At the center, there was administration. Michael worked until six or seven p.m. All I wanted by then was a handoff for that final hour. At bath time, both kids in the tub, slippery and hairless, as I tried to keep one or the other from going under, I would whisper, *Please* come home, come *home*.

The days were long and shadowy, but no matter how well or poorly I felt I had done as a mother, the final hour of the day was the worst. How time dragged at the end of the day. I'd kept the children alive the entire day but feared some unforeseen disaster in the last ten minutes.

Sometimes the panic made it hard to breathe. I felt like an Irish lass caught in the fields at dusk with my apron full of potatoes. Should I drop the potatoes, save myself, and run? Or slow my progress by carrying them carefully through the dark woods?

I could have gotten from that marina to the Long Island Sound in 8 nautical miles. And from there to Portugal in 3000 more.

But I swear I have never <u>once</u> considered leaving Juliet.

No matter how difficult she can be!

No matter how different we are.
I LOVE MY CRAZY WIFE.
(There you go, Juliet, you damned snoop.)

But now. What I wouldn't give to expect him home at all.

The thing is, I <u>liked</u> Harry Borawski. We'd sit at this picnic table that looked over the marina, paging through binders of yachts for sale, or shit-shooting, drinking plastic bottles of warm iced tea. He sold yachts, he'd sold a lot of them, but whenever I came around he never seemed to have anything to do, or he'd given up on whatever that was. He was one of those old guys w/ encyclopedic knowledge about some subjects & huge holes of ignorance about commonsensical things. Big guy, smudged—you were kind of glad for his non-existent wife that he never married her. Sometimes you just have this previous-life connection with the oddballs. And me, I was an easy target, showing up in my tie w/ my memories of my dead dad and 'Odille.' For some reason I opened up to Harry. I told him things I didn't tell other people.

I told him about Juliet.

I think sailing would be good for my wife, I said to him. She struggles with depression. Though she <u>hates</u> when I say that. She had a rocky childhood. She was fine until we had our own kids. I think having kids kicked up the past. It's been a rough stretch of years.

And nobody's around to help us either, I told him. She doesn't speak to her mother. And I'm away all the time. I'm at work or on business trips. I'm no help.

Then Harry says to me, Some of the best sailors are women. Always have been. Some sixteen-year-old schoolgirl just sailed around the world singlehanded. The sea doesn't care who you are.

That's when I first imagined that we could really do it.

That the boat would be good for both of us. And that I could have this dream I'd been carrying around since I was 15.

The sea doesn't care who you are.

Sounded good to me!

Not everybody likes Juliet.

I thought Juliet and the sea would get along.

I knew a woman from the preschool who had divorced and was pretty happy about it. She told me about how she and her ex had calmly strategized their parting, how relieved they both felt. They'd worked it all out before their children were old enough to know the difference.

One cold morning—during the year Sybil was three, before George even came along—I went so far as to see a lawyer. The office was hushed, airless. The secretary whispered my name. It felt so covert, so guilty. I stood there trembling. Sybil was at home with a babysitter. Just a girl from the block, Patty and Charlie's middle-school girl, barely beyond babysitting herself.

Are you OK, honey? asked the secretary.

I thought, What in the world do we *do* to each other? We love in springtime and doubt in winter. We'll blame our heavy hearts on anything.

I'm sorry, I said.

I ran out. I never told anyone.

Harry talked like an Ashtabulian. That is, he saw things like the folks back home. I liked being able to talk about things I couldn't even bring up in the break room at Omni lest some informant report back the presence of an independent thinker. It was good to talk freely & not be censored by the freegans & utopians, you just don't know whose foot you're going to step on. I live in fear of making an honest mistake in conversation followed by some kind of Maoist-style recrimination session. I am genuinely proud of my country & my life & do not understand the awkward silence that follows when I say so.

I'm just a regular person. To be taken at face value. I don't have time to read towering stacks of books before forming an opinion. Maybe the reason I mystify Juliet is because she is overthinking my position. I just want to take care of my family & I don't want anybody taking my rights. I especially don't want anybody taking my rights & then telling me it's for my own good.

I am no Rhodes scholar, but I have an ear for doublespeak. Here's what I want to say to the other side, to the Righteous Left, to the Easily Injured and Offended: You say you want concessions/changes/social justice, but let's admit it, you are never going to quit. Not until your moral victory is complete.

Because that's who you are.

I would just like to hear you say it.

That part of you understands public burnings.

Convert, or die.

Someone is coming up the stairs. In my closet, I brace myself. People keep coming to the front door, leaving things for me, trying to inquire. I've had to surrender my privacy. Which is not as hard as I thought. It makes me feel better to relinquish what I don't need. *Go ahead,* I think, *stare at me, ask me anything, take photos of my house, just don't come inside my closet.*

An old lady enters the bedroom. She's wearing a stiff T-shirt and cardigan and house slippers that she brought with her, on the off-chance that I'm a fastidious housekeeper. She sits on the bed and sighs. Our eyes meet through the crack between the bifold doors.

Hey, hon, she says.

Hi, Mom.

It's almost time for Sybil's bus, she reminds me.

You'll walk up and get her, right?

Sure, sure, she says, looking uncomfortable. It's just . . . you might want to come on out of that closet before she gets home. It's just a little unusual. For a child to see, that is. If you ask me, it's a perfectly reasonable thing for *you* to do. But for *her* . . .

You're right, I say. I agree, I should come out.

But I don't move.

After a moment or two, my mother says, Would you like me to leave you alone, Juliet, or—

It's fine, I say. In fact, stay a minute. I'd appreciate it. Thank you.

This surprises me, that I want her near. She's been living with me and the kids for a full month, since our return. She came the moment I called. But there is a palpable awkwardness while we try out this new intimacy.

Don't let anybody tell you how you should feel, my mother says, after a pause. When your daddy left, it felt like a death. I did not want to feel better. And that was my right.

Another favorite line of poetry comes to me.

there are so many little dyings that it doesn't matter which of them
is death

January 27. LOG OF YACHT 'JULIET.' From Cayos Limones. Toward Naguargandup Cays. 09° 32.7′N 078° 54.0′W. NE wind 10–20 knots. Seas 2–4 feet. NOTES AND REMARKS: Crew has been busy this morning! During engine check the First Mate burnt her finger checking engine oil. Another small setback when Bosun spilled her Rice Krispies into the bilge.

Today we head deeper into San Blas. Our destination is an island called Corgidup. Why Corgidup? Because Corgidup means "Pelican Island" in Guna and Sybil loves pelicans. The first amendment to the CONSTITUTION OF THE YACHT 'JULIET,' which is written in invisible ink on the back of the Parcheesi board, says, "All crew haveth the right to make spontaneous changes to itinerary at random." You want to play coconut football in your underpants? You want to sit &

watch ants carry tiny fractions of a leaf across a log? Well then, while aboard 'Juliet,' it is decreed you must do those things.

Going to be brisk out there today. Everybody is tethered and in vests. In a minute, we will make the next leg of our incredible journey. We will head her into the wind & hoist the mainsail. Then we will feel that ancient pull.

Like plugging into the cosmos.

The little dyings are so much harder. The interstices.

Look at me. Even though I'm safe, back in my comfortable home, I'm still acting like a refugee—scavenging, foraging, guarding my small space, waiting out the end of the war.

I'm going to *survive,* I know that. Someday, I will talk about this calmly and insightfully. And for a good many years after that, I will go about my days, washing and dressing and caring for this body, but only out of obligation, out of the prolonged obligation to stay alive—I want to say "for the kids," but I know that even if I were childless, I would keep surviving, keep eating and drinking, going on. These actions will filibuster my mortal end, which I will be permitted to achieve only when my body gives out.

Because, as it turns out, we don't really *die* of broken hearts. Sadly.

II

'm in the grocery store when I run into one of my friends from
the Church Basement School. She's a person I once cared about
very much. Our daughters both attended the Basement School
when they were toddlers. I used to look forward to seeing her
standing in the autumn sunshine with her fabulous hair full of
cereal particles. There was a group of us, mothers who congre-
gated early outside of the school in the afternoons, waiting to pick
up our very young children. . . . The Church Basement School
was not its real name. It had a nicer name, one that escapes me
now, because all I can remember about it were the enormous red
Episcopalian doors, and the way the mothers would stand grate-
fully close together, in the cool shade of the stone arcade, talking
quietly and sometimes breathlessly, often jiggling an infant.

By that point, I had missed the submission for my dissertation twice, but lacked the courage to quit. So whenever I showed
up early to wait outside the doors of the Basement School, it
was in order to avoid the horror of neurotic self-confrontation.
Apparently, others had the same need. A rotating four or five
of us. Mordantly funny women stinking of peanut butter. We
were strangers except for the fact that we already understood
one another better than our own spouses did. And that we were
committed to not letting anything make us feel better. Over time,
we all grew very attached to one another.

She sees me across the fruit display, this person to whom I was
once very attached, and her face looks stricken. She drops what

she is holding and reaches out to me, like a child, a yearning child. I am unsure of how to respond, because between us sits a rather large wooden plinth full of apples. Red ones, golden ones, displayed in careful pyramids.

Juliet! she gasps, almost inaudibly.

It was a risk to visit the grocery store, I know. I went back and forth, but after counting the days I've spent sitting in the closet, I grew alarmed. I usually send my mother, who agrees to any errand. She sits at the bay window in the kitchen like a firefighter with her boots ready. Whenever I enter the room, my mother closes the local paper and waits for me to speak, this woman I barely know. She has grown intuitive, knowing. The fact that she no longer colors her hair was one of the great shocks of my life, which is saying a lot. She used to be so careful with her appearance, and rightfully so, especially the splendor of her remarkable head of red hair. Now it's threaded with gray.

Standing over the apples, my friend is still holding out her arms. Tears are streaming down her face.

Oh, Juliet, I am so *sorry* about what happened.

She must have read about us in the paper. She must have cried then, too.

She is reaching toward me. But the thing is, I can't remember her *name*.

Maybe we were not as close as I remember.

What do I do with my hands?

Feb 2. LOG OF YACHT 'JULIET.' Naguargandup Cays. 09° 30.41′N 078° 47.57′W. NOTES AND REMARKS: We have found it. We have found paradise.

Birth and death are fixed points, and middle age gives you a good view of both. Michael had dreamed of sailing around the entire world in one year. My ambition was to survive the year without personally sinking the boat. We compromised on roaming the Caribbean coast east of Panama. But once we entered Guna

Yala, we never again thought of it as a compromise; a sailor could spend his life in that place alone.

We came across them in the late-afternoon light—a chain of small, sandy islands, each one about the size of a baseball diamond. They looked like so many other islands in the territory. Palm trees tilted toward the crashing surf like bouquets of tulips, and forgotten human artifacts—a fisherman's cold fire, broken eyeglasses, a single shoe—lay scattered in the sand. We knew that each island belonged to *some*body, but the owners never posted a sign, never left a name. The Guna do not consider themselves Panamanians. They do not speak Spanish, unless to trade with outsiders; they do not believe in selling or buying land, and they do not use money. The coconut harvest was their currency. This implausible economy had preserved the place, and we roamed it like embarrassed ghosts. Truth is, we had blundered into the territory, on our way east to try to tick through Michael's list of port cities. But Guna Yala had already blown open our provincial knowledge, and we were humbled by all we did not know, all that can only be known by boat.

Good conditions for arriving, Michael said. We'll be able to see straight down.

He started the motor, and the boat rumbled warmly. He stepped up to the mast and freed the halyard.

But it's still hairy here, he warned me. There are shoals all over the place. Absolutely no route to enter from this side of the cays. Juliet, honey, look at the chart. You'll need to be really vigilant today, honey.

In my experience, *shoals all over the place* was simply descriptive of Guna Yala—hundreds of islands sitting on a shallow ocean shelf. A sailor could see variations of depth by the color of the water, which was a patchwork of blues—the incandescent turquoise of sand, the mother blue of deep water, and the purple discoloration of coral heads. These colors were a map that was misread at the boat's peril. It was often my role to hang out under the lifelines and eyeball the whole process so that we didn't run aground. Michael didn't trust the GPS. I thought he was crazy until it blinked out in the middle of a field of coral heads.

We weren't purists. We used the GPS. We used our SAT phone until we lost it overboard in the Golfo de los Mosquitos. We used our iPad if we got reception, and we definitely used our autohelm—promiscuously. Like many novice sailors, I developed an emotional attachment to the autohelm, which labored on like some unthanked sub-wife, the quiet, accommodating third hand that we needed desperately.

While Michael lowered the mainsail, I went to the cockpit and switched off the autohelm. *Juliet*'s wheel hummed in my hands.

Sybil was sitting on her hands in the cockpit, gazing at her father, whom she had begun to idolize since we'd started to sail. He knew the name of every rope, clutch, or valve. He was a wonderful new stranger, this Captain Michael. Or was that *other* man the stranger, I sometimes wondered, the one who used to sit with a bag of Funyuns propped on his belly, the TV flickering across his irises, a man who never knew the name of her teachers or friends?

Corgidup, he shouted, flaking the mainsail. How did you know that means Pelican Island, Juliet?

I read it in the book you gave me, I told him.

I *love* pelicans, Sybil reminded us.

Will you please bring us a little downwind, honey? Michael called. We've got to go *around* the leeward edge of that little *dup* there. There's a deep channel between these two islands. Good, good. Is Corgidup inhabited?

Well, there's the pelicans, I said.

Uh-huh.

I had to smile. Michael wasn't really listening. He didn't really care whether or not Corgidup was inhabited. He was tucking the sailcloth vigorously into the cover, the tip of his tongue sticking out.

You're just trying to make me feel useful, I said.

What? he said. I can't hear you.

Uninhabited, I said. The guidebook says that Corgidup is only inhabited during the coconut harvest.

Wonderful, he said. We'll have the whole place to ourselves.

Our first morning here, the light poured in through the hatches & we got a good first look at Naguargandup. We hurried thru chores & filled up 'Oily Residue' w/ masks, flippers & lunch & headed to shore.

Corgidup was too small (& by the way, no pelicans). So we motored to the bigger island, Salar. The kids ran & dodged through the palm trees screaming. Juliet & I stood there in the wind & suddenly I think we both felt the same thing for a change. We both knew the same thing and we didn't have to say it or name it. To me, that's love.

Salar is a perfect, 4-person-size island. A corner for each of us. Sybil loves to climb the tilted palm trees. Doodle favors the bathwater-warm basin hidden between the island & the broken coral heaps. It's the coolest baby pool you ever saw—

For people who have been unhappy for long periods of time, happiness can feel vaguely uncomfortable. They do not quite know how to submit to it, or whether or not such a submission is wise.

On Salar, I did not immediately recognize the feeling—a sumptuous lightness, a nervous vibration, summons to laughter. I watched Sybil in the tree. Georgie, standing bowlegged, squinting in the sunshine. The wind rooted in my mouth, hair, and lungs.

I was still struggling to describe the wind. *Nosy* wind. *Avid* wind. *Silencing* wind. It had so many variations. In the canopy, it rustled the hem of Sybil's sundress. It filled her skirt full as a bulb.

Childish wind.

I had always wanted a tree-climbing girl.

> *I needed you. I didn't want a boy,*
> *only a girl. A small milky mouse*
> *of a girl, already loved, already loud in the house*
> *of herself.*

We spoke very little that day. We'd lose track of each other, then spot each other in the stippled shade. I was playing in the sand with Georgie when I looked up to see Michael watching me. Just watching me, leaning against a nearby breadfruit tree, a look on his face I'd never quite seen. Soft, with no pretending. Tender, impartial. We stared at each other across this space until, shyly, I looked away. When I looked up again, he was smiling. As I said, we hadn't been in a great place before the trip. I think we'd both been very worried—in suspense.

But now, look, he was smiling.

Thank you, he said.

Sometimes, when I fear that I was not a good wife, I think of this moment.

Georgie charged into the foliage, and the spell was broken.

I laughed and followed, unhurried, through the reddish palm trunks until we reached a fire pit. Charcoal and fish bones. *Look,* I said to him, and drew a black streak on his bare arm. He stared at me in awe and copied on my arm. Then he was off again, stumbling past a thatch fishing hut, where brittle fronds hissed in the wind. He tunneled headlong into the invisible resistance of the wind. I had to jog when I lost sight of him.

*Dooo*dle, I called.

But there he was, at the end of the island, where the surf crashed upon crushed coral heads.

Occasionally I would turn and look for *Juliet.* I could see her through the palms, her anchor chain loose and relaxed, deck tidy, and mast barely stirring. She nosed around in a circle, forgetfully waiting for us.

It was *like* love, what I'd begun to feel for the boat by then.

But as with love, I questioned the feeling.

I have never known when to let love hold my weight.

Feb 5. LOG OF YACHT 'JULIET.' Naguargandup Cays. NOTES AND REMARKS: Big day for Sybil! Till now she's ridden my back tadpole-style when snorkeling. Today exploring Salar she pushed off & didn't look back. We swam all the way out over the coral heads side by side. You think those things are rocks? I asked her later. It's all <u>alive</u>. Fish represent just a tiny percentage of sea life. Proportionally, it's almost all invertebrates. This includes sponges, jellies, corals, snails, & urchins. Massive orange brains of sponges, or ones that look like red reaching fingers. Urchins of every color. Did you know that urchins appear immobile, but they are actually slowly scraping rocks with their teeth? All of it is alive, gnawing away, gnawing at life.

Time passed. Disappeared. We stayed in the lee of Salar and lost track of the days. Gradually our provisions dwindled, but for some reason, we didn't worry. We moved from fresh to canned. Spamghetti. Potatoes roasted over a beach bonfire at sunset, a dish the children considered the height of luxury. Michael and Sybil snorkeled ever farther. They created lists of all the marine life they'd seen. They'd sit and develop theories and trade bottle caps. Michael tied a knife to a stick and spent entire days trying to spearfish.

And what did I do? I began to read again.

At first I just read the soggy paperbacks I'd idly picked up in Portobelo. A couple of British mysteries. A biography of Vasco da Gama. And then one day I dragged my research books out of a locker, where they sat behind Sybil's collection of exoskeletons. The book jackets were as familiar as faces. The pages were covered with my own handwriting.

I've always been a reader, ever since I was a child. But after I dropped out of the graduate program, I didn't touch a book for months. Opening a book was connected to a sense of disappointment. The fact that I refused to read left me exposed when George was born. Without my books, I had nothing to interpret but the baby, who wanted a mother, not a poet. My only other text was myself and my creeping despair—a condition resistant to cerebral analysis, since the depressed brain functions as a kind of double agent, appearing rational and faithful but secretly work-ing for the enemy.

Listen, when I worked at Omni, I never really saw the kids. Which, to be honest, was OK with me. I'm just trying to be honest. When I got home from work, I just wanted to sit around & watch some kind of ball move around some kind of field. I couldn't really handle their problems & I know I couldn't handle Juliet. I was a carbon copy of my dad, or at least what I remembered of him, doing my part, earning a living, trying not to yell etc. etc.

What did I do today? Today, February something-or-other? I sat in the middle of the ocean, miles off the coast of Panama, trading bottle caps w/ my daughter. She wanted my Jarrito. No, I said, I'll give you my Stag. I have a million Stags, she said, spilling them onto the sand. I want your Jar-rito! I hold the precious orange bottle cap to the sky. And I was like, NEVER (wicked laughter)!

I don't know. People were so worried about the kids out here. And maybe they're right. Maybe they know something I don't know. But let me ask you, When was the last time your dad spent an entire morning listening to you?

I could never give it a name, my condition. I would have said, "I'm depressed," if that had felt sufficient. But I felt *more* than depressed. I felt that I *was* depression. A swallowed woman. Besides, Michael was right—I hated jargon in any form. "Inner child." "Support system." I'd rather not speak at all if I had to use those words.

I could only tolerate the way the poets described sadness.

Anne Sexton, confessional poet of the 1960s, was incapacitated by spells of depression, which started after she had children. She loved her children, but care of them drove her to the brink of madness. Motherhood made her feel "unreal." Nobody was pre-pared to talk about a mother's depression. In 1956, Sexton learned to write sonnets from a TV program. She conned her way into a poetry class, during which she furtively used her high-heeled shoe as an ash tray.

Not long after, she wrote a poem called "The Double Image."

> *Ugly angels spoke to me. The blame,*
> *I heard them say, was mine. They tattled*
> *like green witches in my head, letting doom*
> *leak like a broken faucet;*
> *as if doom had flooded my belly and filled your bassinet,*
> *an old debt I must assume.*

Ugly angels, I thought, yes, *that's* what they are.
They are not devils. Devils, I could disregard.
You cannot do this, my angels told me.
You miscalculated, they said.
You are prone to miscalculations. Untrustworthy.
You cannot even trust your own thoughts—look at you.
Still struggling to resist the naked truth.
You are not mother material, they said.
A mother is a house.
A mother is a house at night, with everyone safe in bed.
I lived in terror of my enemy. Because of course I understood that the angels were not *real*—my enemy was worse than that. My enemy had no form, no gender, no name. Even the evilest people had *names*. I didn't know what had come over me. I had been fine . . . well, I had held myself together. I had held myself together all my life. Then I became a mother, twice, and I was not fine.

I was the opposite of fine.

My first bout occurred after Sybil. I didn't know how to describe my state, or to whom. I didn't have a way to speak about it at all. Back then, I blamed winter. I blamed Michael. I blamed myself. The angels came, swarmed around me for months. I held on. I swallowed my story. But then they left. And I forgot.

After George was born, everything was OK for a while, just

long enough to get comfortable. Then my moods darkened. The small things that a house contains—the objects one props in corners for the hell of it, flowers or a photograph or a bird feeder or a trinket from vacation—upset me, and I packed them away. I let the cleaning go—I barely had a handle on it anyway. I started to have trouble sleeping. Sleeplessness is not unusual, but you should know I'd always been a champion sleeper, famous for nodding off no matter what bedlam surrounded me, so I had no weapons against it, and once the angels returned, I remembered how they had behaved the first time around, noisiest at night, lecturing me in the darkness. *A mother is a house . . . A mother is a house with everyone safe in bed . . .* I found myself starting to get very disorganized, late to get Sybil to preschool, sprawled beside baby George on the floor during tummy time, wondering how he'd gotten there, and why the poor child was being forced through such a humiliating exercise.

I hid this all from myself and from others. But I remember the moment when I was found out. It was early spring. We'd almost made it through winter. George had just started to pull up on things, and I resolved to get my head on straight. To regain control. In a fit of spring cleaning, I decided to go through Sybil's old baby clothes. Maybe there were some things I could use for her brother.

Michael had just come back from another trip to Akron, where Omni had a regional office, and with some help from my Basement School friends and box wine, I'd made it through all right. I figured that this time around, I was armed with my past mistakes. I wasn't in a lonely city, I wasn't trying to be Helen Vendler. I was giving myself a little more amnesty. You know, yelling was OK, Oreos were OK. It was too much work to try to be special, to flatter oneself with special accommodations. I wasn't going to buy into that. This time around, I swore I was going to be a good enough mother. A one-foot-in-front-of-the-other sort of person.

The seasonal shedding of clothes is a rite, the way one has to put away the outgrown items, and usually stumbles upon last year's outfits. The shoes are bittersweet—tiny little sneakers with Velcro tabs, rubber toes, cartoon characters, or dirty glitter, the grooves still bearing the grit of distant playgrounds, sand lodged under the insole. Evidence of last year's child. After all, children grow in inches and the rest of us inch toward the end.

What's wrong, Mommy?

Sybil was standing in the doorway in her tutu. Bathed in a slice of daylight, hand on the doorknob. Dirty hair, no underpants.

What do you mean?

Why are you crying, Mommy?

I'm not *crying,* I said.

I put my hands to my face. I took them away—salt water.

I was still crying when Michael got home. I simply could not stop. It was almost mechanical. As if I were literally broken. Michael helped me into pajamas and got me into bed. Sybil wouldn't leave the doorway.

Don't let her *watch,* I told him. Take her somewhere *else.*

After that day, the day of endless crying, she always knew when I was sad, and this made me sadder. Because I couldn't *hide.* I couldn't just be alone with it. It wasn't my own sadness anymore.

She wouldn't let me stay in bed. Schooled on fairy tales, she had an instinctive distrust of sleeping women. She wouldn't give up on me, not even for a second. Peering over the edge of the bed, she would open her small hands, and show me an invisible prize.

Mommy, she'd say. Do you want to read this story I just found in the sky?

I loved the idea of being loved by my daughter.

But in practice, it only frightened me.

What was the promise she was trying to secure?

You know what you are, Mommy? You are the *sun.* You are a *present.* You don't even have to wear a pretty dress. You are ex-tastic.

Oh, Sybil, I would say. Thank you so much.

But inside: *Do not say these things.*

I get it, I'd never be out here if it weren't for Dad. But now that I'm out here, I sometimes laugh out loud realizing what a hack sailor Dad actually was. We sailed around Lake Erie in big, sloppy loops. He never knew what the weather was, couldn't read the clouds, didn't care. He was probably learning at the same time as I was. That was the kind of thing my dad did. That's what made him brave & also confusing. How many times one of us almost got brained by an accidental jibe. Dad pretended that ducking from the swinging boom was a game.

He was essentially a fun-loving guy. He was often referred to by others as a "jokester," a "prankster"—a "real individual." At his funeral, everyone had funny stories. I hope I never go to a funeral that funny again.

There was only one subject that made my father grow solemn, & that was the subject of Ronald Reagan.

By God, did my father love Ronald Reagan. Dad had entire speeches committed to memory. They made him tear up. It was the one thing you weren't allowed to joke about—that Ronald Reagan was no longer president, and there would never be another Ronald Reagan.

"Freedom is never more than one generation away from extinction, Mikey," he'd say. "It must be <u>fought</u> for, or one day we will spend our sunset years telling our children what it was once like in the United States where men were free."

My mother was apolitical. She went along with Dad because she trusted him in general. My mother was always "washing her hands" of things. Well, you go ahead & do that, Mikey, but I wash my hands of it. When I was little, I used to cringe when people said I was like my mother. If my father was a real individual, what did that make me & my mother?

Sailing was something that could bring me & Dad closer. I figured he would tell me things I needed to know when we were sailing. But mostly he told me long stories about the funny mishaps of friends of his, or cousins, or people he met once. Plus, the chop was often so bad on Lake Erie we were pretty busy keeping the boat upright.

Years later, when I got interested in boats again, I don't think Harry Borawski was a coincidence. As Harry put it, the sea is the only place where the government can't get its damned hands on you. At sea, you can remain an American, but also escape the massive, unaccountable conglomerate that is the modern American government. Harry replaced Reagan with James Madison. "If angels were to govern men," Harry would recite, "then no controls on government would be necessary. But government is administered by men over men, Mike. So you must oblige it to control itself."

Poor James Madison. Because the American government is currently its own largest creditor, debtor, lender, employer, consumer, contractor, property owner, tenant, insurer, health-care provider, and pension guarantor . . . You see my point.

I've always been around people who try to give me words to use. It must be something about me. I must look like I need a script. This was also true with Juliet. She left me speechless. It wasn't just her sex appeal, which is ample. It was that she seemed free. Confident & herself. A real individual.

I didn't even realize we were politically far apart until long after the kids were born. Until then, let's face it, I was like my mom. Apolitical. I didn't think freedom had anything to do with politics. And then this election happens and everybody chooses a corner.

I don't know, I just cast the vote my dad would have cast. He was gone, but I didn't want his influence to die too.

Imperfectly, I guess, but he taught me how to be a man.

You make your way. You handle it. You don't wait around for a savior. You don't allow yourself to be a victim.

And when all else fails, you make a joke.

I miss him.

Duck duck duck GOOSE.
Mother mother mother GHOST.

The dead talk back to you out here, they really do. I can almost hear him muttering. Chuckling. Cheering us on.

Because even though he's been dead for years, I know exactly what he'd say about things today. He'd be thrilled we are out here w/ the kids. Instead of hamstringing them by being helicopter parents & training them to be scared, priming them for victimhood. Because guess what, trouble is coming. In every life. It marches toward you like storm systems. So why not teach your kids to deal? Or at least admit that you don't <u>want</u> them to deal so that they literally can't live w/out you?

And boredom? My dad thought boredom was the start of all great things. If Sybil says she's bored, I say, Great! Time to take apart the outboard motor on the dinghy. Great, let's get on your mask and you can help me scrape barnacles. Great, go help your mom plunge some laundry.

We are all needed on this ship, I remind her.

And the thing is, she <u>understands</u>.

In some countries (in our own country), kids Sybil's age are changing their baby brother's diaper or hunting for food in the backwoods. My own dad died when I was 15 and for a while there me & Therese ran the show until our mother decided she wanted to live again. Did we fall apart?

This, from Anne Sexton's diary: *My heart pounds and it's all I can hear—my feeling for my children does not surpass my desire to be free of their demands upon my emotions. . . . What have I got? Who would want to live feeling that way?*

So Sybil's missing a year of school. What kid wouldn't want to? I couldn't stand school. I couldn't sit still. There wasn't anything wrong w/ it. It was Ohio. It was the 1980s. It was a normal small-town American school. One level, brick, ugly, flagpole, etc., connected hallways modeled after the Pentagon. Day in & day out, I filled out pie charts, reduced fractions, learned about the Pilgrims. Holy Christ, did school bore me. School was the postponement of life. I survived it by playing so violently after school that I needed the next day to recover. Only if I were very sore could I sit still for that long.

All this came back to me when I found myself suiting up my daughter for the same thing. Kindergarten: the first of 13 years. Sure, the details are different. Now the sneakers light up, and we celebrate "winter" instead of "Christmas," but it's basically the same thing. You know, sit in a circle, stand in a row. Indoor voices. I understand—it's civil society. I don't really have a problem with circles or rows. It's just—

I remember studying my mother's body. I remember a deep, worshipful attentiveness toward all the parts of her, from her soft décolletage down to her painted toenails, which were like candies. I remember her closet, as I've said, touching the silks and smelling the wools. I remember waiting for her to call for me, from the bottom of the stairs, turning my name to four syllables, as I've heard certain birds do with a single tone, just for the pleasure of it:

Ju-lee-*eh*-et.

Strange, to have been so familiar with her voice. And then not to hear it at all for many years.

Out here, the sea is the kids' school. Any single reef in Guna Yala can teach them more than I learned in 13 years of science class. Take the fish alone (and fish, there are mind-blowing varieties), more different species, they say, than all the other vertebrates combined. They mill & weave around these coral heads. Syb & I watch them underwater, then we look through our Audubon Field Guide, checking off what we saw/bragging/making shit up.

The fish have bizarrely human attributes like big noses, or sad eyes, or grumpy frowns, big, little, skinny, humpbacked . . . it's like you're walking through Westfarms Mall on a Sunday, but it's underwater and everybody's a fish. The color combinations themselves are endless, I might even say gratuitous. Blues, reds, yellows, periwinkles & flashes of silver.

Like people, some fish prefer to move around by themselves & others move in groups. Walls of blue tang pass by like a drawn curtain, while a single suffering flounder scuttles below. Others just mob, sticking together but at odd angles. Discoveries abound! We never seem to crack the code.

My parents were muted people with moderate expectations. Even their arguments, in the long, slow buildup to their separation, never reached a full passion. Their hobbies were ordinary, like gardening and watching quiz shows. But every once in a while, when I was little, they used to have these big parties. Folks would emerge from the woodwork—coworkers, and parents of kids I knew—and they'd all get ritually drunk.

I would sit under the table and pretend I was too good for it all. But secretly I loved it when an upside-down face would lift the hem of the tablecloth and exclaim, *Juliet, O Juliet! Wherefore art thou Juliet?* I remember their collective roar. Anyone who laughed like grown-ups laughed, like harlots and farmhands, did not deserve an honest answer.

However. I could always hear my parents' voices rising above the din. Not only because they were my parents and I was hopelessly attached to them, but because I believed they stood guard.

I felt mothered under the table.

Which is why it's so awful that he found me there.

Lionfish are an invasive species, but you've got to give them respect. They can kill you by just brushing your skin. I met a guy in Limones who described it to me. He was free diving & he grabbed hold of a reef to pull himself down, which you're not supposed to, it was just a temporary lapse in judgment. Next thing this guy knows, there is this huge lionfish shaking its poison pajamas in his face. As it swims away he realizes he's just been sideswiped by one of the most venomous creatures in existence. He realizes that he's got to get back to his boat before he has a reaction, but the hull of his boat just looks so damned far away, in another world, a world which he starts feeling nostalgic about, remembering how sunny and full of laughter it was, which terrifies him because he's already thinking like a dead man. Somehow he gets to the boat by pulling himself underwater along the rode. His wife & another cruiser in the anchorage drag him aboard & the last thing he remembers is the squelch of his shorts on the settee and him thinking, Damn it, I hate when the settee gets wet.

But I already said I wasn't going to talk about that.

Sometimes you're fighting the current so hard & still barely moving. Other times you don't feel a thing, you just slip out to sea, like a leaf.

Yes, I remember reading on Salar. The welcome surrender of reading a book. Why had I ever punished myself by stopping?

At my feet, Georgie was developing fine-motor skills by picking up hermit crabs from the tidal pool. His big head hung heavily over his torso.

We look alike, Georgie and I. He got my dusky skin tone, which looks jaundiced in northeastern winters but is immediately flattered by the sun, and my cedar-brown hair, which, thanks to the trade winds, was developing a permanent uprightness. Even after a bath, as soon as it would dry, his hair would start to stand, tilting leeward.

'Rab, he said, holding up a specimen. 'Ood 'rab.

Is it a good crab? I said, trying once again not to worry about his scant vocabulary. Is it *your* crab?

Doo 'rab, he agreed, and plonked it in his bucket.

Then I noticed that I had lost track of Michael. That I couldn't remember when I had seen him last. I could see Sybil, snorkeling close to shore. But I didn't see Michael anywhere in the cove.

Sybil stood up, water dripping off her hair and her swimmy shirt. She lifted her mask, spilling out several cups of seawater.

Are you having fun, my little beauty? I called out.

What?

Are you having fun?

I was talking to the fish, she said.

What were you saying?

I was saying, Don't be scared! They look scared.

Do you know why they gather around you?

No.

Because you protect them. You are bigger than their predators. They figure no one will bother them when you're around. You're like the fish protection program.

Well, she said, fitting her mask down tight. Better get back to work.

Hey. Where's your daddy?

He went out.

Out? What do you mean? Where?

I don't know.

> There are so many wrecks all over Guna Yala you can almost navigate by them. In some places the masts literally stick up out of the water. There's this kind of trench humor about it among cruisers.

I couldn't see him anywhere. Nowhere.

Sybie, I said. Come up here, please.

She slumped. Why, Mommy?

Because I said so.

Do we have to *leave*? We just came *over*.

Sybil. Don't exaggerate. We've been here since breakfast.

Is it lunch?

Sybil. Come up here *right now.*

But my *fishes*—

Do not give me crap right now, Sybil, I said. We've got to find Daddy.

Daddy went out.

Where?

He's at the reef. There's a wreck.

You didn't *tell* me that, Sybil. How far out? Which way?

She shrugged bodily. I cursed Michael under my breath. It was very unlike him, though. He was so by-the-book. Oiling this and pumping that and checking this. But not telling me he'd gone out, out to the breakers? I picked up Georgie, who, in the middle of tending to his crabs, looked outraged, then began to cry.

Sybil Partlow. You come up onto this beach *right now.*

She marched out in her flippers, trying to look defiant.

You sit right here and *don't* move.

I charged into the trees, then doubled back.

Here. I ripped open a granola bar and gave it to her. Don't budge.

There's nowhere *to* budge, she muttered. I'm on an *island.*

I carried a whining Georgie through the trees to the opposite side of the island. When we stepped through the palms to the shore, we were hit with roaring wind, the same wind that barely shifted the leaves at the cove. The wind stopped Georgie's crying immediately. The blow always put things into perspective.

Wind, Michael had told me, *wind is free!*

I didn't see him snorkeling at the outer reef. But I did see an *ulu* with two figures in it. I waded out as far as I could, thinking I might ask them, but they were too far upwind to hear my voice. I watched them for a moment, scanning the surface, until Georgie writhed to get down and the two of us slopped back to the beach.

Hey, Michael said.

He was sitting right there, his back against a palm, his flippers stacked beside him.

What the *hell,* I said. Where the *hell* have you been?

What? His expression changed, contracting around my voice. Snorkeling, honey. I've been snorkeling.

Where, in fucking Cartagena?

He lowered his eyes to his sand-encrusted legs, then squinted back up at me. The sky had clouded up with a hazy brightness. He looked uncomprehending. I softened.

Why didn't you *tell* me, Michael? I said. You should have told me. I was *scared.*

I sent Sybil back. Didn't she tell you? I saw you. I thought you saw me.

You *didn't.* She *didn't.*

George squatted down to stare at his father's sandy leg.

Deh, he said. Deh-deh.

That's right, buddy, Michael said. Daddy.

What's wrong? I said.

Nothing, Michael said.

Nothing?

Nothing. I just feel—

Sybil crashed through the palms. She had shucked her swim shirt and stood with her arms crossed over her naked chest, in a huff.

I *told* you not to move, Sybil, I said.

I don't have nobody to play with. *Play* with me.

What, Michael, I said. Talk to me. Are you hurt? You feel what? Sick?

He looked up.

Changed, he said. I feel changed.

February something-or-other. LOG OF YACHT 'JULIET.' Have you ever seen the way water lights up near the break-ers? Because of the bubbles. It's like a night sky during a snowfall. I drifted out today. Far out. I couldn't see anything but the bubbles & my own stark white arms. Couldn't see the bottom. Just some shapes that changed w/ my imagination. Eventually I saw a shadowy bulk below, smooth.

I've already swum over the stern before I piece it together. Foredeck, cockpit. I half expect to see the crew walking on deck, mopping in slow motion. The light gives the whole scene a supernatural glow. Suddenly my heart is pounding. I can't regulate my breath. I have to lift my face and spit out the mouthpiece, kicking to get high enough out of the water, which this far out bites my face with salty chop.

Then I hear voices. Nearby, two Guna sit in their ulu. A man and a teenage boy fishing. They appear to have been there for a long time. But the current does things like that. A shell game of near and far.

The boy lifts a hand and waves.

Hey! I shout. I'm hysterical, relieved to see two real people—my first in days. Hola! Qué tal!

Qué tal, says the boy, wiping his forehead with the inside of his wrist.

The man smiles and just looks at me. I am close enough to see sweat on his temples. Neither of us says anything. He pulls on a rope a couple times, leans over, and checks his pot or cage. I don't remember how to say "lobster" in Spanish. After a while, I realize they are watching me again. I feel an alertness, a reminder of all that I cannot see. Something shudders below me.

I know what it is before I put my mask back in the water. In the valley between the sunken boat and the sea shelf, moving like a corporation of shadows, swim a pod of reef sharks. They pace back and forth over the wreck.

I swim a little closer to the ulu. But I can't look away.

For a long time, I don't.

I sat under the open hatch. On our bed. Frozen. We were back safely on the boat. But I had been frightened. Michael didn't understand. For him, fear was a charge. A confirmation that he was alive. But for me, fear was intolerable. To feel unsafe—intolerable. *Familiar.* Suddenly I realized how insane it was that a woman who felt this way agreed to move onto a sailboat.

The father & son come back in the evening. They spent the day in a hut on Corgidup. I watched them through my binoculars. After they emptied their nets, they disappeared somewhere w/in the island in the p.m. to rest. Maybe they own these islands. But they don't seem to mind us being here. Funny. What would I do if some dude & his family set up camp in my backyard? I'd call the police is what I'd do.

By the time I think to tell Juliet that we have guests, the ulu is already drawing up beside 'Juliet.' The boy holds up something heavy and asks, Piña? I should know the word but I have to lean over and squint. Oh, I say. Do we want some pineapple?

I almost start to cry. You bet we do! Yes, I say. Sí! Por favor. Mucho piña! Gracias, hombre!

I almost go overboard reaching for the fruit. We haven't seen a grocery store in a month, since we left Porvenir.

I ask them if they have anything else to sell. Other fruit or maybe lobster or fish to eat? Lobster, yes, they say. They know the English word. They will be back. Will 'Juliet' still be here?

Yes, I say. We will be here.

Iggi watchee? asks the boy.

The Guna don't have their own word for "time." In order to talk to the merki, to do business with us, they had to borrow one of our words. They point at their wrists. They say "iggi"—Guna for "what"—and "watchee"—Guna for ridiculous merki tool of self-enslavement. Iggi watchee? I am always embarrassed to be asked this question. After the last time, I tucked my watchee under the aft berth mattress.

I grab my empty wrist.

I gave up time, I tell them.

The boy and the man exchange a glance.

Any watchee, I say. All watchee.

They don't try to disguise their laughter. The boy wears a worn tank top but the father looks like he could have just stepped off the green, handsome, and in a collared polo.

I point to my chest and say, Stupid merki.

No, no, they say. Buen hombre.

I lean down into the companionway & holler for Juliet. We've got the engine running to charge the batteries and the girls can't hear in the galley below. Juliet's making paper snowflakes with Sybil.

Can you please come up and help me? I say. I'm dying out here.

When Juliet steps on deck, her turquoise tunic fills w/ wind. Her dark hair thrashes against either shoulder. She is like a fallen scrap of sky. The three of us stare.

I clear my throat.

We have visitors, I say.

Hola, she says, smiling.

She speaks Spanish like a pro, due to her Puerto Rican grandma. Despite the fact that Spanish is not our guests' actual language, it seems to be the best channel for this confab. Juliet talks in Spanish with them & I just watch.

The man and his son warm to her immediately. She presses her hair down with the back of one hand & smiles. In the dusk, she's brown as a nut. Her big eyes are sleepy-looking. Ah, I think, there she goes again, collecting boyfriends. They talk for a while. I watch her.

I know her. I've known her since I was 21. I fell in love with her so hard I shattered some bones. But there were times back in CT when the sound of her voice made my skin crawl. Because every time I heard it, I was getting either instructions or criticism. I tried to stay intimate physically, but it's tricky having sex with your critic. It may feel great but it's just not ultimately in your best interest. I can only imagine what she thought of me.

It hurts me to think of the things we've never talked

about. Look at the care we take w/ our secrets, when we're so sloppy w/ everything else.

The Guna father makes a joke, & Juliet laughs her big laugh. I join in, halfhearted.

You don't need to punish someone like Juliet.

That would be redundant.

I remember the halyard bumping against the mast like the tongue of a bell, and the boat swaying, pushed by the currents and their cross-purposes. It was brightly dark on our bed, the moon watching our nakedness through the open hatches.

Ménage à trois: man, woman, moon.

Making love on the boat lent the love act added closeness. Under the low ceiling, we were nose to nose, many-elbowed. Michael's body was shadowed blue in the moonlight. Already, he was touched with age. Age grew from his ears, fouled his chest hair. But at sea, a little gray seemed favorable. My sexuality had been blinking on and off like a light with faulty wiring for years, *years* after the kids were born. Some days I walked through the world with absolutely no desire, like a doll, and then, as if possessed, I'd be consumed by lust, triggered by something embarrassing like the image of Tom Brady shirtless on the beach, blowing into a conch. That night at sea, it didn't seem to matter how far away I'd wandered or why. It didn't matter how tangled sex was for me on a good day—not under that moon. I wanted him.

He saw me. He bent down. He cheated open my tiny door. And I became like the spirals of bioluminescence you can stir up with an oar in certain dark lagoons.

Feb 15. LOG OF YACHT 'JULIET.' Naguargandup Cays. NOTES AND REMARKS: No more piña, no more naranja, not even any more banana, a pretty boring fruit that sounds delicious right about now. Today we sail to the mainland to re-provision. Sybie & I up early. Feasting on oatmeal boiled in shelf-stable milk. I figured I would take the opportunity to show her how to use the VHF. We sit at the nav station, side by side. Morning blazes through the hatches.

Every once in a blue moon, I say to Sybil, a boat has an emergency. And the crew has to make a distress call. If so, you use this. I hold up the VHF handset. You've seen me talk on this, yes? Yes. Well even though we can't see them, lots of people are out there listening to the main channel.

Sybie says, I already know what to say. Mayday! Mayday! she shouts. We're taking in water! Help!

Shh, I say. Your mom is sleeping. Good start, though, I say. Let's practice. But not with Mayday. You absolutely can't joke around about that.

OK, she says. This button? Yes, that button, I say. Hold it down. Let's see if we can find somebody. Just for fun. Say the name of your boat. You have to say it three times. Then you say, Over.

This is 'Juliet,' she says, into the handset. Over.

You have to say it at the same time you push the button down, OK?

OK. 'Juliet,' 'Juliet,' 'Juliet.' Over.

Very good, I say. Now wait.

We listen. Nothing. White noise fills the cabin.

Oh, Daddy, she says, sighing. There's no one out there. We are totally alone.

I laugh, thinking, God, she sounds just like her mother.

We're just practicing, I say. No biggie. But now we have to wait two minutes before we try again.

OK. She swings her legs violently. We wait.

Then we hear it.

'Juliet,' this is 'Adagio.' Over.

Sybil's face lights up. Hey, Daddy! That's us!

It gets me every time. A response from beyond.

It's a man's voice. Friendly, a little sleepy. Lightly accented.

Sybil screams, Hello, 'Adagio!'

Over, I prompt.

Over!

'Adagio,' I say. This is 'Juliet.' Switch to six-eight. Over.

Sybil and I both stare into the static.

Roger, 'Juliet,' replies the voice. Roger six-eight. Over.

I scroll through the channels with the knob.

If you are signaling Mayday, I tell her, you don't have to switch channels.

But she has already grabbed the handset. Hello, 'Adagio!'

Hello, 'Juliet.' Am I speaking to the Captain?

No! She roars laughter.

You don't have to shout, honey, I say.

My name is Sybil Partlow and I'm seven years old! Over! I'm learning how to use the VHF in case we start to sink. Over!

Hold on, 'Juliet,' the man's voice responds. I have someone you might want to talk to.

Hello? says a new voice.

I prod her. Say something, Sybil.

Hello? This is the boat 'Juliet.' Good morning. Over.

Hello. My name is Fleur and I'm seven years old.

Sybil throws down the handset, runs across the saloon, and climbs on top of the settee. She does a pull-up to peer out the portlights, her bare feet clawing at the bulkhead.

Where are you, little girl? she shouts.

Sybil, I say, laughing. Use the VHF.

She drops, runs back.

Hello?

The other child is laughing, too. What's your name again? she asks.

Sybil. Sih. Bull. Sybil Partlow. From the United States of America!

I'm Fleur and I'm Dutch. Fleeeeer. Do you want to come over and play?

Do you have any dolls? Sybil shouts. My favorite one fell overboard <u>years</u> ago.

I pull up to the house and sit behind the wheel for a moment. It is late afternoon. The topmost corner of the house is lit with sun, like a dog-eared page. I can see the row of arborvitae that line the backyard, also dipped in sunlight. The backyard was the reason we bought the house six years ago. I wanted to try to grow vegetables. There was plenty of room for Sybil to play. We liked the brook at the back edge of the property. All day and night it could be heard gurgling, reciting a watery rosary through the curtain of trees. And because of this brook, there was a surprisingly good show of bird life. I could sit beside the stream and watch starlings bathe among islands of mint.

Now, I drag myself out of the car and gather the groceries. I'm certain I've forgotten many items in the rush to get through the checkout after seeing my friend. The heft of the bags is reassuring. I must have bought *something*.

I walk inside and push off my shoes. My mother sits at the kitchen table, reading the paper. Her hair is wet.

Did you get a bath? I ask.

Mmmm, she says, rising to take the bags. Your friend Alison came over with another casserole, she says.

That's nice, I say.

She left a note.

OK, I say.

Do you want to read it?

No thank you.

She stands next to me at the counter. Let me put these away, she says.

OK, I say.

But then she stops and looks at me. Are you all right? Did something happen at the grocery store?

I look at her closely. How in the world does she know this?

What do you mean? I ask.

Never mind, she says, taking out the groceries. The preschool called while you were out, she says. They say George has a slight fever. They say not to worry—it's very slight. But he may be coming down with something. Do you want me to go get him?

The news hits me hard. I have lost my ability to absorb shock, even the smallest surprise. I'm worried for George, but also I am afraid. Because it means that, per the commandments of the preschool, George will need to stay home from school tomorrow. And I won't have time to sit in my closet. I'll have to move around and appear competent.

I stare out the kitchen window for a moment. I try to focus on the nuthatch that clings to the feeder.

Yes, would you mind? I say to my mother. Could you please go pick him up?

It's what I'm here for, my mother says, reaching for her keys.

I put my hand on top of hers.

I want to thank you, I say.

It's no problem.

I want to thank you for being here. For coming with almost no notice. For, for—I don't know what I'd do—

Please don't thank me, Juliet. Please let's not say another word about it.

Can you "run from your troubles"? Of course not. You run from one kind of trouble straight into the arms of another. But maybe what I didn't know, I mean when I was a kid, was . . . certain troubles are built right into you. I mean contradictions. For example that 99% of the time our self-interests are at odds w/ any kind of social contract. We are hardwired for deceit & treachery but we keep hoping that the ones we love will live safe & innocent lives.

III

Eventually, we'd hit bad weather. This was *guaranteed*, and yet there was something so cheerful about that peacock-blue Caribbean sky, we simply forgot. It was not hurricane season. I conveniently assumed this to mean it would never storm, but rather that cloudless days would be peeled one by one from God's freshly minted pile.

Well you know what they say. It always gets deeper before it gets shallower.

All right, crew, Michael said, addressing us from the cabin top. We have spent a week—or two, or three, we've lost count, actually—in this fair paradise of Naguargandup. We have runneth out of banana. We also needeth propane and gas for the dinghy. And our clothes stinketh and we must findeth some freshwater for laundering—

Daddy, said Sybil with a laugh. She looked up at me, her eyes bright. Daddy said stinketh.

We also must sail the seas to find the Princess Fleur, who wants to play with Sybil.

Yaaay, she yelled. Find Fleur!

But before we departeth, we should say farewell to our favorite island—he turned and, one hand around the mast, made a deep

bow, and I was glad there wasn't anyone else in the anchorage—
Bottlecap Island, he intoned, otherwise known as Salar, or in certain circles, Home Run Island. Maybe it's the water. Or maybe the breadfruit flowers. Something here makes a man kneel at his wife's altar—

It was my turn to protest. Michael, I said.

But never mind all that! Goodbye to all that! Although I will say, I felt very certain of my wife's love last night. Thank you, Bab Dummad, Great Father of the Guna. Or actually I should probably thank a female deity? Nuit? Frigg?

Michael—

No matter, I will die a happy man. OK, crew, here is your safety briefing. Be safe, OK? Don't be a dummy. All right? Kids remain in the cockpit tethered and no asking Mommy to go below for dumb reasons. OK? Now, repeat after me, crew. Goodbye, Salar!

Goodbye, Salar! Sybil and I chanted.

He turned and bowed to the next island.

Goodbye, Corgidup. Even though we never saw one dang pelican.

Goodbye, Corgidup!

Goodbye, Ukupsui. I have no idea what to say about you!

Goodbye, Ukupsui!

Are you ready, cockpit? That's you, Bosun.

Yes! screamed Sybil, shrill as a parrot.

Are you ready, helm? That's you, sexy.

I'm ready, Mr. President, I said.

And are you ready, young George, to—to—stare out into the distance while teething on a rubber giraffe?

He's *ready*! piped Sybil.

Juliet, can you keep the wind slightly to starboard? What's our depth?

Seventeen feet, I read. Eighteen. Twenty-five.

OK, honey, put her on auto for a sec. You can slack the vang and mainsheet.

Can I do it, Daddy?

Stay seated, Sybil, I say. Michael, you've got her whipped into a frenzy.

Michael unwrapped the halyard from the mast cleat and in two long strides placed a couple of wraps on the winch beside me, giving me a lecherous wink.

You're really losing it, Partlow, I said.

He began to hoist the sail.

I need another wrap or two on the winch, darling, he called over his shoulder. Thank you! See, you knew exactly what I meant, Juliet.

To my right, Georgie was strapped into his car seat, talking to himself over the sound of the engine. Sybil, studying her father, was bouncing lightly on the cockpit cushion to my left. The very act of raising sail felt like a novelty to us all after so long at anchor.

Go, Daddy! she shrieked. Daddy's so strong.

Juliet, downwind, please. OK. *Down*wind.

Sorry, I said, squinting. The telltales are right in the sun.

Don't use the telltales or anything, he said. Use your own instincts.

Sorry. Sorry, I said.

He climbed back to the cockpit, grabbing a winch handle.

Stop apologizing, he said, grinding away. I thought you were a feminist.

I ignored him. Should I turn off the engine now? I asked.

What do *you* think? he said. You've got to know this stuff, Juliet.

I don't need to know this stuff, I said. You're here.

What if I *weren't* here?

I stared at him; the idea offended me.

We're in the middle of the ocean, I said. Where else would you be?

Look, cried Sybil.

The mainsail was filling. We all stopped to watch it curl open like a huge orchid, until, taut and bellied, it was still. *Juliet* responded. At the helm, I felt vigorously lifted, beautifully manhandled, like a child on a carousel horse.

I turned off the engine. It was always better to hear the silence of sailing. The silence gave way to wind. Wind, wind, wind. And the gurgle of gentle seas against the hull. Michael cleated the halyard and stood there looking forward, hands on hips, his tank top flapping. I remained at the helm, where, of all places, I was comfortable. Sybil stared backward at Salar, our island, which was quickly far astern. After a while, she took out her princess coloring book and lay on her belly on the cockpit floor with her markers.

We fell silent, nosing into blue water. North, the view opened up. Nothing broke the seam of sea and sky. We confronted a categorical flatness by which we understood the huge distances that surrounded us, even when we had forgotten they were there.

What a boat. When she sails, she <u>sails</u>. She breathes to life. She grips the wind. Then you can feel her dig in. You can feel her shovel the sea aside. Like she's a steam train parting the snow, two tall columns of spume on either side.

A sailor wants to be worthy of his boat.

Watching the surface of the sea is mesmeric. Time stretches. The surface is thrown into shadow or bedazzled by sun. The wind textures the water, rendering it visible. As a gust approaches, you can see it roughen the surface, a stampede of hastening ghosts, footprints skipping over the swells and disappearing just before the cool force of absence blows through you.

I'm going to catch a fish today, I told them.

They ignored me. Michael was reading his *Twelve Bolt Bible* and George was asleep and Sybil was writing a letter to the president.

A nice juicy bonito, I said. Or tuna. Rub it all over with some salt. Garlic. Lots of lemon juice.

We don't have any lemons, Michael said.

Stop talking about *food*, Mommy, said Sybil.

I sighed. To my disbelief, I was becoming a decent fisher-woman. My ability to catch the occasional fish under way was a cause for celebration aboard. Not least of which because Michael and the children liked to watch me wrestle the thing onto the floor of the cockpit: woman versus fish.

What I miss most is lettuce, I continued. I never thought I would crave *lettuce*.

I miss hamburgers and French fries and chicken patties and chicken tenders and pizza and cake and ice cream, Sybil said.

Finally, I rose. I went astern to check my fishing line.

I stopped cold.

A huge, humped cloud loomed behind us. Just an hour before, when I'd set the line, the sky had been blue and uncluttered, with a couple of cumulus tufts sailing away. But as if to assert its very right to change, the sky was now unrecognizable. I stood there gaping, as the cloud covered the sun, casting *Juliet* into shadow.

Michael! I cried.

It's just a squall, he said, suddenly beside me. A thunderstorm.

I stared at him.

You're scared, I said.

She's staring at me like she just realized I am a fallible human being & an inexperienced sailor & is now re-evaluating a long list of assumptions. I'm thinking she's about to lose it. I promised her we'd be safe.

I'm gonna go below and put on my tether and turn on the VHF, I say. I can probably get the sail down before this weather hits.

Juliet says nothing. Her gaze falls behind me, on the kids in the cockpit.

Juliet, he said. It's *normal* to run into squalls. It's strange we haven't sailed through one until now.

But she says, How come we weren't prepared? How come we didn't see this coming? I tell her we are completely prepared (while a fork of lightning cracks astern). We prepared for months before we came out here. But we'd better move along now, babe.

Can't we sail *away* from it? I asked him.
  No, he said. Not now.
  But we could make it to the coast quickly.
  The coast is full of rocks, Juliet.

     And she's like: I want to go toward land!

We don't have time to get there and anchor, honey.

     You don't <u>know</u> that!

Look there, he said, pointing to the open water. We are completely scot-free to leeward. Nothing in our way. Nothing to bump into. No reefs, no other boats. We are in a perfect position. We can just bob along. Boats are *made* for this, he said. We will bob along like a corked bottle.
  I groaned, terrified. A *corked* bottle?
  A bobbing bottle, he said.
  Daddy? Sybil said. Why's it dark?

     I put my hands on her shoulders and give her a friendly little shake.
      I will reef the mainsail, I say. You will get the kids below. You will shut all the hatches and ports. You will make sure there's not a bunch of shit on the counters. We will ride it out. It'll be over in no time. It's a culo de pollo. Short and strong. They happen down here at this time of year.

But I was frozen. Frozen.

Daddy?

Now, Juliet, he said. Do you hear me?

And just then, as if to bring the point home, the rain began to fall.

I throw the mainsheet off the winch.

For some reason, I seated the kids around the saloon table. The appearance of normalcy? I'd given both children a handful of soda crackers and a plastic cup of water. Sybil's eyes had grown two sizes. She stared at me devouringly. We could hear Michael's crashing footfalls on deck. I felt some sense of accomplishment: We'd managed to put away all the crabs' eyeballs, bottle caps, and sea stars that were lying about, which presented me with the possibility that we would be fine because we had followed protocol. Georgie looked from his sister's face to mine. He reached for a soda cracker only to discover the crackers were *marching toward him.* He stared in awe as they jumped, one by one, over the edge of the table and into his lap, followed by his cup of water, which soaked his WHALE OF A TIME t-shirt. He looked at me, offended, but did not cry. Then, like astronauts training for liftoff, we were rolled backward, until we were pressed against the bulkhead, looking up at the galley, and beyond that, through the portlights, the stormy sky. Above the protestations of the boat—the grunting, the squeaking—was the sound we had grown to live by, amplified: wind.

Roaring wind. *Annihilating* wind.

Damn you, Michael, I whispered. Get the sail down.

I heard the contents of the entire cabin shift, unseen boxes and bottles sliding and crashing into barriers. It all held, except for one locker that flopped open and ejected plastic dishware onto the sole. Plus a row of cookbooks and Audubon guides previously tethered with a bungee, which came tumbling toward us, each one slamming into the benches below our feet. Don't cry! I told the children. Don't worry! But they weren't crying. Georgie was lying with his back against the bulkhead, looking confused. I wrapped my arms around him and looked up. The starboard portlights were *underwater*. As if we were videoconferencing with the tortured sea. I remembered the term Michael had used in the past for the boat's heel. He liked to call it *getting tilty*.

Watch out, Partlows, it's going to get a little tilty!

Meanwhile my daughter was climbing *up* the floor of the boat. She moved like she'd done it before, shimmying from the settee to the doorway of the V-berth. She stopped to look back at us and wiggled her fingers. *Come, Mommy!*

Movement in that kind of a heel is a trial. You are pushed down not just by the angle of the boat but the boat's very speed, as if you are in a sports car taking a curve.

Georgie put his arms around my neck. We followed.

Juliet's V-berth had two bunks, one on either side of the boat aft of the bow. The children loved their bunks. Each bunk had a lee cloth, a kind of apron that protected anyone from rolling out, and when the lee cloth was raised, the children made little worlds there. Sybil's was filled with discarded clothes and coloring books and stuffed animals that rolled their plastic eyes with the rolling boat. Both children jumped into Sybil's berth, and just like that, they were cocooned.

I slid down to the floor, my back braced against the bunk.

Breathe, Juliet.

I hung my head down between my legs. The bow of the boat rose—I clung to what I could—hung briefly at that implausible angle, and then plunged, planing down the other side of a wave I could not see.

The one sailor-like quality I had was an immunity to seasickness. I was proud of that. But in the V-berth, bobbing up and down *like a corked bottle,* my effort not to vomit eclipsed my fear of capsize. I fumbled for a peppermint in the damp pocket of my shorts. Head between legs. A corked bottle. *It's going to get a little tilty!* Rain drilled the deck, a sound matched only by the crashing of the sea against the hull. The waves sounded as if they were full of rocks. You think, *There is only fiberglass between us and that?* Michael had placed a plastic cap over the companionway and thankfully he opened this now, letting a column of wind rush down into the cabin. He shouted, cheerfully, Hold on below, crew! The jib is furled already and now I'm going to reef! She's doing great!

I glanced at his dripping hair and forehead. Then he was gone again.

The reef lines are color-coded. Red for the first one, green for second, then blue. But with the rain drilling me in the face I forget which is which. Plus where the hell is the boom topping lift. You've got to kind of squint up into the rain & shake the sheets (must be a better system). I should have secured the topping lift first—now the boom sags. Live & learn. When that is done, I return to the reefing lines. Then I remember red is first because red is for panic. God bless Harry. He said he would find me a boat that was easy to single-hand. I remember thinking, When will I need to do that? Anyway, it takes about a half hour but I get the sail reefed. Then I've just got to trim the mainsail, which means scrambling forward to the mast on the cabin top, which at the moment is like a big tilting Slip 'N Slide, then back to tighten the mainsheet in the cockpit. As I'm on my final pass I somehow knock the winch handle & it tumbles out onto the side deck, where it's stopped by the toerail. I scramble for it on hands and knees. But just as I lunge out of the cockpit, the boat heels again. The winch handle skids all the way down the side deck like a pinball down the chute, then plops smoothly over the transom. Sinking down plumb with suicidal heaviness. To join the blanket of winch handles that cover the ocean floor.

I curse the sea & boats & mankind & rain. I am so wet I can feel water going into my ear canals & up my anus. The boat labors on. She is unfazed. What a boat!

Michael, the boat says to me, sometimes we are sailing and sometimes we are <u>being</u> sailed.

I HEAR YOU, 'JULIET'! I shout into the blinding rain.

I am not unhappy.

She made so many sounds under that kind of stress. You could hear her shifting, groaning, pushing back against the wind. Underwater, her pendulous keel dropped. She straightened up. It was like she was remembering who she was. Recovering her self-esteem. The boxes and bottles shifted again. My body felt just a little lighter.

The sound of waves crashing lessened and I could hear the hum of the engine. Michael was motoring into the wind. Still, the sea gnawed away at us.

Holy mother of God, I whispered, holding my head.

A hand groped for me. Such a small, strong hand. She wrapped it around my neck, pulling me closer.

It's all right, Mommy, she said, from behind her cloth. We did good. We saved *all* the sea stars.

The sea is thrashing. Furious. The sea has lost her mind. Bizarre to see how something so serious & steady turns into a pit of chop. Like there's a million sharks feeding under the surface.

I'm sure I'm not the first sailor to suspect that sinking our boat would make the sea <u>feel</u> <u>better</u>. That swallowing our tiny vessel would satisfy her for just a second.

Then, the wind began to diminish. Light crept in through the hatches. Even below, I could feel the barometric pressure ebbing away, leaving a strange, purged feeling. A hollowness.

The children peeked out from behind the lee cloth.

Hey, I said. We made it through our first storm, Partlows.

Sybil swiped aside the lee cloth and hit the cabin floor. She ran through the cabin and up the companionway, banging on the plastic cap.

Daddy? she shouted.

Georgie climbed into my arms.

Bo go, he said. Deh-deh go.

We picked our way through the saloon, stepping over books and plates.

Air. Sky. The surprise of a cluttered shoreline. A Cessna raced down from the sky to an unseen landing strip on a verdant island off our starboard.

Michael stepped into view. He looked exhilarated.

Can you believe it? he said. The storm blew us right to Narganá!

I stared at him. He stood in several inches of water in the cockpit, his red windbreaker gleaming, his hair mashed to the sides of his temples. He looked as if he'd been swimming with his clothes on. A raised bump shone on his forehead, starting to purple. *Juliet*'s cockpit was soaked. My new cushions were gone. Sybil stomped in a puddle several inches deep.

He stepped toward me, taking Georgie out of my arms.

How are you doing, buddy?

Bo, says Georgie. Bubble good up. Oodle up!

Really? he said. Did you and Bubble go up and down?

Michael looked at me guiltily. How was it down there?

Juliet steamed ahead, toward the marina at Narganá, as if nothing whatsoever had happened. The jib was furled, and the rain made her deck gleam.

It was a little tilty, I said.

Back in Bocas, the night before we were going to sail across the Golfo de los Mosquitos, I learned about the tormentas. I'd spent five or six hours trying to install a new compressor. We were ready to sail, but I kept thinking there was more to be done, that it wasn't <u>perfect</u>. We weren't <u>perfectly</u> ready, so I went to the marina bar to have a beer & try to calm down.

The marina bar was just a square slab of wood lined w/

stools. The bartender was hardly ever there so you could just reach on in and grab yourself a Stag. The night was mild. Gusty, though. Christmas lights swung in the wind. The bar sat on a patchy field some distance from the outbuildings. I grabbed a beer & drank half of it in one pull. Everything during rainy season felt hurried. You never knew when the sky would open up & drill you in the skull w/ rain.

The man appeared suddenly. There were no streetlights. At the dock hung one interrogation-bright light, but then there were just these gaps of night hiding everything else.

Hola, he said, taking a seat across from me.

It was Señor Know-It-All, the bully from the boatyard. I took a long, squinty pull of my Stag before answering. Either he didn't remember making fun of me before or he thought we were cool.

What's up, I said.

You go to sea soon? he said. Your boat look really—he gave an admiring tsk—really good. She a nice boat.

Thanks, I said. You guys did great work.

Yeah, they see everything, my guys. They see every kind of boat. Every kind of problem. He reached down into the bar, pulled out a beer, popped the cap off against the bar. Everybody stop here in Bocas. So people make sure, they ask us. What's going on? Where they are charging you money? Where they pirates? Where you go get stuck? Yeah. I think everything OK with you. Except you rename the boat—

Yeah, you told me that already.

And also, it's stormy season.

Well, it's not <u>hurricane</u> season, I said.

Still storm season, he said. No hurricanes, still storms.

Suddenly, I couldn't stand to sit there anymore. After all that work, I had failed to adequately install the compressor— it wasn't right & I knew it—I had 10 minutes for a beer before I had to get back home to an angry wife & kids w/ rain-induced fungus growing in between their toes. The next morning I was about to sail them all across the Golfo de los Mosquitos.

Thanks again for the advice, I said.

No problem, he said.

I patted my shirt pocket to pay. Nothing. I patted the pocket of my shorts. I had forgotten my wallet.

My friend pointed his beer at me.

Don't worry, he said. Honor system. You pay whenever you like. You pay in a couple years when you come sailing back the other way. Come right out through the Canal and come over here and have a beer. Tell me how it was. Say, What's up? Here, he imitated my voice. What's up? He said again, amused. What's up? Remember me? Dave Cowboy?

For some reason, I found this funny too. He did a pretty good imitation of me, speaking in an exaggerated, frat-boy gurgle.

What's up, he gurgled. Remember me? I owe two dollars for a beer I drink ten years ago!

That's good, I said. You'll have to play me in the movie.

At this, he laughed too, slapping the bar. I think we both felt better.

I stood to go. He looked sad to see me go. It was probably a familiar pattern with him. He wanted an audience so badly but he was such an intolerable asshole nobody would hang around long enough. He stopped chuckling & nodded my way.

So, you going around the world, yeah? he asked, trying for sincerity.

I don't know, I said. Probably not. I only have a year.

Just hanging around the Caribbean? Nothing wrong with that. You a lucky man. You got your lady wife and your boat wife. That why you rename boat. In case the woman leave, you marry the boat.

OK, I said, finishing the last swig, gripping the bottle neck extra hard.

No, en serio. Be careful of storm, he said. Seriously. You could have chicken ass.

Chicken ass?

The storm. Tormenta. Chicken-ass storm.

I started to laugh, wearily now. That sounds—I got to tell you, that sounds funny, man.

Not funny. His expression clouded over. The storm is not funny.

I believe you.

You asshole if you think that funny, he said.

Friend, I said, leaning hard on the counter. I am asshole. Just ask my wife.

With that, I turned away and started my tired march up the hill to Juliet & the kids.

Culo de pollo, he said to my back. Remember.

I waved without turning.

Everybody want to anchor! Don't anchor for culo de pollo. Anchor is worst. Just go in the open. Lots of open. OK?

When I didn't respond, he said, loud enough for me to hear, Hijo de puta.

Why couldn't we ever keep it going, Michael and I? Why couldn't we convert the small moments of success into a season? I look into these windows now, up and down this suburban block. It's evening, but not yet dark. The windows glint, opaque. I can't see in. How do others do it? I hold my breath: The evening is hushed. If they argue, they do so very quietly.

February 17. LOG OF YACHT 'JULIET.' Narganá. 09° 26.47′N 078° 35.24′W. NOTES AND REMARKS: Sitting on deck waiting for sun to rise, trapped on the mainland. All night long me & Juliet have been tossing & turning. We forgot about bugs. Here on the mainland, bugs rule the world. The houseflies are big as prunes w/ wings. They crash against the lockers all night long. But it's the mosquitoes that kill you. The boat has turned into a torture device. Open the hatches = mosquitoes. Close the hatches = suffocation. Open the hatches just a crack = death by disco music. Bum! Bum! Bum!

Bum-da-bum! From where I sit (lying inside the sail cover on the boom) I can hear the actual dialogue of an episode of Law & Order from somebody's house ashore. It's like Sam Waterston is <u>inside</u> <u>my</u> <u>head</u>. I'm in Hell.

It's been a little stressful. We fought. You don't know quite what to do w/ the adrenaline when you sail through bad weather. But the thing about Juliet is she <u>hates</u> being wrong. If she thinks that you've won an argument she keeps doubling back to it. Trying to make connections between the argument she lost & any unrelated thing.

So we're walking through Narganá, which is a real shit town, it's true, looking for provisions, & we're both feeling pretty sympathetic to the people, because they have high spirits, very friendly kids, even the dogs on the rooftops wag their tails. But also they live in squalor, surrounded by trash, empty chicha bottles. Which is just depressing given that their traditional cousins are out at sea living in the wind & talking to their ancestors & ignoring the uaga, the strangers, the merki—us. But these mainland Guna have just given all that up. Their history. Their independence. Their sea.

Sybil & George walk the dirt streets looking serious. I want them to see this. I want them to know how lucky they are to have a big home back in CT. But I am the uaga and it's not my goddamned business what these people do. Honestly you could convince me they are happier than us.

But Juliet has to get into it.

A beautiful island, she says. Except for there's trash all over the place. Toilets emptying into the sea. But thank God there's no government regulation, though, right, Michael? They might not have sanitation, but at least they have their liberty.

(She says this like a dirty word.)

Oh, I say. I didn't realize class had started. Is this Moral Superiority 101?

Very funny, she says.

I pick up Doodle and set him on the other side of a puddle.

I thought we were guests here, Juliet, I say. I didn't realize these people are just our teaching tools. And the poor primitives don't even know it.

A stray volleyball rolls toward my feet. I go over to the game, where a bunch of teens watch me smiling. I lob it back over the net.

Provisions are limited. We round up a bunch of lemons, bananas, & root vegetables, which is a depressing haul. We grab a couple boxes of cornflakes, shelf-stable milk. I buy the kids some shiny Mylar bags of this bright green cotton candy & Juliet gives me the stink eye. We're all pretty bedraggled & the adrenaline is leaving us. Also maybe we miss Naguargandup. Maybe we're starting to wonder if that wasn't just a fantasy. Being there and feeling the way we did. Giving up time.

We find a place that serves Guna bread so we order like 50. Miraculously they also serve chicken tenders. Sybil starts to levitate w/ happiness. Juliet sits there nursing her beer and I think, OK we're good.

But Juliet can't let it go.

She snorts and says, I thought you loved the sea.

What do you mean? I say. I do.

So how do you justify your hands-off approach to taking care of it? Deregulation and all that?

I sigh. Well let's look at your own example, I say. You're upset that their toilets empty into the sea. You want these people to get flush toilets? Flush toilets are huge water-wasters. What they're doing here is "greener" for the planet, you just don't like the looks of it. It makes you feel bad.

It's called empathy, she says. It's called concern. Since when is feeling concern for others a bad thing?

Since politicians prey on it in order to justify taking your liberties—

Liberty, liberty! she says. I have <u>plenty</u> of liberty.

For now you do, I say.

And she just kind of groans.

Mommy and Daddy, Sybil says sternly. Eat your food.

Juliet signals for another beer.

You only talk about liberty, she mutters. You mean your own.

It simply took a long time for our differences of opinion to matter. We were both aspirational white people from frigid, working-class, landlocked towns. Our families were both middle-middle class, on a good day. We both went to Kenyon, for Christ's sake. Our college friends went on to be journalists, lawyers, or well-read businesspeople. There was no reason to assume we didn't vote the same way. But Michael had this way of hiding in plain sight. He didn't like confrontation. So I was totally shocked when he told me who he voted for in '16. His conversion had been so quiet.

You didn't even warn me, I told him.

You wouldn't have left me alone until I changed my mind, he said.

I couldn't forgive him. I really couldn't understand it.

He was such a softie. As a daddy, he was a pushover. Lenient. His children were his little angels. People liked him. Dogs liked him. But as he got older, sometimes I sensed, in the way he spoke, glinting from between his words, a mercilessness. There was an inner chamber inside Michael, where in the inevitable crises of man or nature, he planned to go without us. He loved us, but in "the arc of history," we didn't matter. Not *specifically*. He believed in self-reliance above all. But how does such a man accept his place in a *family*—a loud, disorderly, many-fated whirligig, a force by which each member is alternately nurtured and deformed? I don't think he philosophically approved of families, but he was too sentimental to swear one off.

His most-often cited ideological source was his father, a man who had been the traditional and undisputed head of the family until he died in a car accident when Michael was fifteen, at which point his mother panicked and stayed in bed for a couple of years. No one had ever prepared her for a life alone.

What bothered me most was Michael's loyalty to it, this vision of life that even he recognized was quaint and obsolete. Things had *changed*, the world *changes*. Car manufacturing moved to Mexico. We elected a black man president. Change is constant. How else to read the kicking and screaming except as a collective white-male temper trantrum?

Unlike a lot of people, Michael *understood* history. He knew a lot about it. He'd been the kind of kid who enjoyed reading books about wars and knew the names of every general. He'd wanted to major in history, but in a sacrificial memorial gesture to his dad, who'd wanted him to be a good provider, he majored in economics. And yet, despite his education, despite his knowledge of historical context, he just seemed inexorably drawn back there, to some ambered past. Not because he thought it was better or right, but just because it was his.

I knew he was conservative in his economics. Frankly, I was sure his theories on that score were right. Economics bores me; I'll never understand. But from his point of view, Americans were growing less and less capable of austerity, and self-reliance, and he'd developed this disgust about it all. During the Yes-We-Can years, I had more hope than he did. Me, Nancy Negative. My hope disgusted him too, on some level. My hope was just a symptom of liberal ascendance. He believed that politicians would manipulate my hope in order to take away people's liberties, and that people were stupid enough to be complicit. He was naturally an upbeat person, but the changing tide made him very dark.

Slowly, over the years, without ever really talking to me about it, he developed this sense of persecution. In Connecticut, no one understood Ashtabula, Ohio. No one appreciated its values and its lessons and its past. No one even knew where it was. Michael didn't give a damn about the NRA, he didn't care if someone wanted to change their gender midlife. But he hated liberal "groupthink." He felt like he'd be written off by friends or coworkers if he had the slightest discrepant opinion.

So he dug his heels in, and inched farther and farther away, until suddenly we were standing on opposite sides of an enormous breach.

Liberals love change. Therefore, if you resist any change, you are simply a Neanderthal, & at that point the liberal power structure is just waiting for you to die. What about the possibility that you are a skeptical person who needs to hear a convincing argument before putting your traditions on the line? My God, I remember hearing Bill Clinton talk about NAFTA and me thinking this doesn't smell good. I was 17 years old! I was not even a grown man yet and I saw it coming.

Did I stand up and say any of this during college? No. I was such a pushover at Kenyon. I'd do anything, say anything, whatever was being said or done. Mom said Dad would have been so proud of me getting into a college like that, etc.

I thought the point of college was to take part in inquiry, but I soon became aware that I was supposed to sit there and soak up The Truth. The Truth as decided by some old dudes dressed completely in corduroy. I mean head-to-toe corduroy. How can you act all countercultural when you live in one of those colossal houses on Wiggin St. & you have what amounts to employment for life?

A couple pseudo-conservatives hung around the Econ Department. Otherwise, agreement was total. I got so angry about it later. I'd been made to swallow ideas that worked against my self-interest. Juliet acts surprised. Why does that matter, she wants to know. It matters because fighting for my self-interest is what makes me a rational being. It's everything.

I understand that things have changed since 1776. But read the Constitution, people, that's the seed of our country. What would Juliet think if somebody came along and started rewriting Emily Dickinson's poetry? Adding periods, switching words around . . . She'd start a holy war is what she'd do.

There was this awkward moment at a party in the neighborhood, not long before we left for Panama. I was standing in the kitchen drinking wine and talking to some of the other neighborhood parents. I didn't know them well. I was bored and on my second glass of wine.

The people in the kitchen were talking about a recent controversy at a birthday party. The parents of the birthday boy had told the parents of a party guest that a game of musical chairs was planned. The guest parents had balked; awkward negotiations followed. So-and-so was not allowed to play musical chairs. Several of the parents in the kitchen agreed with the conscientious objector—musical chairs was a traumatizing childhood game. It struck at the heart of the fear of exclusion.

Just then, Michael walked in, holding a Coke.

What's the new forbidden thing? he asked. Kids aren't allowed to play musical chairs anymore?

Too Darwinian, said one of the other dads.

Holy Christ, Michael said with a laugh. We're turning our own kids into marshmallows.

Well, I said. Let's be honest. Musical chairs is really just a drill for budding capitalists. It's about controlling supply. I don't think the world needs more cutthroat capitalist assholes.

There was a pause in the laughter. Michael eyed my drink and doubled down.

Well unless *somebody's* a capitalist, Juliet, you're not gonna have hours of leisure time to surf online for household goods. They won't be *made* and you won't be able to afford them. Oh, and our parents and our adult kids will be living with us, by the way. You'll be supporting them like they do in most of the world.

I snorted.

People can be so inconvenient, I said.

I rolled my eyes at the woman beside me. She looked away. I sensed the tide shifting against me. I took a swig of wine.

I say we should deport them, I announced.

Who? asked one of the dads.

All the children and all the old people. They're a burden on the economy. I think we should deport all Muslims, Mexicans, queers, old people, and children. No—not *all* children, just the ones who don't get a seat in musical chairs.

I laughed, but I was the only one. Michael was looking at me, stony-faced.

You just mock my positions, he said. That's all you know how to do.

I can't *fathom* your positions.

You've always thought of me as stupid. Why can't you admit it?

The room got very quiet. Others shifted uncomfortably, looking for a solution.

I don't think you're *stupid,* I said. I just think you're blind. It's different.

Christ, he said. How can I talk to you? You make me feel like an ant.

He walked out of the room.

Feb 19. LOG OF YACHT 'JULIET.' Puyadas. 09° 48.3′N 078° 51.6′ W. NOTES AND REMARKS: Today we rendezvoused with the yacht 'Adagio.' She was a sight for sore eyes. They raised us this morning on the VHF. Turns out they were a stone's throw away. There are four crew aboard 'Adagio.' Tomas, Amira, & kids Nova (10) and Fleur (7). All Dutch citizens but Amira is Moroccan-born. Tomas is very funny. It's been weeks since I talked to anyone but Juliet, especially a guy. OK to call this a relief? He showed me all around the boat. She's <u>steel</u>. Square portals. And double-masted. Looks like something out of a storybook. I said, Well at least you'll never meet yourself coming and going.

Finally me & Juliet agree on something. We will hang out here w/ 'Adagio' for a couple days.

Only good thing about Narganá was a strong WiFi signal. I finally checked my email on Juliet's laptop. Could not believe the amount of backlog. Almost all from Harry Borawski, who has sent me one email (or more) per day since we left Portobelo. I read a half dozen of his emails, then my eyes crossed & I told myself I'd take care of it at our next port.

I wrote to Mom & Therese too. I apologized for being long

out of touch. I told them about how everyone is doing, w/ special emphasis on the successes of the kids. I didn't mention marital strain—they wouldn't be surprised.

"The world is beautiful," I wrote. "Freedom is possible. Don't let anyone tell you otherwise."

Maybe that was all we needed, some other people to talk to, some space between us.

They were so attractive, these tall people on their strange boat. They stood waiting for us outside their wheelhouse, the wind pressing the fabric of their clothes against their bodies. Ahoy! we shouted.

The little girl strained over the lifelines. *Hoi!* she cried.

Immediately there was a rapport among us I have never felt anywhere but among sailors. I settled with beautiful Amira in the closed cockpit, relishing the ice with which she filled my tumbler, and the heavy slabs of pineapple on a chipped plate. Nearby, the girls squealed. Fleur's voice was high and plaintive, difficult to hear. She spoke in a Dutch-American patois that somehow Sybil understood. Her older sister, Nova, spoke English with Continental clarity. She moved among the grown-ups with her hands clasped behind her like a scholar. What book? she asked, while the adults conversed. Who died? What happened?

I went into labor in the Philippines, Amira was explaining to me. I gave birth in a lovely hospital in Manila for a couple hundred dollars. We set sail a week later. Fleur's known nothing but life on the boat. She is a mer-child. Nova, however, can still remember our apartment in Rotterdam.

You've been everywhere? I asked.

Everywhere? Amira laughed. *Nee.* But a lot of places.

Which place did you like the best?

Amira sighed. Jesus. I don't know. I loved New Zealand. We stayed there for several years. While Tomas worked as a sailmaker. The children even went to school there for a time. Have you ever been?

We've only been sailing four months, I said. Clinging to the coast of Panama. We're not real sailors.

Of course you are!

Michael's the sailor. I'm the tagalong.

Amira looked solemn, so I tried to qualify. Well, I can fish, I said, blushing. And recite poetry. I'm sorry to babble! I haven't spoken with another person like this for months. Plus, you've got this very steady, disarming gaze. Your children are lovely. They don't miss life on land?

I don't know. Nova! Amira called to the girl, who stood nearby on deck. Do you miss life on land?

Nee, she said. Makes me dizzy.

Amira laughed. I think there's no going back, she said. For better or for worse.

Has it brought you closer?

Thoughtfully, Amira smoothed the wrap around her legs.

The children are best friends, she said. They go off in the row-boat for hours together. There is no need to compete for our attention. They have it.

But what about you and Tomas? Sorry. Is that too personal a question?

She was quiet for several moments.

We were very ambitious when we first started out, she said. Marching around the world. Not stopping to linger. Within our first month at sea, Tomas wanted to make a long passage to the Marquesas despite predictions of foul weather. I did not assert myself. Needless to say, we spent days being tossed around like a toy. The children were sick, Tomas was sick. For some reason only I did not get seasick. There was an ingress somewhere. We took on water. I was the only one who could pump. This is true loneliness, I thought. And then I realized that the loneliness was not new at all. That, in fact, I had been lonely for a long time.

Because?

Because my husband and I did not know each other. We did not know how to help each other or work together. And yet our fates were bound. By a *theory.* I mean our marriage. The arrangement was illogical.

Papa! cried Fleur, on deck.

Daddy, look! echoed Sybil's voice.

I saw my daughter swing past the wheelhouse, a baby Tarzan on a vine.

Ah, they are flying, explained Amira.

Flying?

On the rigging. The children fly all day long. How lovely. Look at your Sybil. So *strong*.

Amazing. I laughed. Is that the halyard?

We watched the children orbit the cockpit for a moment, shy in the silence.

When I turned to Amira, she was looking at me. She dabbed pineapple juice from her wrist.

Marriages have failure points, just like boats, she said. You sail a boat through rough weather and the failure points are revealed, yes? Or would you rather not know?

Her gaze was level, kind. I only looked at her.

If you would rather not know the failure points, she said, do not go sailing.

I'm v. curious about how folks stay out here so long. How do they make money? I decided to ask Tomas. He's a sailmaker. He works when money runs out. Amira has a blog. With sponsors & everything. She writes about the cruising life & cruising w/ kids. Some advertising revenue. They make the bare minimum. This is clear. Enough to stay afloat. But they don't care. They genuinely don't want <u>things</u>. Just more time.

Otherwise they are kept very busy by caring for 'Adagio.' Tomas says there is nothing on his boat that has <u>not</u> broken. I ask, What about the mast?

And he says, Great, I guess that's next. Thanks, friend.

He starts joking about how maybe he'll come over & tear our sail in the middle of the night so he can get some work.

Christ, please don't, I say, it's brand new. That mainsail cost me ten thousand bucks.

I tell him, Just between you and me, I am way over budget. I want to make my own decisions but I've got a—there's a guy. A stakeholder. I never should have involved him, but . . .

Tomas looks at me, waiting to help. He's such a good person, I can tell. I honestly think sailing purifies people. There's so much less bullshit.

Never mind, I say. I have nothing to complain about.

You can tell me, says Tomas.

But I don't tell him. It's my own fault, having a debt. I hate owing others. I also hate complaining. Complaining is a form of taking.

Maybe I'll just sell the kids, I joke instead. You know anybody looking for some nice, healthy Caucasian children?

Ha, well there has been a depreciation in value for American children lately. Sorry.

I don't even bristle, he's that likeable.

Nobody understands what you are doing in America. We think you have lost your minds. You were a shining beacon, much admired, but you did not like this? So you decide to . . . what it's called when you pull down the pants and show your . . .

Mooning, I say.

You have mooned the world, Tomas says with a laugh.

Do we have a nice ass? I ask him.

No! Tomas roars with laughter.

Just then I see Sybil swinging past the deckhouse. On the halyard!

Tomas says their kids learned to use the vertical space on the boat long ago. They used to hang Fleur from the mast for hours, while they cleaned the deck or did other chores. People would say, Is she being punished? And they would say, No, no, she's very happy up there.

We watch his older daughter take a turn. She's almost as tall as her mother. She swings out so far it's crazy. I think, I would have loved this, as a kid.

I say to Tomas, These kids are so lucky.

People don't understand sailing families, he says. They think we are dragging the children along. But it would be much easier for Amira and me to live on land and get away from them whenever we like. Send them to school or leave them with babysitters.

Suddenly Fleur and Sybil decide to fly at the same time. They sail across the deck holding the same rope. Screaming. Their skirts whip in the wind & they are laughing.

Careful! Tomas shouts. Don't hurt the Americans. They will sue us!

It's morning. Georgie sleeps off his fever in the next room. My mother has just left for the bus stop with Sybil. Out my bedroom window, I watch them walk away together down the sidewalk. Sybil is wearing her galoshes, the ones that squelch, and a bright yellow jacket. She looks like a swordboat captain dressed for heavy weather. My mother throws her gauzy scarf over one shoulder. The spring wind plays with it. I lose sight of them.

I stand there at the window, looking at the empty length of sidewalk, worrying that I should not have made Sybil enter school so late in the year. But I came back to this town specifically to make things normal.

Normal.

*Nor*mal.

What an abnormal word.

It feels large and fatty in my mouth.

I step from the window. Where was I? Ah, yes, another day to stay alive. To host a pain so large that it crowds out selfhood. To my credit, I have extremely low expectations. I make the bed. Well done! I go to the window to see if my mother's coming back yet. For one dazzling moment, I fear these few minutes alone in the house with Georgie. The house feels huge, absurd. I push open the closet door, sink to the floor upon my pillows, and feel immediate relief.

After a while, the front door opens. My mother shuffles in. I hear dishes clinking in the kitchen. I sit very still and listen to her movements. An hour passes.

I go into Georgie's room to check on him. I lean over his bed and watch him breathe without strain. His face is turned decidedly toward the filmy light through the window. Does he dream of the boat? I touch his forehead. Warm, not burning. His eyelids flutter.

There is a form of dizziness that makes the sailor almost unable to exist on land. The inner ear gets so used to motion that stillness is intolerable. I remember the first time I woke up on land, at a hotel in Kingston after I got the news about Michael. As if it wasn't bad enough to try to figure out how I had gotten there, as if it wasn't bad enough that I had to face that shattering first day as a widow, the room started swinging like a picture on a hook. I clung to the mattress. Even now, as I stand upright, dizziness washes over me. I hold my head in my hands.

Are you OK?

I jump, hand to heart.

My mother watches from the doorway.

You scared me, I whisper.

Sorry. Everything OK? How's George?

Fine, I say. He's sleeping.

I leave the room on tiptoe and close the door behind me. We stand there for a moment in the hallway.

He's always been a good sleeper, I say.

You were too, my mother says.

Was I?

Oh, yes. You could fall asleep anywhere as a child. At the dinner table even. Once, at the beach, you wandered off and fell asleep behind a sand dune. We were beside ourselves with worry. Until we found you there, snoring.

I lean against the wall, remembering with fondness.

Michael never slept, I say. He only needed a couple of hours of sleep, tops. But he never got tired. He was so efficient. When you think about it, sleeping seems so indulgent. I mean, why doesn't the sleeper *produce* anything? Like an egg, or silk?

My mother laughs softly. We hear pistons. The garbage truck is inching up the street.

You shouldn't worry about George, she says. It's just a fever. It must be hard not to worry it's something worse. But it's not. Don't worry.

I look at her quickly. For some reason, this offends me. She has gone too far.

I think I'll lie down for a little, I say.

All right, she says.

At the door to our bedroom, I turn around.

Oh, I say. Today is Sybil's doctor appointment. After school.

You mean the—the—

She can't say it.

The psychologist, I say.

The child psychologist, she says.

Yes. Of course, the psychologist wants to talk to me too. She needs context.

But so soon? my mother says. If you don't feel up to it, Juliet—

Is it soon? I say, sincerely.

I feel like a hundred years have passed since our return.

Our bedroom. Why do I still call it that?

IV

❧

February 22. LOG OF YACHT 'JULIET.' Snug Harbor.
09° 19.66′N 078° 15.08′W. NOTES AND REMARKS: What's
the saying? If you want to make God laugh, have a plan? We
had to leave our friends & keep moving. Our plan was/still
is to take our time heading to Colombia. Stop here & there,
find more paradises & more sea stars & go upriver and see
the cemeteries at Sugandi Tiwar . . . But provisions in Narganá were too thin. We realized we needed provisions ASAP.
Juliet said that soon we were going to start gnawing on the
bulkheads. So we cruised here to Snug Harbor to plan our
first real crossing. To Cartagena. And then? The sound of
divine laughter.

Snug Harbor. I remember standing at the bow trying to read the
water. Knowing that *Juliet*'s keel was clearing the reefs by a hair.
Michael was shouting from the helm. It was always worse when
it was blowing. The wind flustered me.
   What? I screamed. *I can't hear you!*

Anchoring brings out the worst in us. From stern to bow
you've got 40 ft. between you. It's hard to yell w/out sound-
ing angry. Then, as soon as you start goofing up, a crowd
forms.

The sun was high, but there were no bright contrasts on the bottom, only variations on the color brown. That was new for me: mud. *Juliet*'s prow raced along. I could see my own shadow squatting on the bow, trapped in the shadows of rigging like a spider in a web.

> There are 3 other yachts in the anchorage. Despite its cozy English name, Snug Harbor is not a popular stop for foreigners, so it's just bad luck. As me & J argue, each boat empties onto the deck. I guess there's nothing more entertaining than watching a married couple work their shit out in a high-stakes situation. Part of me isn't really here. My head's not in it. My cruising guide is belowdecks. Snug Harbor . . . Did the guide mention a coral shelf to the southwest or southeast of the island? The GPS lags, then resets. No shoals yet. I turn the goddamned thing off.

I can't see the bottom! I shouted to Michael. The bottom here isn't sandy!

What? he shouted back from the cockpit.

I said it isn't sandy! It's muddy. It looks deep, like deep water.

But that's the bottom, Juliet. The depth meter is reading fifteen feet.

How many feet?

Fifteen!

Don't *yell* at me, I said.

I'm not yelling! he yelled.

What about the GPS? I asked. Look at the GPS.

It's useless in a situation like this, honey. It's much better if you—

Damn it.

What?

Reverse!

Reverse, Daddy.

Quiet, Sybil. Reversing!

He kicked her into high reverse. The large coral head just

ahead of us edged farther away, the surf washing over its fat, slippery hump. I could imagine *Juliet*'s keel, blindly trusting under the water.

What the heck, honey?

Well we were a couple feet away from running aground, is the thing, Captain.

OK, we're reversing. Please don't use that term with such irony, Juliet.

Which term?

Captain.

Don't be mean, Mommy.

Stay out of it, Sybil, Michael said. And stop *singing,* please. I need quiet in order to hear Mommy.

I turned and cupped my hands around my mouth. *Use* the GPS, Michael. I am not clairvoyant. I can't *see* these things, I'm telling you. Not against a muddy bottom—

You are more reliable than the GPS, Juliet.

But the GPS doesn't get scared, Michael.

You're saying you can't navigate because you have *feelings*?

I gave a shriek of laughter. Well, if you want to know what it's like to have feelings, I can tell you sometime!

Don't *yell,* Mommy and Daddy, Sybil said.

Stay out of it, we both said.

We looked over at the nearest boat, where several figures sat in a shaded cockpit. We were giving them a very good show.

Hi there! Michael waved.

No one answered. It was a spotless, expensive Beneteau. From the listless, fashionable figures in the cockpit, we could tell it was a chartered boat. The kind where the captain has to wear white shorts and tell stories about surviving ninety-foot waves in the merchant marines. I hated them.

I took a deep breath and stepped onto the cabin top and hugged the mast. Sybil was sitting in the cockpit next to her brother, whispering in his ear.

What are you *doing,* Juliet? Michael said. You've got to stay on the bow.

Listen, I said. We're going to have to get awful close to that boat to get through here. They're kind of blocking this entry. Should we go around? Go somewhere else, maybe?

Michael considered, thrusting her into neutral. Sybil peered up at us, on edge. But I already knew that he wouldn't concede. He'd take us this way on principle.

Ack, he said. We're here already. It's not our fault they don't know what they're doing.

OK, it's definitely a tight squeeze, but do they need to panic? The passengers of the yacht blocking our entry start throwing over their fenders and shouting, Watch out! Watch out! Someone even gets out an air horn and we get a couple deafening toots in the face as we try to thread the needle, which sets George wailing. But I know 'Juliet.' She's slimmer than she looks. I watch my wife on the bow. Something about the screaming rich Americans calms her down. Looking like a conqueror, one foot on the bow pulpit, she lets us come another foot or two toward the yacht, calm as a cucumber. At the last possible moment, she waves me hard to starboard. We're inside the reef.

We dropped anchor in the easternmost area of the anchorage, clearly the rolliest part, because no one else is there. But we were the least popular boat in Snug Harbor, so it was a good match. Then we had to debate which anchor to use for mud. By the time we found a good holding, we were all exhausted. Georgie was crying with hunger and Sybil was sitting below looking out of the portal like a prisoner. Michael had this thing about testing the anchor. We'd set it and check it ten times, but then he'd pull back on it under power, "just to be sure."

Please, let's stop, I said to him. Please. The kids haven't eaten. There's no wind. But no, Michael insisted on testing the anchor. He reversed. The rode went taut, but just as he shifted back into neutral, something gave.

What the hell? Michael hollered. What the *hell*?

Juliet produced an unfamiliar rattle, then she immediately relaxed. The engine was on, but there was no propulsion. The feeling was palpable.

Michael checked the wash. None.

He dove down the companionway and opened the engine hatch. I stood on deck looking at the sky, trying not to think, trying not to worry. We're in Snug Harbor, I told myself. We're snug. I unbuckled Georgie from his car seat and he climbed into my lap. Both children fell silent and watched Michael's movements with funereal gazes. They always sensed when shit hit fan.

Michael came up the ladder slowly.

It's the transmission, he said.

What about it?

Kaput.

Then I remember something: not my first dead transmission. Aside from the Westsail, my dad's one other flourish was the purchase of a 1984 Pontiac Fiero in white. I used to drive it around Ashtabula with my best friend Nate in the passenger seat. The car was a lot slower than it looked, but Dad was so proud of the thing. He told us not to race it. So we raced it all the time. Stoplight to stoplight through empty nighttime Ohio intersections. One night, the Fiero started sticking a little as I shifted gears. Like it was having doubts. Then, as I was trying to gun it from first to second, the gear shift came loose & started flopping around in my hand. Turned out it was the clutch plate. Me & Nate had broken it. So when 'Juliet' quits in Snug Harbor, that's why I start praying, <u>Please</u> let it be the clutch plate. Because it could be so much worse.

It was our hottest day in Guna Yala. There was no breeze in the anchorage, and, sitting in the bald sun, we got a taste of how hot it would get when the Caribbean summer started. Nothing stirred in Snug Harbor. Our neighbors were all belowdecks, probably drinking Moscow mules in the air-conditioning. Georgie played in the baby pool we'd set up in the cockpit so that we could concentrate on worrying. Sybil lay on her back in the shade of the bimini top, not minding the lack of cushions, nibbling attentively on a candy necklace, one of our last items of food. Michael and I sat in the cockpit perspiring, trying to figure out what to do. Midway between ports, we were perfectly stuck.

Oh, great, I said. Missionaries.

What? Michael said, dreamily.

Missionaries. Look.

Because there they were, white shirtsleeves and all, motoring toward us on a dinghy.

Well, this day is just going from bad to worse, Michael said.

Why're they all dressed up? Sybil asked, peeking out of the cockpit.

Michael and I looked at each other. He was wearing his muscle shirt, and his unwashed hair had clotted into soft blond spikes. I was wearing one of his T-shirts over a sarong. And the children, forget it. Sybil was topless, except for some Mardi Gras beads. She was wearing shorts over pants. We had to laugh. I tugged Sybil's shirt on.

Jesus Christ, I said. What a sight we are.

Don't use our savior's name in vain, Michael said.

Hello! called out one string bean of a boy. We heard you are having problems!

Oh, I said. They want to help.

Can we come alongside, *Juliet*?

Uh, sure, Michael called back.

Another boy threw a line and Sybil quickly tied it to our cleat. There were three of them in the boat, nearly identical in dress and buzz cuts. One boy lifted his sunglasses. He looked older than the others, but still very young.

We're based in Playón Chico, he said, just on the other side of Snug Harbor. I'm Teddy, this is Mark, this is John.

We introduced ourselves and explained about the transmission.

Rotten luck to need a repair out here, the older boy said. But you have options. We have a local guy who flies out of Narganá. He could fly you back to Panama City to get parts, if you like.

We were just contemplating what to do, Michael said. We're stumped.

Rotten luck, the boy said again. He seemed genuinely sorry.

Even if I got the part, Michael explained, I couldn't do the repair myself.

The boys nodded somberly.

But you can sail, said another boy, hopefully. I mean, your *boat* is sound.

I looked at Michael, who seemed lost in thought.

The way they used to do it, added the third. Plenty still do. Like the Guna.

My husband's a really good sailor, I said. He could sail us to Cartagena without a motor. It's not far.

Michael looked at me, surprised.

I can fly on the rigging, Sybil announced. Want to see?

Either way, we still need a *zarpe,* Michael said. We can't sail out of Panama without a *zarpe.*

For that you want to go back to Porvenir, Teddy said.

Michael squinted. Why?

The guy at the border of Colombia is a jerk. Excuse my language. They'll give you an exit permit in Porvenir, no problems.

That's a good idea, I said.

Porvenir is upwind, Juliet, Michael said. It would take forever to sail without power.

I shrugged. You'll have to go alone. By road.

Michael scoffed. And leave you guys *here*?

All six of us took a look around at the harbor. Placid and uninhabited. Egrets posed in the trees.

We can give you a lift to Tigre, Teddy said. Boats head to Porvenir all the time from there.

We could keep an eye out for your family, another boy offered. What with little kids aboard and everything.

Thank you, Michael said, looking sad. We'll think hard.

Good. So . . . The boys glanced at one another. Would you mind if we said a prayer for your boat?

Well, Michael said with a sigh. That can't hurt.

Teddy stood and grabbed *Juliet*'s side stay. The three bowed their heads.

O Father, Teddy said.

I slapped Michael's arm. He bowed his head too.

You are always there, Father. For Your love reaches everywhere. Above the clouds, beneath the sea. In the brightness of day and through the dark starry night. I know Your hand will cover me. Upon the heavens, or over bridges, in deepest valleys, rocky cliffs. You keep me safe. You watch over me. I choose to put my trust in Thee.

I looked up, but the boys were still frowning in concentration.

If my boat breaks down, I know that You will guide me, O Father. You will not leave me on the waters alone. You will show me the way forward. I give You my fears and anxieties and You will teach my heart to trust. And in turn, I will love You and spread Your word, O Father. Amen.

Finally, their faces relaxed and they looked up at us. The clouds had passed overhead and they stood amid glittering water. They appeared satisfied, even relieved.

We'll stop by later and see what you've decided. Would that be OK?

Sure, Michael said. We really appreciate your concern. Thank you.

The boys motored off, leaving Sybil gazing at their wake.

What's a missionary? she asked.

Missionaries are people who want everyone to believe in their God. They are here to "save" the Guna.

What's wrong with the Guna?

Nothing is wrong with the Guna.

I believe in God, Sybil said. *I* believe the missionaries.

Fine, I said, smoothing her sweaty hair. We need all the help we can get.

Dear God. Did you know that jellyfish have their mouths in the same place as their anus? Dear God. Did you know that you can change from a girl into a woman but not from a girl into a rhinoceros? We came from the monkeys (as you know). We lost our hair. But if you want to be a rhinoceros you have to wait for the next life. I believe we come alive over and over again. This is just the first life.

O God, are you just in the sky or also in the water? I think the water too. When the boat is going fast I look over the side and I have seen you looking back at me, O Father. Did you find my Baby Nugget, O? She is wearing a red dress and a white skirt and she's got big excited eyes. I don't always tell the truth, Father. I tell the truth but my bones lie. Baby Nugget fell overboard. I should not have been playing with her on deck, O Dear One. Also I pinch my brother when Mommy isn't looking. Dear God the Father. Please protect the China childs in China and the Australia childs in Australia and the Guna childs in Guna Yala and watch over my daddy on his journey, O Lord.

We debated for hours. Whether I should go to Porvenir w/out them. I'd be gone for 2 nights. One to get to Porvenir and then the other to re-provision in Sabanitas.

I don't like the idea of this, I tell her.

You think I can't handle things by myself, she says. You encourage me to sail but deep down you don't really think I can handle things by myself.

I shrug. I don't take the bait. I tell her I don't know which part worries me the most. Once I come back with food & an exit permit, we still have no motor. I will still have to sail to Cartagena w/ no motor. The kind of thing even a seasoned sailor would be nervous about.

She studies me. I've known you for years, Michael, she says, and you've always been able to keep your head on straight. I admire it. But out here, it's more than that. You're a <u>sailor</u>. You understand the sea.

I look over at her. Her cheeks are pink from the last dregs of Narganian wine. Her eyes have a bold, low-lidded look.

She's got her hair tied up in a backward bandanna, knotted at her forehead, like Rosie the Riveter. I stare at her for a moment, trying to recall who she reminds me of.

Then I remember who she reminds me of.

She reminds me of Juliet.

I'll go, I say.

When we lived on the boat, my gift for sleep returned. Long days in the sun and wind left me limp on our berth, lying as I'd fallen, the amniotic swish of the water in my dreams. Meanwhile, Michael's energy reached a new pitch. He seemed to dispense with the need for sleep altogether. In my thick slumber, I would sense him leave the berth. I could hear his footsteps on deck. But the next minute, there he would be again, lying on his side, staring at me.

The night before he left for Porvenir, I went above to find him. I missed his body in the bed.

He was sitting on the edge of the cabin top, his back to me, writing. The wind was strong offshore but the wall of jungle absorbed it. The sky was free of clouds, lambent with moonlight. Polaris shone fixedly over the mainland. I considered saying his name, but I didn't. I considered calling him back to bed, but I didn't.

It's tiring to carry the weight of eternally unsaid words.

They get smaller & smaller. Juliet is holding George in the cockpit but Sybil has climbed up the mast partway & hangs just below the spreader. Juliet waves. She prompts George to do the same but he squints into the distance because he can't see me. The sky is overcast but blinding. I blow kisses. But within seconds of clearing the anchorage, young Teddy kicks up the outboard & I nearly smack my chin on the stern.

I take a seat beside the motor, as if sitting this far astern will keep me closer to Juliet & the kids. When, in fact, as we veer around Snug Harbor, following the shore, I lose sight of them instantly.

My Christian friends exchange me like a package on a dock in Tigre. I thank them & say goodbye & hop onto a dented plancha. I begin retracing my steps. Sailing backward through our journey. Undoing. The motorboat slams westward. We pass Culebra Rock, Spokeshave Reef, Puyadas. Farther on, sooner than I expected, we thread through the Farewell Islands, & soon after that, we arrive at the crowded shoreline of Narganá, where we stop & pick up a crate of coconuts & a dead peccary (the stench makes my eyes water, even after we've returned to our suicidal speed along the coast). I'm relieved when we veer toward the coastline, & I don't have to relive the journey, w/out 'Juliet.' Because the motorboat reveals just how inefficient sailing really is. In one day, I will travel a distance that took us months. And they have been, let me tell you, the best months of my life . . .

Watching the palms & the mangroves & the villages & smoke slide past, I realize that I've found the feeling I came here for. I don't know what freedom is, but I know what it's not. It's not the life we had back home. Years of my life spent waiting to turn right into the vast Omni parking lot, pulling my weight even when bored to tears, trying to be a decent person and coworker and not some boozer or flower-stomper. But no matter what I did, I kept being reminded, by my own countrymen, that I am an exploiter/polluter/oppressor. When, from what I could tell, the rewards of my privilege included awkward networking lunches with friends who'd lost their jobs during the recession, staycations, & the luxury of not getting shot by the cops during routine traffic stops. Had I actually <u>enjoyed</u> oppressing others, had I gotten off on my alleged exploitations, it would all have made a sick sort of sense. But I stopped feeling <u>good</u>. I stopped feeling that I had a potential to <u>be</u> good or noble.

No one out here makes me feel like that. The sea is an equalizer. Anyone can survive & anyone can die. We all suffer through the same weather, not just the sailors but all those who live in fragile housing by the sea. My family & I inhabit 44 feet of space. Other than peeing into the sea, we leave it untouched. We burn less gas than we ever would traveling in a car. At sea there are only minimal rules of coexistence. You stand on or you give way. You keep a look-out at all times. You carry the burden of your own life.

I suspect there will be a time, not long from now, when I will have to realize this isn't real. I'll go back to Omni. Back to the right-turn-only lane. I am overwhelmed, if briefly, with vertigo. At the thought of my blinker glowing in the rain. As if it's the very definition of insanity.

In front of me, a father lifts the tarp he's put over his children to protect them from the spray. The gesture hurts me. I miss the kids.

The guys driving the boat are modern Guna, as unsentimental as any New York City taxi driver. They blow past an old fisherman in his ulu at such close range he nearly capsizes. Their shirts flap arrogantly in the wind.

Red T-shirt. Yellow biplane. Dead peccary. The hills of the San Blas range rise and fall to port. I guess I nod off, my forehead wedged between my thighs.

I wake up surrounded by water. We've taken an offshore passage. Never one that a nervous merki would choose. We are surrounded by blue water in a tin can of a boat. So over-full that the gunnels look level with the water. None of us are wearing life vests. I turn around to see an island in our wake. To other foreigners, it looks like any other island, interchangeable. But I can recognize Salar.

Give me your Jarrito!

Never!!!

Someone shakes my shoulders. I am in the way. A nylon sack is handed down. The boat bobs beneath a concrete dock, dripping w/ seaweed. The sky is dimmer.

Siéntete, the driver says. Sit. He shoves the bag under my seat. I feel the creature in the sack probing my leg. The slow death shuffle of a lobster.

W/out ceremony, we rip back out to sea. The plancha is like a bee cross-pollinating the islands, each one shabbier & more crowded than the next, the closer we get to port.

How far to Porvenir? I shout over the wind. Eh? Says the driver. Porvenir? I say. He shrugs, gestures w/ his chin. I squint to see the flash of glass. SUVs, buses & cold concrete buildings.

Civilization.

The longer we stayed in the remotest of places, the more easily we felt crowded in. I felt it too; we were changing. We were learning things we couldn't unlearn.

Before Michael left, we sailed *Juliet* east of Snug Harbor, into a tiny, empty anchorage surrounded by a collar of jungle, where he thought we'd be safer. I assumed we were totally alone, but moments after Michael had motored off with the missionaries, I heard the splashing of a paddle.

Hello! came a voice. Hello, friends!

It was Ernesto, the *sahila* of Gaigar. At least that's what he told us. There was nothing to suggest that he was or he wasn't. He lived alone in a thatched home just inside the mangrove. I remember his gnarled hand wrapped around *Juliet*'s lifeline, balancing expertly on the seat of his rowboat—a fat old bucket with oarlocks and all, unusual for these parts.

Nobody ever anchors here, the man lamented. It is so shallow. Only special sailors see the way through to the holding where you are. *Juliet!* You are a genius. And you sail with no motor.

Oh. I shrugged. No, the transmission broke. That's why we didn't use the motor.

Excellent! Ernesto cried. You can stay here in Gaigar while you repair.

I looked down at him, a squat old man with bowed legs. His skin was old and sun-stained, but his teeth were bright white. He offered a handsome smile.

Pardon me, *Sahila*, I said, hand to my chest. But how do you speak English so perfectly?

His face assumed a grave expression. No Roman or *gringo* was ever as criminal as the Spanish, he said. No one ever pillaged the earth as well as the Spanish pillaged us. They committed the first ecocide in history. He lifted a finger. Therefore, I refuse to speak Spanish. I will not have it spoken in Gaigar. This leaves English to communicate with the *uaga*. Unless—he smiled again—you speak Guna, my queen?

No, I said. I'm sorry.

Also, he added, I've got a sister in Miami. I learned English there.

The old man turned to Sybil and asked her, Do you want me to teach you how to read?

I *do* already, Sybil said, saucily. I can read any book. I'm homeschooled.

No, said Ernesto. I teach you to read the mangrove. Come visit me later, friends!

Then he rowed away. His shoulders were those of a much younger man.

Been standing in line 2 hrs for my permit. Watching the port captain talk to a local man for so long that I feel like I know him. I watch his expressions. His habit of digging in his ear w/ a knuckle. They laugh, having a great time. Sometimes they even fall silent & look out to sea. Nobody in line says anything. It's like we don't exist. Hey, buddy, I say, gesturing to the line. The guy gives me an ironic salute. We all keep waiting.

This building is as spartan as a barracks. Dogs trot in & out in a line from tallest to shortest. The dogs are more organized than the people. The day turns balmy. Men driving SUVs back and forth to Panama City stand smoking. Finally, I put my pack down and sit on it & write.

I've got to be <u>patient</u>. They are <u>fine</u>.

After our visit from Ernesto, Sybil and I couldn't sit still. Suddenly it seemed unimportant that we had no transmission, and that

Michael was away. We'd been invited to Gaigar! By the *sahila*! Sybil donned her safari hat, tan with a neck flap, packed a butterfly net, her Strawberry Shortcake notebook. I dressed Georgie head to toe, slathered us all with bug repellant, and grabbed our pole—a six-foot-long wooden rod.

By the time we set out in the dinghy, the sky had clouded over. Low, skudding clouds obscured the bottom of the anchorage, but as soon as we passed beneath the first overhanging tree, the water became transparent, revealing a map of roots.

I turned off the outboard and raised it. The absence of the sound left a particular, interrupted silence. We coasted into the center of the mangrove.

Listen, I told the children. What do you hear?

Georgie gaped open-mouthed at the swamp.

I hear bugs, Sybil said.

Bugs whirred around the boat. First, a cloud of tiny flies no bigger than snowflakes. Georgie reached out to grab at a beetle with pendulous legs.

Hands inside the dinghy, I said.

I heared something plop, Sybil said.

We turned to see the ripple on the water.

Something jumped, I said. I wonder what.

We poled past Ernesto's house, the only structure in sight. It was a large, hospitable-looking hut, the thatch roof whispering in the breeze. We saw no movement through the cane walls.

Maybe he's gone out, I said.

Gone out *where,* asked Sybil, staring at the jungle.

I assumed I would be nervous in Michael's absence, but in the mangrove, for some reason, I felt calm. The children and I fell into a peaceable silence, watching the shadows of leaves and seabirds cross the flat surface. What calmed me was the absence of wind. It's hard to find privacy on a boat, but the one presence a sailor can never truly get free of is the wind. Even belowdecks, it whistles, questions, and tears.

The banks of the mangrove formed a solid wall of vegetation. Cool exhalations came out of the jungle when we brought the dinghy close enough. The roots of the mangroves multiplied as they forked outward, diving into the water in huge, complicated knots. Sybil and I made a game of trying to follow one root all the way back to its trunk. We were still doing this when Georgie suddenly pointed into the canopy.

Deh-deh! We ignored him. Deh-deh! he said.

Be quiet, you, said Sybil. I'm *con*centrating.

We nosed farther toward shore, close enough that the vines started poking our hair. I became aware of the snake too late. By then it was overhead, hanging in bracelets from a branch. I screamed, poling the dinghy backward. The snake leered at me and dove into the swamp. Georgie looked on, wide-eyed.

Deh-deh, he explained again.

I put my hand to my heart.

Sybil was rattled. Why can't he just say *snake,* she huffed.

'Nake! said Georgie. 'Nake!

Guess you just taught him how to say it, I observed, heading out into the open water as fast as I possibly could.

The commotion roused Ernesto.

My friends! he said, stepping through the curtain of vegetation, buttoning his shirt. Welcome to Gaigar. Excuse my tardiness.

I found myself grinning. Hello, *Sahila.*

What is the name of your tender? called Ernesto.

Oily Residue, I replied.

He put his hand to one ear.

Oily Residue!

The *sahila* asks for permission to board your *Oily Residue.*

Sybil looked at me and snorted. Why's he talk like that?

He's a chief, I said. He can talk however he wants.

If you bring your vessel to my dock, he shouted, I will show you Gaigar.

I rested the pole across my legs. The old man stood there in a rumpled linen shirt with a blossom through the buttonhole, knobbed legs sticking out through *merki*-style running shorts, his skin cleanly shaved. I realized he'd gussied up for me. My pulse, to my chagrin, quickened.

Georgie stood and charged across the dinghy.

'Nake! he cried toward shore.

Ernesto put his hands on his knees. Did you see a *snake*? Doesn't your mother know not to wander under the fig tree? Watch this.

Ernesto stomped the thin board on which he was standing—his dock, I presumed—and immediately several smaller snakes thrashed away through the sargasso weed.

Cool! Sybil said. We're coming!

He gripped my hand hard and strong, stepped down into the dinghy, and sat beside Sybil. He directed me across the swamp without turning his head. He was probably too old to do otherwise, but I liked to think he was respecting my right to captain my own vessel. Guna women learn to sail in girlhood. I had seen beautiful women with tippy, overloaded *ulus* fitted with sails crossing open water in high winds.

The jungle looks like one but it is many, Ernesto was saying to Sybil. See this plant. Growing from the trunk of palm. No, not that one, this one. See its leaves. Big. Wings. Like stingrays. This is why it is called *nidirbi sakangid*. Stingray fin. This plant cures dizziness. Do you ever get dizzy?

Never, Sybil said.

Or that one. That one your brother will like. *Bachar.* To treat snakebites. Look there. You see that big tree, young man? Leaves like open hands. This is the *beno*. Boil the *beno*, you cure the skin. Look at our friend *ari*. Do you see the iguana, friends?

We all strained to look up at the tree, tipping the dinghy. Ernesto moved to the high side, laughing. None of us could see the iguana.

Ari is very lazy. Some call him branch hen.

Where *is* it? cried Sybil.

So you *can't* read, Ernesto teased her. Not everything.

'Nake! said Georgie.

Your brother has seen it.

'Nake!

Not fair, Sybil said. He calls *everything* 'nake. Oh—she gasped—I see it!

The creature clung lovingly to a branch, shaking its soft spines.

I see what you mean about reading the jungle, I said. You really have to look closely.

The old man smiled, flattered, but did not say more.

We nosed along. The sun slipped to the stern of the dinghy. The children were quiet. Hot, yes, but also spellbound. Until I sailed, I never would have known that children could be so brave. Which is not to say they did not whine at sea, that they did not cry at the worst times, or need their crusts cut *just so,* but as it turned out, they had a deep capacity for witness. In a way that I could not, they *became* the sea, they *became* the swamp. Their experience was total, without footnote. That day in the swamp, I felt unaccountably happy for them, and for myself as a child, because I knew that I must have been that way once too.

I remembered the loss of childhood too well. But I often forgot the long years it was mine.

When Ernesto put his hand on my arm, I had to dry my eyes with my wrist.

Madam, he said, his eyes full of concern.

I'm fine, I said, and placed my hand over his.

Do you ever wonder where school buses go to die? I'll tell you! They go to Central America, where they are tricked out, painted & forced to climb mountain roads picking up anyone w/ their thumb out. When I boarded the chicken bus in Sabanitas this p.m., it was already full. No one batted an eye as I snuggled in w/ 5 sacks of groceries. I could feel the exact shape & cup size of the breasts of the woman standing behind me, but she didn't seem to mind. Then her breasts were replaced by the hard belly of a gentleman who'd given up his seat. Had to struggle not to fall forward into the man in front of me, who stood holding onto nothing like Jesus as we tore through the one-lane roads back down the other side of the mountain.

Small pleasures. The sensuality of clean hair. Waist-high in Ernesto's swamp, where freshwater streams entered the mangrove, Sybil and I submerged our bodies in freshwater for the first time in months. Water cold as May. Beside our pool, Georgie swung from a liana. After months of sprinkling ourselves off the transom with a showerhead, bathing in the freshwater felt religious. We'd become used to having hair stiff with salt. It rested heavily on our backs like saddle blankets. But not that day in Gaigar. In Gaigar, we were clean.

They tell me, No more buses back to San Blas tonight. Ningunos. Portobelo is the end of the line. I find a hostel with a crumbling façade hiding behind a couple jacarandas. OK, I love Portobelo. We spent Christmas here mere months ago. It's just not as close to getting back to Juliet and the kids as I'd like. The front room of the hostel is filled w/ backpackers. Americans. They laze on the couches like invertebrates, the girls' legs spread open & lolling on top of the boys' legs. The boys are so used to this paradise of flesh that they punch their smartphones, ignoring the legs, their biceps shining w/ sweat in the dim light.

As I enter, everyone looks up at once.

Hey guys, I say, putting down my overstuffed grocery bags.

One of the boys gives an ironic salute.

I get a small single room at the end of a dim hallway, painted peach like the inside of a conch. It's early evening. I'm tired. I try to put myself to bed. But whenever I close my eyes, the bed sways. Opening my eyes stops the motion so suddenly that I have to physically brace. The room is too <u>still</u>. Everything is too <u>itself</u>. The bureau is a bureau & the chair is a chair & nothing moves. I sit up, overcome w/ nausea. I crank open the window & dip my face in the air. Some local teenagers gossip nearby underneath the jacaranda. Two girls & a boy, teasing one another, no different from kids you'd find in Hartford. I watch for a while. The boy has his eye on the bigger girl. He keeps glancing at her low-slung jeans.

I get dressed and go outside.

Portobelo is a beautiful, crumbling colonial town. Once important, it is now mossy & forgotten. The Spanish used it as a launching ground to pillage the riches of South America & send them back to King Ferdinand. Shadowed ruins of the Spanish fort remain on the hillside. After we survived our first overnight sail across the gulf from Bocas del Toro, we made landfall here & the kids played on those old cannons for hours.

Hey, I say to the teenagers, half out of loneliness. Teléfono, por favor? Teléfono público?

The big girl turns & looks at me, w/ the adoring smile for the boy still on her face. I almost catch my breath. She's radiant, standing there against the cold, weepy walls of the conquerors.

Por allá, she says, her smile dimming.

The phone is obvious, just on the other side of the small plaza.

Muchas gracias, I say.

I stand in front of it for a moment before dialing. It's evening in Connecticut too. He picks up, fumbles the phone like an old man would.

Hello?

Hello? Is this Harry? It's Michael Partlow.

Michael Partlow, Harry says. Where the hell have you been?

In Panama, man. Just where I said I'd be.

I've been trying to reach you for two months—

You'll never believe it—

I wrote emails. Called you a hundred times —

Get this. The SAT phone fell overboard. Like hours into our first sail.

Harry says nothing for a second.

I'm at a payphone in the middle of nowhere Panama. Harry?

I'm here, he says finally. How's the boat?

Beautiful.

How does she sail?

Oh, she's very balanced. Besides, it's so calm down here. My seven-year-old could sail her.

(Pause.)

That's good to hear.

She's a wonderful boat.

Well that's great. You're going to make a bundle on the resale.

I look across the plaza. The kids are still there, eyeballing the world. Now another couple enters, novios. Dressed up for each other. Combed. Serious.

I'm getting attached to the boat, Harry.

He says nothing.

You should see her, I say. I've fitted her with a new mainsail, new wiring, new paint. We lost a couple cockpit cushions in a storm but otherwise she's—

She's a great boat.

She is.

But she's not yours, Michael. She's mine too. Remember?

I laugh, nervous for the first time. Well, ours. She's ours.

I wouldn't press the point, Michael, if I had been able to <u>talk</u> to you. This is a fully wired world. You could have sent me an email. There's WiFi at every damned port. It's not possible to disappear anymore.

That's not how you talked when you were trying to sell me a boat, I point out.

You work in insurance, he says bitterly. You're supposed to be predictable.

Well I'll buy you out, if the arrangement upsets you—

That's not what I—that wasn't the—

But I hesitate to give cash to you right now, I say. We spent so much in Bocas, getting her ready. And now—

What?

A new transmission. Possibly.

There is silence on the other end. The teenagers have turned to look at me. It's as if they can smell drama.

Look, Harry says. There's no need to make any decisions

right now. We've got our agreement. And you've got your good life and very nice home. Which you put up as equity if there was any default in the loan, you remember. So. When you are ready, any time before your year is up, sail her back here, let me resell her at a profit. I get my money back and give you what you paid <u>plus</u> what you put in. Don't you see I'm trying to make you a bundle? I had a guy come in just yesterday from Greenwich, looking for a boat like 'Windy Monday.'

That's not her name, I tell him.

What?

I renamed her. She's the 'Juliet.' And don't tell me it's bad luck to rename a boat. I don't give a shit.

OK, OK. I'm not trying to rile you up, Michael. I just wanted to make sure you weren't going to slip away with our boat.

You just said disappearing was impossible.

She's <u>our</u> boat.

We are co-owners. But <u>I'm</u> the Captain, Harry.

Yes. You are the Captain of—what's she called again?

'Juliet.' She's the 'Juliet.'

We were dressed and waiting. I wore a white sundress with spaghetti straps. The evening breeze rooted in my skirt. Sybil hung out over the lagoon on the bowsprit and peered toward Gaigar. Ernesto was coming for dinner.

Is Daddy in Porvenir now? Sybil asked me.

I hope so, I said.

Will Daddy get a new transmission in Porvenir?

No, Peach. We have to sail to Cartagena for that.

She seemed surprised—aghast, her hair falling into her eyes.

We have to *leave* Guna Yala? she asked.

You don't want to leave, Sybil?

Ever, she said.

Ever? You mean you don't ever want to leave *Juliet*?

I don't want to leave *Juliet* ever.

Really? You don't miss home? I asked. You don't miss Audrey and ballet and your own room? Or Grandma visiting, stuff like that?

She stared at me, trying to remember. I saw her expression soften.

I *do* miss Grandma, but—

Deh-deh, sighed Georgie.

He's coming back soon, Georgie.

Sybil grabbed the halyard. She pattered across the coaming, then took a slow, meditative flight around the mast, landing back in front of me.

Where will Daddy stay tonight? she asked.

In a hotel in Porvenir. At least, that was the plan.

Can he call us on the VHF to say hello?

They don't have those in hotels, Peach. That's for talking ship-to-ship. And remember, our *real* phone fell overboard. So . . .

Sybil drew her long hair behind her ear. I had not seen it so clean and silken in months.

Sybil sighed, pressing her cheek against the mast. I *do* miss Grandma, and I miss my room. But I *don't* miss Audrey. Audrey cheats.

Well, sometimes even friends disagree, I said. People are complicated.

I like the sea, Sybil said. I agree with the sea.

I like the sea too, I said. I'm trying to learn not to be afraid. You're never afraid?

She turned and scanned the view, her bare shoulder blades lit up with a golden last light.

No, she said, and I knew it was true.

Georgie pointed.

'Toe! 'Toe! he cried.

He'd spotted Ernesto astern, rowing toward *Juliet* from the direction of the village.

Hello, *Juliet*! the old man cried. *Bienvenue!*

His voice echoed in the jungle. A troop of white-faced monkeys cried in response.

Ernesto threw his painter on deck and Sybil tied him to *Juliet*.

I offered my hand, but the old man had already stepped out of his boat and onto the transom. Sybil tugged on his shirt.

Guess what, she said. I speak Guna.

He laughed. The *merki* children know more about Guna Yala than the Guna.

By the time the transaction shook out, it cost a little more than I estimated. OK, a lot. OK, I was dead wrong about most of it. I didn't factor in the costs of the surveys, the repairs, the permits, the upfront money for the slip in Bocas, everything else but the boat. I'm <u>never</u> that guy. Head-in-the-sand guy. The one who rents a slip for his 40-footer only to be told the boat is 44 feet in <u>overall</u> length, at which point he has to admit to his wife that he simply had not understood the acronyms on the listing sheet. I work in insurance. We are detail people. I guess I just fell in love. It doesn't help how we gender the boats <u>she</u>. In love, I behaved toward the boat just as I'd behaved when I met Juliet. I knew she was smarter than me, and I also knew she was half-crazy. I knew I couldn't "afford" her. Meaning, I suspected on some level that I would never be a satisfying husband to her, but I did it anyway.

Have I lied to her? Sure. I lied to her the moment I represented myself as someone she could count on for a lifetime. How would <u>I</u> know?

She told the same lie.

How could she know she would stop loving me?

I don't know. It's too much to ask. We come from nothing & return to nothing, but in between we're supposed to lead lives of grace and courage?

Read those trees, Ernesto said to me, pointing. Those two leaning over the water.

I laughed. Is this a test?

Yes, he said.

The evening was quiet, some birds mewling in the trees. Georgie was asleep in his berth, and Sybil drowsed in my lap. The old man and I sat in the cockpit, drinking warm after-dinner whiskey from Michael's "medicinal" flask.

That's a palm tree and—I tried to remember—a fig.

The palm and the fig, he said. Very good. In the jungle, as you know, my queen, everything fights for light. Do you see how the fig is climbing up the palm? Using the palm to get closer to the light? As soon as the fig succeeds, the palm will fall into the water, killing both the palm and the fig.

It made me sad. The parable of the fig and the palm.

Were you ever married? I asked him.

Was I, Ernesto, married?

Yeah.

Of course! What do you think? I had a queen of my own! Do you know that in Guna Yala, when two people marry, the man must move to the island of the woman? And so I did. Years later, when my poor wife left this earth and went to our Father Bab Dummad, I returned here to Gaigar.

Did you get along well, the two of you? I mean, what did you fight about?

Fight? Ernesto looked at the sky. I didn't trust her people, he said. Her people were sick with money. They sold anything they found. Sacred things. They taught their children Spanish. They are Western, her people. We fought about that.

Ernesto sighed heavily. In Guna Yala, we do not study our own language anymore. That is considered "dialect." We force our children to study Spanish. The mother tongue is replaced with Spanish. To help the little Indian become *less* Indian. Why should the Gungidule study Dule, they say, if he already speaks it? Well, I say, why do the great universities of Spain have Spanish departments? Look at me. I must teach *merki,* because my own people think I am crazy. I am not crazy. I am Ernesto, *sahila* of Gaigar. I am no *cholo.*

What does that mean, I asked, *cholo?*

Cholo is a civilized Indian. Ernesto will not be *cholo*-nized. I will never be tired of being an Indian. The *uaga* will keep coming forever. Let them come. I'll never be tired. I'll never stop being crazy Ernesto. You want erotic salsa show? Good. Be a *cholo*. You want to kill all the turtles and sell them to the *uaga*? Good. *Cholo*. Without your soul you are a comedian. I laugh at you, even though you think you laugh at me.

He stared hard into the distance.

I used to tell my wife this, he sighed. But she went to Bab Dummad without ever understanding. Now there will always be a misunderstanding between us.

Sybil murmured in her sleep. I smoothed her hair.

My husband and I are very different, I said. We keep arguing over and over about the same subjects. We argue, but we never change each other's minds. We only get farther apart.

I took another swig. *Juliet* swung slowly on her anchor.

He says it's our self-interest that keeps us alive, I said. But if that were true, we'd be better off alone, right? But that's *not* true. The solitary animal dies faster.

Ernesto closed his eyes, listening.

Ah, who cares, I said, and drank again.

I was about to walk away from the deal. The rational part of me said there wasn't enough $ to go around, not w/out selling the house. I could A) buy the boat outright and have no money left for repairs or expenses, or B) take out a loan on the boat, which would mean the hassle of another mortgage, interest, payments from abroad . . . Selling the house was out of the question. Juliet wouldn't even rent it. What if we wanted to come home early? Hedging your bets is expensive. But I didn't walk away.

I was in the car. I was <u>in</u> the car, about to drive away. We'd spent months looking for the perfect boat, Harry & me. Paging through binders at our picnic table. Debating over grinders at the sandwich shop next door. I was beginning to think we were doing it for sport. Maybe just to be together. He seemed like a lonely guy. And me, I had no dad. Harry was nothing like my dad, I'm not saying that. My dad was fit, & vain about it. Harry wore what looked like free shit he'd just taken out of a box, crisply folded sweatshirts. My dad was lively, always up for a laugh or a good story. Harry seemed too tired to laugh. His past hung back there like smog. All Harry talked about was sailing. He understood life via winches & cleats.

But being around him . . . I don't know. Maybe I missed the physical fact of a dad. Maybe I just wanted some old man to care where I was.

Harry had his hand on the top of my car. (I remember now w/ some bitterness.) Like he was trying to keep me from leaving. Weekenders were pulling into the marina w/ coolers. He leaned down & he said, Michael, I will tell you honestly because you've been honest with me, that what you want is a holy human right, and you shouldn't just give it up.

I humored him. I said, What right, Harry?

The right to feel the burden of carrying your own life. Just you and your family and your boat. No crutches, no excuses.

I almost laughed. Who the hell did he think he was? At the same time, I was in total, giddy agreement.

You stay here and you might just give in, like everybody else. To your dependence and your entitlements. Then you're just another placeholder.

We both stared out at the water. You could see how swiftly the Connecticut flowed only when you saw some brave soul being swept by in a canoe.

If you were my son, Harry said, I would tell you to go. Go. And that's the honest truth.

When I reminded him that I was 20K short, he said, Hell, I'll <u>give</u> it to you. I'll pay the difference. You just have to agree to bring her back here in a year. Sail her up here. I'll resell her for you and I'll get the loan back and we'll both make a bundle. Or worst case, break even.

I looked up at him. All I had to do to get my boat was make a lonely old man a promise that I'd come back & hang out w/ him again.

Do that, and I get my dream.

Except for a couple of trips to the grocery store since our return, I have not driven a car in eight months. Now that I am blazing down Main Street via a gentle pressure on the gas pedal, I realize that driving is not the kind of thing you want to think too hard about while you're doing it. The double yellow lines mesmerize, the margins between them and danger on the roadside are infinitesimal. One spasm sideways and you exit this mortal coil. The wheel of a car, unlike the helm of a boat, is so sensitive. You could spin *Juliet*'s wheel all the way the hell around before having any impact on her direction. And with the distant coastline in sight, sailing never feels particularly *fast*. Yet any yahoo is allowed to speed sixty-five miles an hour or faster in a car, and the world blurs by like a drunken memory.

Up on the left I see the big red doors of the old Church Basement School. Across from that, the library where we used to spend long daytime hours spanning the oeuvre of *Clifford the Big Red Dog*. Farther on, toward the highway on-ramp, the grocery store, the shoe repair store, the fire department . . . I hold on to the wheel, trying not to let my attention wander.

Maybe my mother was right. It *is* "too soon."

Driving, psychologists, talking, any of it.

I glance into the rearview mirror.

How are you doing, Peach?

Great, Sybil says, automatically.

Her hair, which was neatly braided when she left for school this morning, has loosened around her face. Her eyes look blank, her face heavy. I have picked her up directly from school for her appointment with Julie Goldman, doctor of pediatric psychology. I used to joke with Michael about how I would someday be able to call myself a doctor. I'd be very useful in a literary emergency. *Stand back—I'm a doctor of letters!*

It's OK if you are not doing great, I say. I can handle that.

Her eyes meet mine in the mirror. Ideas brine in her consciousness.

I *am* great, she says at last.

That's great, I say. We're almost to Dr. Goldman's office. If you have any questions about what's happening, you can ask me. OK?

She turns and looks inquiringly out the window, raising her eyebrows.

She pauses, then seems to forget.

The thought of navigating traffic into Hartford made me anxious, so I chose a practice in the outer suburbs. After one exit on the terrifying highway, we slide down the off-ramp and back onto a slower, two-lane road, and travel through colorless neighborhoods until we reach the nondescript office building. I pull in to the parking lot.

Here we are, Sybil, I say.

I smile. Simultaneously I see my smile in the rearview mirror.

Warm, sincere—it shocks me.

Turns out, Dr. Goldman is a woman just about my age. Wearing a loose blouse, stretchy pants, and a long, complicated necklace, she's hipper than I thought she would be. She smiles tolerantly, projecting the endless patience psychologists need to wait out layers of denial. She also looks slightly apologetic, like she's sorry, but she's going to have to crack your psyche like a nut.

I attempt to smile back—difficult. I feel enormously jealous of her self-possession. I envy the way Sybil warms up to her, touching all the dolls and puppets and art supplies that Dr. Goldman keeps in bins below the windowsill. At the same time, I feel relieved for Sybil, who has noticeably perked up. It is not "too soon" for Sybil to talk about what happened. Tears bite my eyes, so I try even harder to smile. The effort has distracted me, and I do not hear Dr. Goldman when she directs me toward the waiting room. She has to say my name several times.

Mrs. Partlow?

Yes?

Now I'd like some time with Sybil. Just the two of us. I'll come get you in the waiting room just as soon as we wrap up.

I like Dr. Goldman, I trust her immediately, but as I look around the waiting room, I am unsure if I can bear the next thirty minutes. First of all, there are no good magazines. I pick up an issue of *WebMD*. From behind it, I observe the only other people in the room. A man and a woman sit side by side, their expressions identical. Their eyes roam the room, unfocused. They do not touch. They are both dressed nicely in business casual. Finally, the woman's eyes meet mine, and I offer my rictus smile.

How do you know if the distances between a man and a woman are those of gender or of personality?

Once, when we were arguing, I remember shouting at Michael, *Your lack of emotional range makes me feel lonely!* And he shouted back, *Then go marry a woman!*

It had been such a nasty argument. But now, sitting in Dr. Goldman's waiting room, it makes me chuckle. Good one, Michael! The woman and man both cut their eyes my way.

Today, Sybil and I are going to tell some made-up stories, Dr. Goldman had explained to me, when I sat trying not to cry. Sunlight fell upon Dr. Goldman and Sybil through the large, clean windows. These stories will help me get to know Sybil, she continued, and will also help us develop a language, if you will. So that when we start to talk about real-life events, we will have some metaphors at our disposal. Stories are just kind of a way *in*.

Oh, I had said. That sounds fun.

Sybil nodded from her beanbag.

Sybil's got a great imagination, I said. Then, helpless to stop myself, I babbled on: She tells *endless* stories. She'll start in the morning and still be telling the same story when I tuck her in. She's my little Scheherazade. But you know, anything to avoid going to bed! Of course, sometimes I wish she could be a little more concise. By the end of the day, it's death by one thousand *cutes*—

I grimaced at Dr. Goldman, who had smiled back patiently, but did not laugh.

All right, Sybil. Well, here we are. We get some time to sit and chat about things. In this room you are invited to talk about *anything* you want. Wonderful things, or things that scare you. I'm a listener. Your mom tells me you like to tell stories. That's a fun way to get to know each other. Would you like to tell me a story?

A story about what?

About anything in the world.

Anything in the *world*?

Yes. Anything you like.

OK. Once upon a time there was a cow but the cow didn't make milk, she made juice. Then she met a fairy named Juice. Her hair was made of laundry. No, wait. Once upon a time there were a *bunch* of fairies. Their names were Cathy, Jill, Junis, and Blatch. They lived inside of a circle. A big, pink circle . . .

[. . .]

And then what happened?

[. . .]

Sybil?

What?

What happened next?

Nothing. Nothing happened next.

V

⬦⬦⬦

Feb 25. Snug Harbor. NOTES & REMARKS: Thank God.
Made it back. Never been so glad to see those suckers in all
my life. Lined up on deck a ragtag crew. Doodle w/ his messy
face & Bosun saluting, dressed like a hobo. Juliet leaning
against the forestay watching me w/ private smile. OK I will
take it. I will try and be worthy of it. Thank you, God.

The fig and the palm.

It wasn't always that way.

Even when there wasn't enough light.

Winter in Boston with no money. Making the best of it, plan-
ning for the baby. Making thrift seem sexy, this was the price
of walking the Cambridge streets where my poetic heroes had
walked. This was the price of not having to live somewhere stupid, like Connecticut.

Then she arrived—a dollop of life. We brought her home,
droopy headed, draped over the shoulder, diapered and zipped
to the neck. We made nervous jokes. We put on funny accents. *I
sink it iz time for un diaper change.*

I wasn't, to my embarrassment, a natural. From the very first
day, I had to *learn* to be a mother. I had to learn not to be afraid
of my love for her. Because love is tidal; it goes out, it comes in,
it goes out. I hadn't known.

Gradually, this movement stopped scaring me, and instead

rocked consciousness to sleep. When austerity measures were taken to cut down heating costs, the baby and I kept each other warm under the blankets. I padded around the apartment in my robe and slippers, excited, like I had a houseguest. I don't have much of a singing voice, but it turns out motherhood opened a trove of lullabies in my memory. Where had they all come from, and how did I know every word?

After one single week off, Michael went back to work at Bingham & Madewell. I didn't mind. I had my *baby*. I studied the clarity of her skin, the angelic amnesia in her eyes. She had the perfect heft, a weight for which there was no worthy metric. I counted her digits aloud, in made-up languages.

I believed that motherhood would allow me to finally cease construction on my heart.

I would finally be able to take the scaffolding down.

And then she started to cry.

Like, *all the time.*

I've <u>tried</u> (to be worthy). But when you are handling a big problem you don't always pick the right solution first. When Sybil got colic in Boston, we had to get out of there quick.

I'd read about Milbury in a magazine, one of those magazines that rates everything. "Best Small Towns in the U.S." I thought, Connecticut, sure. I could vaguely remember a glittering shoreline out the window of the Vermonter, marina after marina, tiny bridges, clam shacks, libraries, & me thinking, Wow, people <u>live</u> here? Like, permanently? That's what I remembered about Connecticut.

But, you know, we don't really "remember."

We cherry-pick the past.

For three months that winter, crying was what our beautiful baby did—with dedication, like it was her part in a war effort. We went out sometimes, when I was on the verge of insanity, which was all the time; we went out all the time, in January we walked the rock-salted paths of Harvard Yard, in February we sloshed through winter runoff, in March we traced the swollen Charles; we were tailed by our pitiful reflection in the storefronts, and only very occasionally did my ears prick up to hear a unique sound, the sound of not-crying. The intervals of not-crying were so brief that I never had time to reach out for assistance, or to make even the most casual friend.

Plus, Michael was gone *all the time.*

Plus, he did not understand how wrenching the sound of a baby's misery is.

It was like my anciently injured self crying out for help and nobody coming.

Again.

Plus, the extension for my dissertation was coming to an end and my mind contained not one single thought about female confessional poets of the mid-twentieth century.

Plus, it's possible we had stopped loving each other.

(Though this seemed like the least of our problems.)

I was genuinely surprised that motherhood didn't heal the wound.

In fact, the wound was worse. Because I was faced with the possibility that I was going to offer no better mothering than I had received myself.

A career reading poetry—I think *that's* what I'd always wanted. I wanted to sit in a corner somewhere quiet, licking my finger and turning the whispery pages of manuscripts. When I think about this fantasy in which I am reading poetry somewhere quiet, and I poke around its edges, I find no husband, no children. I am entirely alone. I am safe that way. The poetry envelops my life. I *am* the poetry.

> I was sure moving out to Milbury would be a magic bullet & fix everything, so when it didn't, I felt more powerless. Started staying up late looking online & stumbled on the

philosophy of survivalism. I got these catalogs. I would pore over them w/ more energy than I gave my Omni reports. The stuff you could buy, to ensure that your family would survive large-scale disaster. Fascinating. <u>Anything</u>. Barrels for capturing rainwater. Seeds. Radios. Bows & arrows.

When Juliet got pregnant w/ George, I signed up on a lark for a Wilderness First Responder course at the Litchfield Nature Center. That's where I met this guy Don Alley.

Are you prepared? Don Alley asked me.

Prepared for what? I said. Is there an exam?

I looked around at the group. We were in a class of 6. 3 males & 3 females. Standing there in the shade in our middle-aged shorts & big knees.

No, said Don. Prepared for social and environmental collapse.

I got this for myself as a birthday present, I said.

Happy Birthday, Don said.

So what are you preparing for, exactly? I ventured to ask.

Most of us here are prepared for anything, Don explained. You name it. Drought. Flood. Asteroids. Although personally I think the most probable scenario is that once we are fully digitized in every area of our life, someone will shut down the internet. Everyone will panic and turn to violence. We'll be like babies being weaned cold turkey. But not me, Don said. Not me and LeeAnn.

We watched LeeAnn single-handedly drag Isaac onto a gurney. Isaac didn't scream like the rest of us when we had to be the victim. He moaned like a woman in labor. He was totally unwilling to cheat by inching in the right direction. He was just two hundred pounds of dying weight.

He's really good, I said.

He's the best, Don said.

Then Don turned to me and said, very intimately, So we know people are already living like primitives. I mean modern people. A guy in Syria, a pediatric dentist or something, with kids, he's already living in a bombed-out version of his life. He's living like an ancient person <u>now</u>. Chopping up his furniture and making fires. Depending on himself. Spin the wheel, and that's you.

I looked over at him through a cloud of gnats. He seemed to hear my thoughts.

Rescue? he said. By whom? Superfuckingman? By the West? You know what Obama let Assad do? ANYTHING HE WANTED. This is Obama, who won the Nobel Peace Prize? Remember the Superdome? Holy shit. Satan couldn't dream that stuff up. FEMA sends you to the Superdome and you're robbed of your baby formula at gunpoint, then raped. Democracy? We kick our democracy around like it's a <u>football</u>. We're too barbaric to be democratic. All we ever do is argue like conjoined twins who can't stand each other. So you're a privileged white man, anointed from birth to prevail? Good for you. In the next life, you'll probably be reincarnated as the seventh daughter of a farmer in Eritrea. THIS is where you find yourself, through no fault of your own and certainly not to your credit, but it's your life. Me and LeeAnn didn't have kids. I think it's unethical to have kids at this stage in history. But I take care of my mother. I've got a generator for her dialysis machine. A cellar full of food, water, seeds. The whole spread. Am I happier? No. I think happiness is an irrelevant metric at this stage in history. FUCK happiness. But am I afraid? No I am NOT afraid, Michael. I am prepared.

Well, meeting Don Alley had an effect on me.

Historically, in me & Juliet's marriage, I'm the sane one. Juliet's the poet, the hothead, the crier. We used to fight about it, how even-keeled I was. Like it was a liability. She'd say, It's not fair, it's not fair, you're so <u>invulnerable</u>.

But after my First Responder course, after George was born, when I started to talk about leaving Omni, when I started to talk about the boat, I bet she missed that old invulnerability . . . I loved the kids. I love them so damned much. But once we had two, it seemed like they were always toddling toward busy roads & otherwise tempting death. When bored, they were like raccoons at night, just tipping shit over to see what would happen, playing in the ash can, or putting pennies down the steering wheel column. It's like they were hazing us. To see how much stress we could take.

I read an honest-to-God parenting book a coworker lent me, said it had helped save his marriage. I didn't remember telling him mine needed saving, must have been obvious. This book explained how important it is for kids to be brought up in a strong marriage. This book said that kids should take a backseat to the marriage, because that lets the kids know that they can't destroy the very mechanism that keeps them safe.

The child is trying to destroy the marriage, but it's a test he hopes to fail.

If I understood the book correctly.

As for the slow progress of my dissertation, I thought the move to Connecticut would help. Less maneuvering and less striving. No more dragging strollers up historic stairwells. Michael had easily found a job working for Omni, an insurance-company-cum-city-state in a corporate park just outside of Hartford. He talked up the regular hours, the company gym, and it touched me to see him try so hard to make it sound great.

We found a solid white house with all-new systems, smack in the middle of a crowded, children-rich neighborhood near a man-made pond. It was strangely easy to surrender the charms of Cambridge for a large, turflike backyard, complete with vegetable garden. Behind our house in Milbury is a swath of undeveloped land where we roasted marshmallows over a rustic fire pit. You could hit the house with a stone, but it still felt secret and faraway. Plus, what with all that suburban square footage, I now had an official study. Bright and square. Not too big or small. Michael did his DIY magic—built-ins, light fixtures. We put far more work into that room than we did into Sybil's nursery, which assumed a beautiful Scandinavian austerity on its own.

Maybe I tried a little too hard with the study. Because I kept thinking it needed something else. A rug. A different rug. More photos. No photos. It took me a long time to realize that what that study needed was *me working in it*.

And yet. After two years away from the dissertation, I didn't understand it anymore. I didn't remember what my point was. I'd take out my manuscript when Sybil was at nursery school and sit there trying to decode the first page. But I literally did not remember it. I didn't remember it mattering. So instead, trying to achieve in *some* area, I became a ninja of procrastination. Give me a delay tactic, I mastered it. I formatted and reformatted my indices. I changed fonts. I moved my desk closer to the window. I debated changing topics. I tried writing longhand. I prayed. Tried kombucha. Sponge-painted the half-bathroom. I bought a pack of cigarettes. I moved the desk back to where it had been. I envied. I hungered. I missed my daughter, who was being cared for in the basement of a church *so that I could finish my dissertation.* Nothing worked.

I'd gone intellectually dormant. OK, OK, not ideal, but not permanent. I could ask for another extension. I was still nominally enrolled in graduate school, and I could make it over to Boston if I needed help.

Connecticut is very peaceful, I wrote my adviser. *I was just chatting with the ghost of Wallace Stevens. (Kidding!)*

The flip side to my new life was: No more standing in front of the open refrigerator at night, sobbing. No more bondage to five hundred square feet. No more fear of dusk. No more beating my head with my own fists in order to restrain them from hurting my own child. No more bargaining with God in the bathroom.

My ugly angels were more comfortable in Milbury.

More space for their molting wings.

Sometimes, I missed Juliet, even when she was right there.
Don't know when this missing feeling started. When she was pregnant with Sybil, she was gorgeous, just <u>colossal</u>. I was so proud to lead her around by the fingertips as she

swayed around town. I cried when Sybil was born! I plastered my office at Bingham & Madewell with photos of this little bald, cross-eyed person. I literally became a better man.

But still, I missed Juliet.

We met senior year at Kenyon. A friend of mine was in a play. I went to see it. The gods smiled, I sat next to Juliet, who was eating a package of Red Vines & laughing w/ the boy on her other side. We'd never spoken, but after a semester of sitting across the room from her in our Ethics class, watching her take endless notes, I'd imagined talking to her many times. When I was actually faced w/ her, the real, live Juliet Byrne, all I could think of to say was that I hoped it didn't sound too weird, but did she know that she made a little circle w/ her mouth when she was concentrating really hard?

She stared back at me. The lights went down.

Then things got even more awkward. Turned out, my friend's play involved him pantomiming having sex w/ a horse. Naked. I mean, there he was, standing onstage, in front of me, his cock in the stage lights. He wasn't a close friend, really. The point was, he had this whole other life I didn't know about. A life in which he stood onstage showing the world his cock. And nobody else seemed to mind. The others in the audience watched him. They were moved. To them, his cock was just part of the play. His cock wasn't important except that it was part of the play.

I'm not sure what it says about me, but the whole thing made an impression. I mean, I was about to graduate. But where had I been? Hanging around the Econ Department, clinging to the lifelines, agreeing w/ everybody. While other people were gathering in theaters & basements & cafés throwing off their fetters. Juliet made an impression on me, in her stupid coat & her bangs so blunt they looked like she'd gone at them with a handsaw. She laughed when she thought something was funny, even if no one else did. She was something else. Literally. I mean something <u>else</u>, not a "girl" or a "girlfriend." It's like she was impatient w/ all gamesmanship & was just like, listen—yes or no.

Ironically, I could understand Sexton's poetry even better when I was kept from writing about it. She was, after all, a suburban housewife, with two little children and a husband who frequently traveled for business. She plonked away on her poems while her children listened to records.

But how could I explain this to my adviser back in Boston? Especially after my second extension passed, with no results. That I loved poetry. I loved its density. Its suggestiveness. The shadows it cast. I loved the trance it put me in. I could feel my brain stretch when I read poetry, my preconceptions literally cracking up like ice in spring. When I read poetry, I had no body. And for somebody like me, this was a particularly welcome relief.

My adviser, however, would have been horrified that this was all I could come up with. *Love? Trance?* She was clearly awaiting the death of poetry with great excitement, so that she could autopsy it and publish the results.

Nobody had told me, back when I was a star undergraduate in the Kenyon English Department, that loving poetry functioned in inverse to the ability to finish a dissertation about it.

Juliet let me take her out sailing once back then. On a small keelboat I rented for the day on Lake Erie. It was very choppy, just like I remembered. She kept shouting questions over the wind. Are we going to tip over? Are we going to drown??? Juliet has a strong body, so even though she never sailed, she looked like a natural pulling in the lazy sheet . . . I could only stare. Gobsmacked.

When we were docking, she jumped off the boat first. I thought she was running away. I shouted after her, When can I see you again?

Are you kidding? she shouted, reaching back for the dock line. You'll never get rid of me now!

During those first years in Milbury, those baby-versus-dissertation years, the only thing that could truly exhaust me—the only thing that was as crazy and disorganized as I was—was the internet. I relinquished golden hours of scholarship to reading online consumer reviews for products I had or was considering, until I would feel an irresistible urge to add my opinion, and to watch the *likes* add up, until I could no longer ignore the fact that more people would benefit from my opinion on an acrylic throw blanket than would ever benefit from my thoughts about confessional poetics.

I think that was the beginning of the end for me.

> Who knew that, years later, I'd come home to her lying on the floor, crying. What's wrong? What's wrong?
>
> I don't know.
>
> Sybil standing in the doorway. Is the baby OK?
>
> Yes, yes. He's asleep in his crib.
>
> Sybil kneeling down, patting her shoulder. It's OK, Mommy. Do you want an ice pack, Mommy?
>
> We got her into bed. I fed Sybil dinner, read to her, tucked her in. Then this voice in my head says, Hey, maybe you're the problem, that ever occur to you, Einstein?

Could I decide that rejecting my literary studies was a matter of principle? After all, some of the poems I pored over were solipsistic, artistically undisciplined, occasionally whiny. Was my primary subject, Anne Sexton, even a good poet? This was debatable. Her subject was herself—her own desire and her own madness.

And poetry, what did it *do* for anyone? Could a poem dig a hole or heal a wound or bake bread? The creation of art is predicated on an unconscionable looking-away, even if for the small duration taken to create it. As Theodor Adorno put it, *To write poetry after Auschwitz is barbaric.*

I would stop loving poetry. This unseen self-deprivation would be my protest.

That's about when I started going to the marina. Once or twice a week. In the middle of the workday. I was just there to hang out w/ a 60-year-old man w/ a hard gut, but somehow it had the whiff of the illicit. I'd come up w/ one excuse or another. My team leader pretended not to be irritated, because irritation was not part of the corporate culture at Omni. But soon we were having some pretty tense meetings. Arguing over small, irrelevant things. Maybe I wanted her to fire me so I could finally have my excuse to go sailing.

I used to look at Juliet at night while she slept. How many times I almost woke her up to tell her everything. I didn't have the balls. I guess, in the end, I was afraid to talk to Juliet.

How could a grown man be <u>afraid</u> to talk to his wife in the privacy of his own bedroom, you ask?

It's like a sailor who doesn't tell his shipmate that water is pouring into the hold.

Then I realized nobody gave a shit what I did, one way or the other.

Should I have tried harder? Been more honest? A better communicator? Sure. But listen, part of the problem with Juliet is, she's really exacting. As hard on others as she is on herself. And very hard to argue with. All that unused academic training. I couldn't talk to her when she got all wound up. When she got wound up, she was like John Calvin at a poetry slam. My <u>wretched</u> insensitivity <u>inflamed</u> her! My actions were <u>indefensible</u>! She couldn't <u>bear</u> my <u>indifference</u>! I wanted to be, like, Juliet, do you even remember what we were talking about? Because I don't. And if you think those words have a place in some stupid argument about how we take care of our comfortable home or our healthy, appropriate children, you need to get out more.

Can you talk your love away?

Because I love her & I think somewhere she still loves me.

The truth is, we just can't get the timing right.

We can't seem to love each other in the same way at the same time.

I shut the logbook.

I step out of the closet, blinking, and try to come back to this world, this room. From the light, I figure it's one or two in the afternoon. George returned to school today, his fever having been one of those things.

Just then my mother walks into the bedroom carrying a basket of laundry.

Oh, she says. You surprised me.

I'm sure I look strange to her. Standing in the middle of the bedroom. Standing there, doing nothing.

I thought you'd be in *there*, she says, glancing toward the closet.

Oh, I say. Yeah. I needed a break.

I realize I am still holding the logbook. I put it on the night-stand, and I sit down on the bed.

I see my mother glance at it.

That's Michael's logbook, I explain. About our trip. And other things. It's more of a diary, actually.

Oh, she says. And you're reading it?

Of course I'm reading it, I say.

She nods, unsure of what to do with the basket.

I stretch out my hands to take the basket from her. But some-thing in the plaintive gesture breaks me. I put my face in my hands and I sob.

My mother drops the basket to the floor.

She grabs my hands and pleads, Juliet, what *happened*?

This is torture, I want to tell her. It is a torture I'm not sure I deserve.

(But then again, I might.)

Poor Juliet, she says, as I weep into her shoulder. Oh, my daughter. I wish I could take the pain away.

We sit on the bed. I lean against her.

You don't have to talk about it, she says. You can just cry. Cry all day if you need to. That's right. That's right.

For example, back in CT, I'd watch her across the yard, gardening, & something in me would just kind of . . . roll over. Melt. She used to swear at the plants as if they could hear her. She'd bend over those plants in some charitably short shorts, threatening them, not a strain in her posture or bend in the knee, & my pulse would start flying, because she is so real & so well-made & she is my wife, my Juliet.

Then she'd walk toward me. I'd be full of this feeling & about to tell her, when she'd say something like, Goddamned poison ivy. She'd shake a fistful of it in my face. I must have asked you a hundred times to spray this shit, Michael!

The spring days are getting longer. A hint of celestial lilac outlines the houses across the street. I stand looking out the bedroom window. The streetlight clicks on. Its halo, empty. Waiting to be stepped into.

Below, I hear the lilting of Sybil's voice as she asks my mother a question. My mother's deeper voice coos an answer. Their talk is birdsong. I mean, just tone. And there's George too. Clumsy squawking. Soon—any minute—I'll go downstairs. I'll say, Wow, what a wonderful painting, Doodle. You got a Fab Tag in school today, Sybie? That's *super.*

Any minute, I'll do that.

Gambier. January. You'd die of hypothermia without those lampposts they placed all around campus. They lit your drunken way through winter.

I do *what* with my face when I'm taking notes? I asked the boy standing in front of me.

You make this—he rounded his lips, and then reached up to touch them—this little O. Like this.

It was winter, very cold. I wore a man's coat I'd bought at the

Gambier Salvation Army. The friends I'd gone to the play with had wandered away, laughing at me over their shoulders.

I raised my eyebrows.

It's not a criticism, he said, blushing.

I stared at his practical coat, his neatly laced New Balance sneakers.

Wait. You *watch* me during class? Do you think that's OK?

No, I don't watch you the whole time! I just check for you! Like, is she still there? Good.

Why should that matter to you?

I don't know! the boy said, laughing. I'm just a stupid kid from Nowheresville. Clearly an idiot! I don't know why you matter to me.

Ju-lee-*eh*-et, my mother calls from downstairs.

Coming, I say.

VI

It's a new day. I'm putting on a scarf in front of the hallway mirror. The scarf is silk, a bold fuchsia. Michael brought it back from a business trip several years ago. I never found the occasion to wear it. Well, until now. And of course, now it's terribly inappropriate.

My mother walks out of the guest bedroom, rubbing her eyes.

I fell dead asleep, she says. Is it already time for the bus?

Yes, I say. I was going to let you sleep.

She blinks at me. One side of her hair is flattened.

Are *you* going to the bus stop? she asks, incredulous.

I thought I would, I say. I thought I *should*. Try. Go out and face people.

She looks around the room, licking her lips.

Well, sure, she says. I bet that would mean a lot to her.

I see her glance at the scarf.

Self-consciously, I take it off.

Pink washes me out, I say.

I hand the scarf to her.

My mother stands there holding it like a pelt.

Were you reading Michael's journal again? she asks.

I shrug. The clenched smile appears. Jack-o'-lantern.

I was wondering . . . My mother shifts her weight. I don't want to give unwanted advice, but maybe you should put the journal away? Just for a little while. Until you feel stronger. Ready.

But I'm getting to the best part, I say, before I can stop myself.

The best part? She squints.

Of the story, I say. The best part of the story. Which just so happens to be the worst part of my life.

I don't believe you need to *read* that story, Juliet. Do you?

I sigh. You ask good questions, I say. But I really should head to the bus stop now.

One more thing, she says.

I wait, my hand on the doorknob.

My being here, she says. I want to stay. I will stay as long as you need me. But promise me you'll tell me if you'd rather be alone. Just tell me. Under the circumstances, I wouldn't take it personally.

My heart pounds. The truth is, the possibility of her leaving hasn't even occurred to me. I know she has her own place—an apartment in Schenectady, not far from my childhood home and her best friend, Louise. Even though I've never seen it, I can picture the art on the walls, the succulents on the windowsills. I can picture my mother going busily in and out of the front door, retired but living carefully, on very little. Volunteering at the Boys & Girls Club. Visiting ignored New England museums with Louise.

Juliet? my mother says. Have I upset you?

The sensation is familiar. Reminding me of what? Then I remember.

The thought of my mother leaving feels like being out of sight of land.

February 27. HAPPY DEPARTURE DAY FROM CREW OF YACHT 'JULIET.' Port of Snug Harbor. 09° 19.66'N 078° 15.08'W. Time: 9:15 a.m. Course: NW. Wind: SE 10 knots. NOTES AND REMARKS: Full battery power. Running lights functional. Hatches secured. Sheets cleared. Below Bosun and First Mate are practicing engine check. I let them do this because engine does not matter because does not work anyway! Am reluctant to delegate anything this morning as don't want any misgivings about little screwups that end up in crises in the middle of the Gulf of Urabá. J seems sad, so I ask her what's wrong. She says she has misgivings. That's just great, I think. I give her a gentle punch in the arm and tell her we can do this. I program our course into my pal GPS. Back in CT when I dreamed of this, I saw myself sitting w/ paper charts and calipers. I've grown up these last couple months & part of growing up means using all available technology. I check the weather for the millionth time. Fair, fair, fair.

Only needs to hold for 2 days. But still I'm jumpy.

Georgie falls into my lap.

Ready, Doodle? I say. Next stop, Cartagena.

It happened without our noticing. We were so preoccupied by the newness of sailing off the anchor, the sound of the sails and the rigging, which were so much louder without the engine, without the *possibility* of the engine, that none of us looked backward until, without fanfare, the coast had vanished.

Then there were no landmarks, no beacons, no buoys, no docks, no masts, no rooftops, no *ulus,* no cliff sides, no hills, no islands, no fires, no smoke, no sounds, no shapes, no forms in any direction . . . only a lunar absence of mankind. Three hundred and sixty degrees of water.

But like I said, there is no such thing as separate "oceans." There is only one endless, undivided sea.

The lack of anything to look at was like a form of blindness.

This is <u>it</u>. This is what a life <u>is</u>. A journey with no signposts. The seas roll out in every direction. There but for the grace of God

I had to shut my eyes, the view almost hurt. I tried not to imagine us from above. A mere accessory. A little spangle on the sea.

go I

For a while, privately I'd wondered if who I'd become in recent years—skeptical, anxious, angry—was who I really was, or rather the warped effect of a deforming history.

Free. I'm free.

But at sea, like the scholar who pens her last note, I had nothing keeping me from answering that question, nothing standing in the way of self-knowledge. There was only more and more horizon, empty in every direction, an absence of interference, a vista without mediation—pure, terrifying selfhood.

February 27. LOG OF YACHT 'JULIET.' From Snug Harbor. Toward Cartagena. 09° 53.5′N 077° 47.96′W. Time: 8:15 p.m. Course: NW. Wind: SE 5 knots. NOTES AND REMARKS: My first night watch under way. I've never been so aware of nightfall as I am on deck tonight. I watch the east give light to the west & the west give darkness to the east. There is no struggle. For hours I watch the sky trade light. I feel like I'm being let in on something. Watching endless spaces change. You would think this would get boring but it never does. You merely start to think like the sky does. In slow explosions. Tumbling & changing w/out resistance.

Sybil would like me to note that we were just greeted by a huge pod of dolphins. They followed us halfway into the Gulf of Urabá then vanished. Now we watch several mammoth tankers moving way out in their shipping lanes. Running lights hard to distinguish from low stars. You can find companionship in weird places out here. Just now a little seabird came and rested on the stern pulpit. We tried hard not to scare it, but soon as it could, the seabird popped up to the spreader, opened its wings & was swept away.

I tell Bosun, This is it. This is sailing. What do you think?

I love it, she says.

Not a soul in sight. Just us and the sea.

Juliet moves about below as if she is in a cabin in the woods. She is getting George ready for bed. The boat is filled w/ light. A room moving across dark waters.

George was the only one among us who remained clean while we were under way, because he could still fit inside the galley sink. That night, I sponged him with bubbles and I dried him with a towel, all the while steadying myself against the roll. *He* didn't know we were out of sight of land, *he* didn't know we had no motor. I envied that. I tried to be cheerful, but I was scared.

That's when I felt them—there in the middle of the sea— the presence of the ugly angels. The cold wind of their rustling wings. The wan, uncompassionate expressions they wore from their rafters. They came, I should have known, whenever I was scared, insecure; they fed on my shame.

Leave me alone, I said.

Georgie, fingers in mouth, looked at me.

Not you—

I hugged him tight. Then I lowered him into his bed.

When I stood up, I hit my head on the shelf over his berth. Hard enough to see stars.

I would never learn. I would never, ever learn.

Christ. Goddamned Juliet. Can't get on the damned <u>team</u>. Sybil & I are in the middle of a game of checkers when a strong gust tilts the boat. I hear Juliet thump around in the head. The checkers slide off the cockpit table. Sybil scrambles after them.

Sorry, hon! I shout to Juliet. Did that knock you over?

She shouts something back that I can't hear.

It's much more difficult to gauge the wind out here w/out the normal markers. It's not just the lack of a shoreline. The sea itself is different. So massive. It gives no signs. There's some communication between the wind & sea that is too private to understand.

I bring the boat closer to the wind & trim the sail. She evens out.

Crap, Michael! Juliet calls from below. The kitchen sink is filled with seawater!

And I'm like, Did you close the seacock on the sink drain through-hull before we left?

Did I close the seacock on the what?

I guess not, then, honey. Well, wait until it drains out. Or have Bosun help you bail the sink. OK?

Bail the <u>sink</u>? she shouts back. With what?

Listen, Juliet, no offense, but I'm trying to sail the boat up here.

No shit, Michael!

Mommy! Sybil says. That's potty talk.

My wife's face appears below, framed by the companionway. Her look is dark and accusatory.

Sorry to bother you with domestic matters, she mutters. <u>Captain</u>.

I clutch the wheel for a minute. I just stand there, in the cockpit, surrounded by the sea. Then I don't know what happens. I march over & slam my hand on the cabin top. Below, staring into the sink, Juliet jumps.

How about this, I say—<u>you</u> come up here and sail this boat. And <u>I'll</u> bail the sink. <u>I'll</u> make fucking sandwiches and <u>I'll</u> cut fucking snowflakes.

Daddy! That's potty talk.

Juliet looks shocked. She comes to the foot of the ladder.

Don't swear in front of Sybil, Michael.

Don't yell at Daddy, Mommy.

Juliet gives Sybil a pained smile. Sybil, honey, why don't you go listen to a bedtime book with the headphones?

And Sybil's like, No thank you.

But I can't stop. Why can't I stop?

This is the real thing, Juliet! I shout. We are sailing with no fucking power. Excuse my language, Bosun. You have to change your attitude <u>now</u>.

Juliet climbs halfway up the ladder. Where is this coming from, Michael? Are you mad because I left the seacock open?

No. I don't care about that. I've made a hundred mistakes. I want you to <u>sail</u> <u>this</u> <u>boat</u>. For once. To <u>try</u>.

Why, Michael? She's got tears in her eyes. Why does it matter to you so much?

Because you've got to fight back, I say. That's why.

And then I say the thing I shouldn't have said.

For years I've been watching you be a victim. The things that hurt you happened <u>years</u> ago. But it never gets further away for you, Juliet. It never gets further away!

She stares at me with disbelief.

You know why you talk about equality all the time? I yell. You want everybody to be equal so you can never be called out for your mistakes! If everyone's equal, it covers up any personal shortcomings. Like your <u>endless</u> dwelling on the past. Your <u>endless</u> excuses for putting things off. You'd probably say it's all a result of gender oppression. But no! I think you <u>love</u> your <u>pain</u>. It's your <u>poetry</u>.

Juliet looks back and forth from me to Sybil.

I can't believe you'd say that in front of—

Christ, I say, finished. I'm sorry.

Daddy, Sybil pleads.

I'm <u>sorry</u>, I say.

In front of—

I'm sorry, but it's getting gusty up here and I'm . . . Juliet. Juliet!

But she has already disappeared below. I hear our berth door slam.

Shit, I say. <u>Shit</u>.

I lean out over the stern, clutching the rails.

FUCKING COCKSUCKING GODDAMNED BULLSHIT.

I turn back to the helm.

Sorry, Bosun. I just had to get that out.

It's OK, Daddy, she says, but she looks pale.

I take deep breaths. I check the tension in the sails. I check the chart plotter. But I'm shaking.

There's no signal for the weather app, but everything seems fine.

Fair, fair, fair.

What can I do? he used to say. *How can I help?* How about you put your finger in the dam? How about you let me take one shower without turning off the spigot to hear the screaming of children? And if you are not capable of keeping the children from screaming, of saying no, of capping markers, of slicing strawberries the way they like them, or applying sunscreen or bug spray, or coming home on time, or understanding my feelings, or asking me about my work or my dreams or my disappointments, could you at the very least *try* to imagine what it means to be me?

The thing I realized then about men is, they are willing to become stupider in order to avoid feeling stupid. Sensing themselves outplayed in one realm, they develop new, unrecognizably stupid heights of stupidity—a metastupidity—which they wear like a banner, as if being stupid were a strategy, as if it were the plan from the get-go. Their stupidity, they claim, is a necessary tactic used to inure themselves to female intelligence. They have no choice but to become demonstrably, sublimely stupid.

Belowdecks, I threw my face into the pillow and sobbed.

I know, I know. What was I thinking? Not only am I an asshole, but also a shit captain w/ no crew.

But I honestly don't know what happened to the Juliet I sat next to in that dark theater so many years ago. Whoever that girl was, I <u>liked</u> her. She was weird, you know, sloppy and loud, but she was also a fighter. Man, she was pissed off. I knew right off the bat that I would never fully understand her journey, but I loved her enough to go along on it, wherever it led.

I knew about the stuff that happened to her as a kid. I always tried to keep it in mind. But it was the life that came <u>later</u>, after graduate school, after Sybil—domestic life—that was like quicksand for Juliet. She couldn't handle it. I mean, just basic life problems. The less she did, the less she seemed capable of. Atrophy, that's what it felt like. Once I got a frantic call in the middle of a meeting. I stepped outside to take the call. Juliet smelled gas in the house.

Why are you calling <u>me</u>? I said. Call 911!

She'd have these bursts of clarity, of being her old self, & she'd come into focus again. Juliet's always lived in her head. Way the hell in there.

It must be a hard place to find your way out of.

I'm here, I'd say to her in the middle of the night. Look where we are. Look what you have now. All that is over. All that is behind you.

I woke to the sound of the halyard slapping the mast. The berth was dark, the hatches closed. A breeze came down the companionway. Where was I? I felt alone to the point of vanishing. I pressed my hands against the portlights. The black sea rose and fell. I checked my watch. Three-thirty. I peeled off my sweaty tank top and felt my way into the head. There I confronted myself in the harsh light. Lips swollen from crying. A sunspot developing on my left cheek. I brushed my bangs with my fingers. I peed. Splashed water on my face. Sweatshirt. Windbreaker. Harness.

Maybe I'm heartless. Maybe I am literally handicapped.

A man with a heart would never have said those things to her, knowing what she'd been through.

What I don't know about sailing could fill encyclopedias. But I'm cautious, & I'm handy, & I'm respectful of the sea. I can solve problems, & I can stay calm. I've led us this far w/ only a few snafus.

But my wife? W/ her, I'm all thumbs. Juliet is the unreachable waypoint.

It's very beautiful, you must understand, at night on a boat. When the sky is clear, the moon is as bright as a muted sun. You can read the face of a watch. You can apprehend the expression of a person clear across the boat. The moon flatters the sea. It electrifies the spindrift. It animates the clouds, riming their humped edges white. In its lambency, the clouds mount and tumble. Everything churns so hugely.

In the cockpit, my daughter was sleeping under a blanket, her head resting on her stuffed rabbit. Michael and I watched her, not speaking. The breeze was gentle. It grazed her hair.

Burua, I said.

What? Michael asked.

Burua. That's the Guna word for "wind." I just remembered it.

He didn't say anything. He didn't comment on the word *burua.* He didn't know what to say. And I couldn't look at him.

Conditions are perfect, he said, after a while. The sea's really calm. Of course, the swells out here feel giant anyway. Now and again, the wind is a touch shifty.

What does that mean? I said.

Well, sometimes the wind comes around from a new direction. Then the mast starts doing big circles up there. If it comes around, you'll have to steer more to the sails than to the destination.

Fear coursed through me. What does *that* mean?

So. The fuller the sails are, the better they will move the boat—

I know that, I said.

OK, he said, hands open. I honestly don't know what you know. I *know* that. You know that I know that.

What I'm saying is, if you want to steer by hand to keep her moving, you can. If we head a little off course during your watch, it's all right. Just keep her moving. Experiment. Or, if you want to just sit here and stargaze, with the autohelm on, that's fine too. Your only real job is to look around. Every fifteen minutes, do a scan. If you're worried, if you see something, come get me. You might not see a thing. But come get me if you see anything funny.

I nodded.

If you figure out the meaning of life, come get me.

I did not smile.

Once you get used to the moonlight, it's almost as bright as the—

You should get some sleep, I said.

Right. Just an hour or two. That would do it.

He took a step toward me.

Go to sleep, I said. I'll take the full watch. It's my turn.

I tried. I tried to hold the hurt with her. But living w/ a depressed person is hard. It's like being married to the tide.

A depressed person keeps changing. When you leave the room, things are OK, but when you return, she's crying. You never know quite where the depressed person is. I mean, you can't anticipate where she is going to be next.

Sometimes I'd just ask outright. I'd be in the bedroom, dressing for work, Juliet motionless in bed. She seemed awake, but not close to getting up. Meanwhile sunlight would be streaming in around the edges of the blackout curtains. I was worried she wouldn't be able to take care of the kids. Should I stay home? I'd wonder. Should I call my mother? Ask her to come help us for a while? Was she going to hurt herself? I tried asking these questions in ways that wouldn't offend her.

Hey, Juliet, I'd say. Are "the mulligrubs" any better today?

Looks like you're in "the doldrums" again, Juliet.

Got "the mopes" today, honey?

The grumbles?

The blues?

One day she was like, Michael, I'm going to scream if you use one more euphemism.

So I did. I shut up. I mean, I really shut up.

When they went below, I was exponentially alone. As I watched the sea, I could see him move around the cabin, getting Sybil into bed. Stepping in and out of the light.

I'm going to turn off the cabin lights now, Juliet, he called up softly. It's easier to see on deck without them.

Then, darkness. I held my breath in the interval, in which I saw nothing at all. Gradually I could make out the lace of foam on the sea swells, the moonlight being passed from wave to wave, and the boat herself, sails drawing, her deck white as china, her flags and her flywheels and her telltales streaming. For all the improbability of what she was doing, slicing across the sea, she was very quiet. I held fast to the wheel.

Burua. That was the right word. That's exactly the right word. *Burua.*

There were so many kinds of winds. Ernesto had told me that the Guna name each one. *Sagir burua* comes from the Chagres River. And *dii burua.* That is the wind that blows just before it rains.

And this, I asked Ernesto in my mind, what's the name of this wind? It blew almost behind us, at our port quarter. The following swells lifted *Juliet* first from the stern, then beam, then forepeak, but without any splashing, no hard setting down, just a shudder, a sense that a force had passed underneath. Above, the sky held several humped clouds, which wandered, balloon-like, passive. Clouds were the cows of the sky, it seemed to me, remarkable only in their size, their bellies full of moonlight. As a child, in school, we tied our names and addresses to the string of helium balloons. We stood in a field and released them. Whoever's got the farthest would get a prize. I remember watching mine rise higher and higher until I could no longer tell if I was seeing it or imagining it. They had to call me inside.

When I was a kid, my mother's best friend, Louise, was a constant in my daily life. Her first husband died when they were very young, and by the time she hooked up with us, she still lived in their house by herself, no kids, making dark jokes about her bad luck. I could see into Louise's living room from my bedroom window. I could see the back of her head and the book she was reading—on the rare occasions she wasn't at our house, that is. I often wished she and her dead husband had hurried up and had a little girl. Because that girl would have been my best friend. We could have sent messages across on a clothesline. We could have ridden our down-market bikes up and down Morry Road, which dead-ended in a pile of cedar chips between the woods and our house. I liked Louise. I could see why she didn't want to jump into marriage again with just anybody. She was a big-boned woman, quiet except for when she laughed, which was frequently. She and my mother laughed all the time. My mother wasn't very funny. It was as if my mother possessed a kind of humor that made no sense to anyone but Louise. She spoke Louise. And Louise spoke Lucinda.

I was not jealous. I loved to hear them laugh together, Louise's effervescent hee-heeing answered by my mother's conspiratorial snicker. I'd known since I was a young child that my mother was unhappy, and I wanted the burden lifted from us both. I wished my parents were happy together, but they weren't, and so new friendships had to be resorted to.

Occasionally the two women drank too much. Though it's hard for me to square my mother now with the woman I once caught laughing uproariously in the backyard the summer I was ten.

Louissse, I heard my mother say, stretching out the word. There are love stories and there are love stories. Most love stories are horseshit.

You bet!

I leaned my cheek against the window screen, eavesdropping. Behind their low talking, tree frogs.

But some love stories are pretty realistic, my mother said.

I hear you. Yes, Lucinda. I know.

You ever heard the story of Narcissus and Echo?

Tell me, Lucinda. Oh, God. I can't wait to hear this one. Hee-hee!

Well, Narcissus loved his own reflection. He didn't want to talk to *anybody*, just stare at himself. And Echo kept trying to talk to him, but *she* couldn't come up with her own words. She could only repeat what others said. But they were bound to stay together forever. At cross-purposes. Now *that's* a realistic love story, my mother said.

Louise did not laugh.

Within the year, my parents divorced.

Suddenly *Juliet* was making a racket.

Luffing sails sound so animal. Like a giant trapped bird.

Gaw, I said aloud, borrowing a Louise-ism.

It's true—the wind did swing around. I looked up at the mast and saw that everything Michael said was right. The masthead light swung in a dizzy circle and was hard to look at. I turned my head to feel the wind and to hear it in my ears. Sail to the sails, he said. I turned her downwind. The sails refreshed. I took a deep breath; she quieted.

Gaw. That's what Louise used to say, all the time.

Gaw, Juliet, she said to me one day that summer. I've got such a nice new beau.

She blew a cyclonic cloud of cigarette smoke into the kitchen.

Let me tell you, Juliet, honey, Louise said. He's such a gentleman.

(*Gentleman.* The word sets off alarm bells in my head now.)

Move your plentiful bottom, Louise, my mother said. We have to get ready for the party.

A party. My parents were having a party. What else was my mother going to do with that glorious head of hair? It was entirely going to waste on Morry Road in Schenectady. Her corona of sunset-red hair made her look famous. She was just a clerk.

I stopped hard at the memory. I didn't really want to go further. But it does, the sea draws the inner life out. Behind us, our wake was a road that unraveled as soon as it was lain. Watching it emptied me. So much time went by looking astern that I soon realized I'd forgotten my one simple task—to check the horizon.

But there was nothing and more nothing at the seam of sky and sea. For the first time, I felt proprietary. She was my boat too. My *Juliet*. I was the kind of person who didn't want to lay claim. Mine, mine, mine, the children said. Mine, mine, Michael said. Fine, I said. Yours, yours, yours.

I conceded everything, as if it were a favor, rather than a conscious strategy to avoid loss.

And what's your name?

Juliet. What's your name?

I'm Gil. I'm Louise's new friend.

Why are you under the table, Gil? Under the table is for kids.

I just needed a break. So much talking. You think I'm strange.

No.

Is it strange to want to take a break from grown-up troubles?

No, sir.

Who's that?

Caffeine.

That's your bear's name?

Yup.

Hello, Caffeine. I'm Gil.

Hello, Gil.

What are you two doing?

We are watching a movie in our heads.

Ha. Is it a good movie?

Yes.

It's so wonderful to watch you play. You've got such a great imagination.

OK.

Just watching you play has made me feel better about my troubles.

OK.

Do you believe that grown-ups have troubles?

Yeah.

But kids have troubles too, don't they?

Yeah.

Like you can't have soda or candy or anything. I remember how hard

*it is to be a kid, and never get to make your own choices or pick your
own things. Hostages to fortune, that's what children are.*

If you say so.

Can I come back under here later and say hi?

Nope. I'll be gone.

*Ha, that's great. I like the way you put things, Juliet. No veneer. And
you're as pretty as your mother. Except you're not a redhead, are you?*

Not yet.

That's when I realized I was wrong about the clouds. They
aren't passive. They are beautifully plastic and expressive. You
just have to watch them for a long time. They crossed the sky,
large as a continents. The whole mass tumbling and contracting,
reaching and resigning, until somehow the cloud had traveled
the entire sky and snuffed out the moon.

Juliet splashed across the sea in a new darkness.

It's simple: In order to see, you just have to broaden your definition of what *light* is.

There, around the edges of the cloud, was a sweet incandescence.

I thought, *I am not alone.*

I was wondering if you wanted to talk a bit more about your
life on the boat, Sybil. What your day-to-day life was like . . .
Like, did you play with your brother? Did you have chores?

I had chores, sure. Polishing the compass—I liked that.
Scraping barnacles. Did *not* like that. I had a bucket. I filled
it with seawater for the dishes, stuff like that. And we did
school. Liked that. Crab-eye math. Painting. Writing letters
to famous people . . .

That's very cool. Sounds like normal life, but at sea.

Yeah.

Were your mom and dad happy on the boat?

Oh, yes. But they yelled sometimes.

At each other?

Oh, yes.

What kinds of things did they fight about?

Vegetables, rocks, the weather. That sort of thing . . .

What did you do when they yelled?

I singed.

You would sing? That's a good solution.

Sometimes to Doodle. Baby songs. "I'm a Little Teapot," that sort of thing. Or I would read. *Fox in Socks*. Or I would just make up my own stories. 'Cause that's easiest.

Ha. Well, not easy for everybody.

When tweetle beetles fight, it's called a tweetle *beetle* battle.

February 28. LOG OF YACHT 'JULIET.' From Snug Harbor. Toward Cartagena. 09° 75.59′N 077° 10.02′W. Time: 4 p.m. Course: NW. Wind: SE 2–3 knots. NOTES AND REMARKS: It is late in the day of our 2nd day of the passage to Colombia. Slow progress. We really need more wind. Juliet & kids restless. Juliet says to me, If I ever agree to read that damned Fox in Socks book again, kill me please. And you can write that in your little fucking diary!

It is hot as hell. Lack of wind makes it feel hotter. We all feel antsy. Then Juliet looks around & she says, w/ a straight face, I want to go for a swim.

My first thought is, A swim? In the middle of the open sea? But then I realize this might give us something to rally around.

The cat was out of the bag. About how Michael really felt about me, at least. My problem was I worried he had a point. *Did* I love my unhappiness? Was it mine long before it had a cause? I mean, before my great misuse? When I had my babies, did I choose my unhappiness over them?

I was an only child, so I was always wandering around bored and nosey. Once, I overheard my mother talking about me to Louise in the kitchen.

Such a pill, my mother said. I can't do anything to cheer her up.

Well, sighed Louise. They say you can only be as happy as your *un*happiest child.

Ugh, said my mother. With Juliet, I'm doomed.

So I say, All right, crew. Mommy wants a swim. Anyway, it's time for lunch. So we are going to heave-to.

Yay! Sybil says, clapping. What's that?

I look at Juliet, leaning against the cabin top, tugging on a hank of her own hair. That means we are going to—

I know what that means, she snaps.

You do?

Yes. I read all those books you gave me. You—she squints, recalling. You backwind the jib. You stall the boat.

Holy crap, Juliet, I say. I'm impressed.

Good job, Mommy!

I'm not saying I can <u>do</u> it, she says.

The truth is we don't need to heave-to in order to swim off the boat in this light wind. But I have promised myself I would make her practice. She should know these things.

Well, I say, first, we've got to turn her head to wind.

What wind? mutters Juliet.

I laugh, but when Juliet doesn't move, I go ahead and bring the boat around myself.

Finally, Juliet comes to the helm. I hand it over, stand behind her. She tenses but doesn't elbow me in the gut or anything. I explain how we are going to take her through the eye, like in a normal tack, but we won't release the jib. We'll let it back to windward. Then the sails will cancel each other out.

We both stare up at the sails. The jib fills backward across the foredeck.

Look, says Sybil. The jib is inside out!

Slow, slow, I say to Juliet. There. Can you feel the loss of steerage?

Yes.

Right there. Feel it stall? Lock the wheel right there.

We step apart. Like from a burn.

Very well done, I say.

She looks at me hard for a moment. She shucks off her shirt. She's wearing a bikini top I've never seen her wear before. My pulse quickens.

Remember we can still drift, honey, I say. You have to tie yourself to the boat. Take the flotation device.

She looks back at me over her shoulder.

Of course, she says, tucking it under her arm. What do you think, I'm crazy?

I remember driving in the country that fall. With Gil. It was easy, he said, to *nick up* to Vermont from New York State. Cross the border into Vermont and everything's prettier. The same barns and farmhouses but these are freshly painted. And the hay bales are neater. The cows are washed. Why in the world would you let your ten-year-old daughter go on such long drives with a man that is not her father? That part of the story is beyond me. I guess because he'd showed up in a real pinch and that made him reliable. Plus, he did the honorable thing and put a ring on Louise. Of course, everyone assumed he *was* my father. Is it all right if your daughter tries one? said a lady holding shards of maple candy. I loved maple candy. I loved the wet, sugary grit of maple candy, cut into leaves. She's not my— Gil stopped. A flash of shame came across both their faces, the lady with the plate, and Gil. That's when it lodged itself into me. My psychic splinter. My brain yet grows around it. (People do live with that, with shrapnel in their bodies. Muscle envelops the foreign object, like a nail in a tree.) Sure, she can have a piece, Gil said finally. You want a piece, honey?

Then the whole busy world just got right back on track. Thank you! Thank you! We got back in the car. The earth was spinning at hundreds of miles per hour but somehow the car stayed on the road. All the way back to Schenectady.

In his own awful way, I guess he was in love with me.

The drives became regular. Almost every weekend, deep into winter. Whenever my mother and father needed to disentangle their lives—a very complicated task, I now realize—they'd call Gil and Gil would drive me around. Why not ever Louise? They got married in a low-rent ceremony right before Christmas.

When we parked, he'd lock the car door. He didn't have to: I wasn't going anywhere. But the locking got my attention. It drove fear into my heart. I tried to listen to what he was talking about, but it never offered any clues as to what we were doing: good versus evil, man and nature. He would rub my shoulder good-naturedly, play with the fingers of my sweating hands. Sometimes he got very quiet, then he'd chuckle, give himself a slap, and buy me ice cream. Only once did he hurt me. But that one time contained all of the torment of his days. It turned me to ice for years.

You think kids keep the secret. Well, they do tell, just not always in a way that grown-ups can hear. After the day he hurt me, I told my mother what Gil had done. My mother sent me to my room. For a long time after that, I did not tell the story again. I pretended that the story belonged to me, that I was not telling it by choice. The story was powerful. I had shown its truth to my mother and the story blinded her and she sent me to my room, and she never spoke of it again. But neither did she send me off alone with Gil anymore. I was awarded a **real babysitter**—a girl.

I understood that it wasn't a question of believing me or not. I think on some level, my mother did believe me. But she did not want a scene. She did not want the embarrassing misunderstanding to gain traction. She was in the middle of a divorce. She could not afford to lose Louise. I suppose Gil understood that too. That's why he knew I'd be compliant.

See the scars where the forest burned? See the second-growth trees?

God. How woefully insufficient this kind of postmortem sequencing has always seemed to me. So completely beside the point.

Coming up for air, I could see Michael there on the transom. The boat looked totally still, balanced like a white moth on the sea. It was surprising when the float I held on to strained in my hands. The water below me was so clear that I could see down into infinite depth, fractals of light with no end. Vertigo loomed. I had to catch my breath.

Did you make any friends while you were sailing, Sybil?

Oh, yes. I made friends all over the place. Guna friends, American friends . . . friends from Lost Vegas . . .

Can you tell me about your friends?

There was a little girl who was magic.

What could she do?

She could fly. She liked French food. You know, like vegetable soup. Washed burgers . . .

Did you get to play with her a lot?

Not really. I can't remember. But we did play Barbies.

How *fun*.

They didn't have Barbies where she was from. She was from the Neverlands. We said let's never forget each other.

And look, you *haven't* forgotten her.

And we met a man, a king!

A king? In the real world, he was a king?

He taught me the words for plants. He was a *chief.*

You're smiling, Sybil.

What?

You're smiling. It's a nice memory. The memory makes you happy.

Yeah.

It sounds like there were many wonderful moments on the boat.

Yeah. So many. I loveded the boat. Daddy loveded the boat. We all loveded the boat.

Yes, I can see why.

Until in Cartagena.

Hmm. You want to tell me more Sybil?

[. . .]

Sybil?

Yeah?
What happened in Cartagena?

March 1. LOG OF YACHT 'JULIET.' From Snug Harbor.
Toward Cartagena. 010° 06.44′N 076° 28.72′W. Time: 2:15 a.m.
Course: NW. Wind: ZERO knots. NOTES AND REMARKS:
We are totally becalmed. Wind gone. Vanished. I trimmed
the sails tight as tight. I paced back & forth. Gave 'Juliet' a
little slap on the hull. Come on, honey! My voice sounds like
I'm talking in an empty auditorium. Out here there's just no
<u>consciousness</u> w/out the wind.
  I sit on the bow. Legs dangling over.
  Well I'll be damned.
  This brings whole new meaning to the word "doldrums."
  If there were a way to sail w/out wind, sailors would have
figured it out centuries ago. Pray? Sing? Throw everything
overboard? I've heard that in a pinch you can tie your dinghy
to your boat & the outboard can tow you. I look back at 'Oily
Residue,' bobbing astern.
  Or maybe this is punishment.
  Hard not to think of it that way, everything out here is so
damned biblical.
  For example, I got slapped by a fish last night. On deck,
slammed in the back of the head with a fish. I thought Juliet
threw it at me. But it was a flying fish. Juliet wasn't even on
deck.
  I look toward Colombia. The sea rolls on. The lapping of
the water against the hull sounds like chuckling. Somebody
laughing.
  Harry's voice nags me. "She's not yours, Michael."
  Like hell she's not, I say out loud.
  Who got us into this? Me. And that's who'll get us out. Just
two days ago I sailed her off the anchor. Like a sailor in the
Age of the Galleons. My wife standing at the bow. Barefoot,
brown from the sun. Turning for a last look at the land. The
late-afternoon sun catching the red in her hair . . .

She <u>is</u> mine. She is <u>ours</u>.

Harry can't have her.

Christ, the lack of wind is agitating. I can't <u>think</u> w/out it. My worst fear is arriving to Cartagena after dark tomorrow & having to find a mooring in the dark. Soon the sun will be up. Even if we hightail it all day, it's still going to be close. I look back at 'Oily Residue,' drifting back & forth on the water. I bend down & start pulling her in, when out of nowhere comes a breeze.

The mainsail bellies. I run to adjust the trim.

Here! I shout to the wind, giving it yards of sail to fill. TAKE IT! TAKE IT!

There is a soft, ghostly pressure.

And we're off.

I see them standing at the corner. Three women, under a tree. They are so lovely as to appear arranged. Two of them are slender, the third strong and curvy. It is warm and balmy today, and the wind riffles through their loose blouses. The wind is coming from my back. A gusty NE. As they all turn to watch me approach, the wind presses against their breasts, flips open their sweaters, and sweeps their hair from their faces, revealing complicated expressions. In the month I have been back, they have not yet seen me at the bus stop.

I raise a hand. Eagerly, they respond. Vigorous, cheerful waves.

Oh, these protected villages. I used to roll my eyes. House after house is the same. Rectangles with bright doors. Yards give in to yards, except where hedges form a porous barrier. Driveways are tarred smooth. Children's laughter is uncomplicated. As soon as they get off the bus, they shed their jackets and their shoes.

I used to dislike how it made me feel, the neighborhood. How had I ended up in the same kind of postwar suburb that was new when Anne Sexton's generation moved in? An entire section of my dissertation was devoted to the symbolism of the bay window—that large two-way glass through which the suburban female saw and was seen, pined and posed. Try as I might, I could not avoid feeling watched through mine. But watching was how it worked; we watched the children together, children everywhere, even in the trees, the adults inside aware, keeping watch, until eventually each front door was opened and one by one, the children were called in.

I force myself to continue to walk forward.

Juliet! the curvy woman says, stepping toward me first, her arms wide open. It's so good to *see* you.

She embraces me before I can even lift my arms. I feel her warmth through her shirt. One of the other women steps forward and puts a hand on my shoulder. When she smiles, I remember that I'd always found the gap between her front teeth attractive, because she never gave a damn to have it fixed, and always smiled anyway, more than any person I'd ever known.

My friend comes last—Alison. Our daughters love to play. Alison and I embrace. It's the first time I've seen her since our return.

I know I haven't written you a thank-you note yet, I say to Alison. But we ate *every single one* of the casseroles you left us. Every last bite. Straight out of the dish. We didn't even put it on plates. I just want you to know how much we've appreciated it.

I'm so glad, Alison says.

We step apart. Her eyes are wet. She blots them with her sleeve.

Alison, I say, taking her hand. For a week or so there, you left a casserole every day. I got used to it! I would check the stoop. You never rang the bell. You were the casserole fairy.

I didn't want to disturb you, Alison says, laughing. I didn't want you to feel you had to talk.

But that's what was so kind about it, I say. It was so kind, but so impersonal. You know we needed food. And you were right—we did. My mother is an *awful* cook. I'd forgotten. I haven't seen her in years! What she does is, she pours cans of V-Eight into a pot, then adds anything from the freezer. Meatballs. Frozen corn . . .

The other women watch me, their heads tilted.

So anyway, thank you. I don't think you can begin to understand how meaningful it was—

Please, Alison says. I know that you would have done the same for me.

I stare back at her. Her face is so delicately constructed, so responsive. But I almost laugh. I would *never* have done the same for her. That's my point. I might have written her a poem. I might have scarred my arms for her, cut off my hair. But I would never have made her a casserole.

We hear a vehicle approach. We turn, expecting the school bus, but it is not the school bus. It is a police car, sliding our way with its lights off. We track the car as it passes us with a hush and proceeds down the street. A police car on our street is an anomaly. We give it our complete attention. It passes the Reynoldses', the Olivieras', it passes the Lehman-Rosses'.

My house is at the end of the block, just before where the road forks left, toward the pond, or right, toward town. The street has a very slight upward grade, so that my house remains quite visible even from this distance. The police car pulls up in front of my house. Two figures emerge, dark as crows against the sunbeaten grayed tar of the streets, the pale green of spring. They shrug on their coats.

I have an idea, says Alison, as if something splendid has just happened. Why don't I take Sybil to *our* house when she gets off the bus today? To play?

The other women nod vigorously. They are all trying not to look in the direction of my house, a locus of sheer trouble.

Cora has been begging to play with Sybil, Alison continues. It's been so hard to hold her off. Juliet, please.

Finally, the school bus approaches. The wipers have cleared two eyebrows in the dirty front windshield, behind which sits the old reliable matron driver. Am I imagining that she stares at me suspiciously too?

That's a great idea, I say to Alison. Sybil will be thrilled.

VII

M y mother is standing at the front door in agitation, waiting for me. She wedges the storm door open.

Juliet, she whispers. The *police* are here.

Two bodies in dark clothes stand in the sunlit living room behind her. I take my time wiping my feet.

What *for*? I whisper back.

To talk to you, she says. They won't say more. Where's Sybil?

At Alison's house. Stay with me.

We walk into the living room. A broad-shouldered man stands with his hands in his pockets, relaxed and looking out into the backyard like he's thinking of buying it. A young woman with a severe ponytail stands on the other side of the room. She smiles when I enter.

I'm Detective Duran, she says, offering her hand.

Dur*ahn,* she pronounces it. She wears no makeup, and no jewelry. She appears scrubbed clean, leaving nothing to criticize. She introduces the other officer as Detective Ross. He reaches over the back of the couch to shake my hand. The woman asks if I have some time to talk. I tell her I do.

My mother and I settle side by side on the loveseat. If my mother is not allowed to be there, the pair do not push the point. Detective Duran lifts her hands, a kind of fatalistic shrug.

You must be in a very difficult place, Duran says. I am truly sorry for your loss.

Thank you, I say.

Sorry for your loss, echoes Ross, still at the back window.

I always wish I could do more to ease people's pain, Duran says. But we are officers of the law. Our job is very narrow. To uphold the law. No matter what else is happening.

Of course, I say. So this isn't about Michael?

It's not exactly about Michael. It's about someone he knew. We're wondering if you can tell us anything about Harry Borawski.

I blink. I tilt my head, like a bird, to the side.

The man who sold us the boat? I ask.

Yes.

Why? What does he want?

He's missing. We don't know how long, since he had no wife or kids to keep track of him. But he had a regular monthly lunch with some old salts at the local Denny's and he never once in his life missed it. So, when he didn't show this month, they were very insistent. We searched his place, nothing.

That's strange, I say.

We took a look at his emails, Duran says. In the past several months, he sent dozens of emails—

Dozens upon dozens, adds Ross.

To your husband.

Unanswered emails, clarifies Ross.

By the sound of them, Mr. Borawski probably wrote quite a few of them in a state of disorientation, Duran says, raising her eyebrows. So we can understand why your husband didn't write back. But it's curious. As you know, as you probably know, they were technically co-owners of your boat. Your boat, called the . . . Duran shuffles through her papers.

The *Juliet*, I say.

Both of them look up.

The boat was named *Juliet*, like me. Michael named the boat after me.

Oh, Detective Duran says, her hand to her heart. That's so *sweet*.

It's a nice name, agrees Ross. Sometimes boat names are really weird. Like, *Now I'm Poor* or *Never Again*. Like bad *jokes*. Why do people do that?

They both look at me cheerfully. I'm unsure what to say.

My mother clears her throat. So what exactly would you like from my daughter? she asks them.

Detective Duran nods at her. Good point, Mom, she says. Then, to me: Honestly, we're just trying to find the guy. We're thinking maybe he's not even around here. Maybe he went down to Central America to hang out with you guys. We know he'd been to the area several times to buy boats on the cheap. To sail them back to the U.S. and sell them at a profit.

Perfectly legal way to make a living, adds Ross.

Any chance that's what happened? asks Duran.

No, I say. I didn't see him in Cartagena. I've never met him in my life.

Duran gives a short, frustrated harrumph.

Ross takes up the thread. We've got another client of Mr. Borawski's saying he inquired about buying a boat called *Windy Monday,* he says. We did a little digging. That was the name of your boat—

Before your husband renamed it after you, adds Duran.

We weren't selling *Juliet,* I say. I'm not sure why the other man would have thought so.

I guess Borawski told the guy you'd be bringing it back soon.

Well, I say, that was the plan.

Do you think the plan was changing? asks Duran. Was that *still* the plan when your husband—when he—

I look at Duran levelly. I couldn't see into Michael's mind, I say.

It's just an unusual arrangement, says Ross. That kind of gentlemen's agreement. Usually boat loans are done through a bank. Like a home mortgage. Impersonal.

The thing is, Duran says, since Mr. Borawski was still part-owner, even a minority owner, he would have been able to take possession of the boat, if he wanted to be *technical* about it. If your husband didn't keep his word. If he didn't do this one thing he promised.

So we're just trying to figure out if that's what was happening, says Ross.

I look back and forth between the two of them.

Well, the only person who could explain that to you is dead, I say.

Duran winces. Ross looks respectfully at the floor.

Michael is dead, I say again. I claim the words, louder now, hard and dry. I've never said them before. Those three words together. They are an outrage, but this is why I must say them.

If he weren't dead, I continue, he would tell you. He was a very honest person.

My mother grips my hand and squeezes it, as if to say, *That's right*.

And I have plenty of money now, I go on. Michael's life insurance. Mr. Borawski can have it all. He can have the boat too, and he can have anything else he wants. If it weren't for him, we never would have bought a boat. We never would have left for Panama. We never would have sailed anywhere, and my children would have a father.

Then tears come. My second bout of tears in two days.

Please, my mother stands up, waving her hands. Please stop. She's already barely managing. She's got two little *children*—

They stand.

We are *so* very sorry, Detective Duran says.

Listen, says Ross, no one ever wants to see us coming.

March 9. BIENVENIDO A COLOMBIA. After sailing into Cartagena Bay last week, we all got our wishes granted. Because it is decreed in the CONSTITUTION OF THE YACHT 'JULIET' that UPON ARRIVING TO A FOREIGN PORT WITHOUT LOSING ANY CREW OVERBOARD, EVERYONE GETS WHATEVER THE HECK THEY WANT.

What I wanted: a cappuccino. Sybil wanted to run really fast w/out having to stop. Doodle wanted ice cream. Brave Juliet wanted to ditch the boat for a night & stay in a hotel. Turns out she'll get more than that. We just moved into the Hotel Casa Relax while 'Juliet's' transmission gets fixed by an excellent boat mechanic named Arturo. Arturo is one of these guys built like Oscar de la Hoya who also happens to run a side business taking tourists down the Rio Magdalena to Mompox. You could see him wrestling a gator & winning.

As a result of all this, spirits much higher. Cartagena is mind-blowing. What can I possibly say about this city? Impossible to describe. I got robbed of 50,000 pesos right next to the most aromatic frangipani bush. Everybody's trying to cheat you or touch you & you can't walk anywhere safely at night, but it's the most <u>alive</u> city I've ever seen. The richest person lives next to the shoeshine man, who sleeps in his wheelbarrow w/ his feet sticking out. There's this outdoor market called the Bazurto. Big as Milbury but made of stalls. Miles & miles of aisles you can't see the end of. Named after what's sold there. You can buy anything on earth. A whole aisle for women's shoes. An aisle for live crabs. Vendors standing behind piles of fruit so large you only see their heads. Fruits I'd never heard of. Soursop. Slimy cherimoya. Green plantains. Mountains of watermelons. Stacks of dried fish. Hammocks. Jugs. Pig heads. Wholesale perfume supplies. Anything you want to buy on the off-chance you didn't already lose your wallet in the jostling crowd at the corner of Fish & Pork.

I couldn't go to my closet immediately after the police left. There was Georgie to get at daycare and soiled clothes and dinner and then Alison rang the doorbell with Sybil. My mother and I weaved around each other with lunch boxes and baskets of laundry. We've become like married people. Unable to have an extended conversation.

We were thrown into added distress when Georgie lost his stuffed seal with the big blue eyes, without which he cannot live. If he were just a normal boy, on a normal day, maybe the sound of his wailing would be tolerable. But because he is who he is, a boy who has just lost his daddy, the sound of Georgie's crying hurts us too much. We look everywhere. Even Sybil. In cabinets, under beds. Finally, Sealie is discovered behind a toilet.

Then, the second before I lose it, without saying a word to

anyone, I go into my closet and shut the door. I sit down, grab the logbook out of its shoebox, and I read on.

Michael, I say out loud. What. Have. You. Done.

The word "cappuccino" is the diminutive form of the Italian word for "hood," named for the color of the Capuchin monks of 16th-century Italy. But few know that the drink itself originated not in Italy but Austria. The Austrians made their kapuziners out of coffee, sugar, cream & egg whites. Then along came a genius named Angelo Moriondo. What you see atop a modern cappuccino like those sold here at Carullos (by the way, best cappuccino in the world = Carullos) is not egg whites, of course, but the result of Moriondo's magical espresso machine. Duels have been fought over

Christ Almighty, I say.
I flip ahead.

We teach our kids that the Pilgrims came up w/ the idea, but here, as everywhere else in the New World, the arrival of the white man was an unmitigated disaster for the native population. Low estimates put death toll from European-imported diseases at 90% by end of 17th cent. Built on the ruins of that civilization, Nueva Granada was actually a coalition of modern-day Colombia, Panama, Venezuela & Ecuador, all ruled by Spain. Then Napoleon threw King Ferdinand in prison in 1808 and the colonists learned to live quite easily w/out a king.

Two main political parties, Conservative & Liberal, struggled for power for the next zillion years until they decided to <u>rotate</u> <u>control</u> of govt. every 4 years.

Not a bad idea! Must write my senator.

What's amazing & haunting about Cartagena is the way

they never bothered to destroy the past. They even kept the Spanish torture chambers. Which are worth a visit. Sybil & I are partial to the Inquisition Palace. Stone archways, sunlit courtyards w/ palms growing inside, flowering vines . . . Then you enter this dark chamber full of torture devices. Sybil likes the large upright sarcophagus for burying people alive, which you are allowed to stand in (while open). Doesn't bother her at all, she's fascinated. Smart kids like her are always trying to piece things together. They accept all information w/out sentimentally protecting their innocence for Mommy & Daddy's sake. I tell her this is what happens when government takes the liberties of the people away. In the sunlit plaza you can still see the char from bonfires where heretics and witches and crypto-Jews were burned. Roughly 800 people were burned in this city alone, resulting in very bad PR for the Catholic Church because you'd think torture would run contrary to Divine Will, but there you have it.

Does the arc of history bend toward justice? Well there is no <u>arc</u> of history. That makes history sound like it has an ending, like a rainbow. No. It just keeps bending & bending . . .

I jump—there's a knock on the closet door.

Juliet, my mother whispers through the wooden slats. *Juliet.*

In here, I say.

She parts the closet doors and peeks in. Her damp skin looks radiant in the soft light. We stare at each other for a moment.

Are they asleep? I ask.

Yes.

Come in, I say.

She looks doubtful. Come in *there?* With you? Are you sure?

I clear a space next to me, moving my sweatshirt, books, wrappers, laptop. Slowly she maneuvers herself down beside me. Her old knees crack. She swats back the sleeves of Michael's shirts.

We both stare myopically into the logbook. I flip forward again.

He sure did have a lot to say, mutters my mother.

He could be a real windbag, I say.

March 12. Hotter than Hades. Kids spent the day in tiny swimming pool at Casa Relax. A late-afternoon downpour sent us all to the room where there is this exotic thing called AIR-CONDITIONING. We all sat bathing in the Freon . . . sublime. The heat doesn't quit until dusk. Everybody in this state of suspended animation. Too hot for birds to fly, too hot for dogs to bark, too hot for everything but the mosquitoes. Those wait until dark, then they like to make feasts of your ankles. We slather the kids w/ DEET. As for me, I don't like the stuff.

W/ reluctance, got new SAT phone. Will help to make plans w/ other cruisers & to keep in touch w/ Therese & Mom, plus we can be found in an emergency.

Also, finally got around to calling Harry to see how he's doing,

There, my mother says. That's him!

owed it to the guy. But as soon as we started talking, Harry rolled right onto the old track, "Why don't you bring the boat back now, we'll sell her, make lots of cabbage, or you can keep her at the marina, if you don't want to sell, sail her around the Long Island Sound all summer etc. etc." Suddenly I think, Maybe it's not about the money at all. It's like he misses me.

I am processing this thought when out of nowhere he tells me he's coming to Cartagena.

I laugh nervously. I'm like, You are?

Yeah, he says. I love that city. Always thought I might retire there.

When I don't say anything like, Great!! Or, Can't wait to see you!! he gets this kind of wounded tone and says he's got another boat he wants to buy down here.

I won't bother you, he says. He has a hotel where he always stays, he says. In Getsemani.

Before I catch myself, I'm saying our hotel is in Getsemani too.

What's the name of it?

Casa Relax, I say.

Then everything's smoothed over. Like he's relieved just to get this one crumb of information. Now he knows how to find me. And I think, No skin off my back. Call the guy. Hang out w/ the guy. I kick myself a couple times for getting into this fix. Need to convince him to let me out of the contract. Fine. Will do this in person.

My mother and I glance at each other. I skim ahead, but it's just page after page of fine-grain detail about boat transmissions, coffee, the arc of fucking history . . .

Maybe it would be easier to go backward, I say.

I skip straight to the last page of the book, where the pages are blank.

As I turn the pages backward, page after smooth and empty page, the pages compound my grief. I cannot help thinking, *These are all the words he did not write. These are all the days he did not live. This is his silence.*

Let's stop, my mother says.

No, I say.

She puts her hand on my arm.

Obviously, he didn't do anything criminal, she says. We're talking about *Michael*.

I want to know, I say.

This is torture, she says. Juliet.

We look at each other, inches apart.

I turn the page again.

She removes her hand.

It's a drawing. In blue pen. Crude strokes. It's a face. The face of an old man, with a mustache and thick hair. Big blobs mark his cheeks—he's crying. There is no other way to put it—it is a very haunted drawing.

That's the last entry? my mother says. A *picture*?

She sits back.

I grab my laptop.

Harry + Borawski + yacht + sales + CT

There's a dated webpage. Font in bold Wide Latin.

In the corner, a small photograph. Old face shadowed by the brim of a baseball hat. A poor picture. Blurry, with wind. But it's Harry Borawski all right.

My mother peers into the photo. Then she takes the log out of my hands and stares at Michael's ink drawing.

Is this some kind of . . . admission of guilt?

I don't know, I say.

You don't *know*?

I mean, could Michael have killed someone? Sure.

Juliet!

I mean, Michael was a very loyal family man. But he was a bootstrap Republican. He would not have felt bad for some down-on-his luck old guy who was weighing us down. It would not have been *personal*.

You're saying Michael could have killed a man due to his choice of political party?

No. I'm just saying the people he admired were strong and successful and self-reliant, not needy and crazy.

I look my mother in the face.

Even me, I say.

Even you what?

He thought I was weak, I said, shrugging. He didn't have respect for the things I was good at. He thought I enjoyed playing the victim. Up until our last passage, I was also an incompetent sailor.

You're not remembering things right, my mother pleads. He

was gaga over you, Juliet. He thought the earth revolved around you.

I run my fingers over the ink drawing. Harry Borawski stares out of the notebook with puzzled sadness. Michael was not an artist. I'd never seen him sketch anything in my life. But I can recognize the drawing as Michael's anyway. For a moment, I wonder if the likeness is purely coincidental, and that the drawing is not the face of Harry Borawski, but rather Michael's idea of God. His knowledge of God, in those final hours before he died.

I close the book.

I think I'm going to be sick, I tell my mother.

Dear God. I have mean voices. They say, I'LL STING YOU. I have nice voices too. My woman voice. That voice says, Don't cry. Very soft, Don't cry. Did you know that the easiliest way to win is to cheat, God? But I do NOT cheat and I do NOT tattle. But I do cry. I had lots of friends when we lived on the boat. The girl who was magic. Another one who gave me a conch. Some say I am bragging, but I have done many things for a kid. I have swum in a swamp. I have drove a dinghy. I can do a clove hitch. But OK, there are some things I have not done. I will now brag about them to you. 1. I have never watched TV while riding a horse. 2. I have never eaten a waffle underwater. 3. I have never been to Palm Springs. The end.

You see, I never asked questions about money. He allowed me to believe we had paid for the boat. But that wasn't my department, and listen, I had other concerns. It didn't really matter until Cartagena, because that's where Michael ran out of rope. We were sitting at a tiny table in the Plaza de Santo Domingo when he confessed. It was late. We hadn't moved into the hotel yet. We were still living aboard a broken *Juliet* in the harbor, tense and hot and barely speaking.

I was drinking an aguardiente and watching the children, who were playing on the enormous recumbent nude statue in the middle of the plaza. It was easy to love the children when they were playing in the distance.

He said, I owe money on the boat. I took money from Harry Borawski and didn't tell you. But I don't have it, he said. Not without leveraging the house. After the transmission repair, we have enough money for food and fuel, but that's it. I can't buy this guy out. I don't know what to do.

And I said, After what you said to me on the crossing, I don't care. I can barely stand to be around you. Knowing what you think of me.

Michael did not respond quickly.

Finally, he said—and I remember how he said it, gently, We can't give up.

For a moment I did not know what he was referring to, the marriage or the boat. Then I realized he meant both—either. I looked at his face. His was a strong, bony face, with a bracket-shaped crease on either side of a wide mouth. Over the years, I had gotten to know his face better than my own. His face was my constant reference. When I spoke, his face would tell me if what I was saying made sense or not. Its amusement confirmed my sanity. Its softness invited my love. Fear in his eyes warned me. And when I did not know how I felt, or how I *should* feel, I would check Michael's face, and I could read it like text.

There in the Plaza de Santo Domingo, I watched his stricken face. The expression was so new and so unguarded, that for a moment I was more interested in his expression than I was in the betrayal he had just revealed to me. We had known each other almost twenty years. What a strange thing, that I could still be surprised by his face. Finally, he took a drink of water, then looked at me so frankly that I drew my breath.

He said, Honestly, Juliet. Tell me—do you want to give up? Do you want me to let you go?

I opened my mouth, but no words came. An evening breeze was sweeping the heat away, setting the tablecloth ruffs and café umbrellas waving. Other children had joined ours on the recumbent nude statue, while a couple of women stood fanning themselves against the bolted doors of the Iglesia de Santo Domingo.

I could understand how he would ask me that question. Without fully being aware of it, I asked it of myself constantly. Giving up was very seductive. I wanted to be done with the suspense of marriage. I wanted to be done with the unknowns of the journey. Love had such very long odds. It must have been exhausting for him, to have to believe in the enterprise all by himself. He looked exhausted.

Say something, Michael said.

Large tears began running down either side of my face.

I don't want to give up, I said.

He smiled. Michael had a very sudden, mile-wide smile. When he was happy, his smile would take up his whole face. It was like turning on a light.

Me neither, he said.

Then he took the napkin out from under my drink and roughly dabbed the tears off my face. He pulled a chart out of his sack and spread it on the café table.

Then let's go see the world, he said. Harry will have to come get this boat himself if he wants it so bad.

March 19. Club Nautico Marina, Cartagena, Colombia. NOTES & REMARKS. Preparations afoot for a Caribbean crossing to Jamaica. Folks say that's a 5-day sail for a cautious boat. So we are taking our time getting ready. Being smart. We have moved back aboard beautiful 'Juliet.' Transmission humming (thanks, Arturo).

Then as if things could not get better we saw 'Adagio' sail into the harbor yesterday. Sybil screaming w/ happiness. Fleur screaming w/ happiness. Just a lot of screaming. Today Bosun is over there playing with BFF. The deckhand is napping. Me & Juliet haven't been alone for a looooong time.

In the calm of the harbor, I say to Juliet, OK, what is it I've never explained? You've got to understand that I don't know whether I've explained sailing to you well or not. I'm not trying to mess with you. There's just this empty horizon when I try to imagine what you are thinking. I know it feels like the white man's conspiracy to you but that's giving me too much credit. I just need you to <u>tell</u> me. Imagine that we've just met. And there's no history between us.

She nods & thinks about it. She tells me that, in the heat of the moment, she can't remember what things are <u>called</u> on the boat. She says there are so many archaic nautical terms it's like living inside a Renaissance Fair. We decide we should label all the clutches and sheets. That way J can be sure she's opening or closing or easing the right thing. While I label, she watches & listens. Labels are really helpful. Should have done that <u>day</u> <u>one</u> if I hadn't been wrapped up in my own shit.

Plus. Talked to Mom. Agreed Mom will meet us in Kingston in two weeks! She needs a vacation & a break from midwestern winter. Juliet & I need more time together w/ no kids, like normal people on a date.

Also, guy emails us from the Kenyon alumni magazine. He's coming to Cartagena on business and he wants to interview us. He says he writes a column about alums doing interesting things & he thinks the Kenyon community would be inspired to hear about our journey on the boat.

Me & Juliet find this hilarious. Oh, she says. The way you are plunging the head is <u>fascinating</u>.

Could be a wet slog across to Jamaica. The winds come from NE and we want to go N. Must sail close to the wind. The only time you have to push is just off the Colombian coast, where the eastward current can force you off course. I explain all this to Juliet. I explain how the boat might feel different head to wind. Plus we have a new transmission & could always just motor across. Even if there was a squall, we learned what to do getting blown to Narganá & now have protocol for rough weather. She nods. She listens. No overreactions. If we feel close to each other, me & Juliet, we can do anything.

What are you going to do? my mother asks.

I look at her, slowly pulling my mind back to the present.

If the police see this drawing, she says, they'll think Michael did something bad.

Just then the clearest image of Michael comes to me. He's eating sausages in the Plaza de Bolívar. He's licking his lips, eyebrows bobbing.

Juliet?

What?

Why are you laughing? This isn't funny.

I'm not laughing, I say. I mean, not about this. I just remembered something endearing about him.

Well, be *serious*. What are you going to do?

My chuckling fades. I'm already exhausted, but I will not sleep. If I am to exonerate him, I will have to read.

I guess I'll have to let Michael speak for himself, I say. That's the least I can do. Don't you think?

She nods and gets up. I can't take it, she says.

We have to talk about food. OK? We have to talk about bandeja paisa. (A faceful of rice, pork belly, fried & salted plantains . . .) We have to talk about sausages. Forget it, I can't even talk about the sausages. I could write poetry about the sausages. OK, let's talk about rolls. You pass the bakeries w/ their doors open & the smell lures you in. For about a dollar you can get a dozen. Then there's always some guy selling lemonade out of a fish tank on a cart. Turns out, lemonade tastes better out of a fish tank. We get lemonade & rolls & sit there on wrought-iron benches watching the world go by.

I know we're tourists, but you never feel like one as a sailor. We're all just a bunch of people. The world doesn't belong to any of us. I'm almost physically incapable of paying for a ticket anymore. So instead we just walk around the seawalls, which are pink due to being built out of coral. The churches are pink. Everything is pink & yellow, even the cubes of spiced and salted mango on a stick that Juliet likes.

Plus of course she also likes her aguardiente in the evenings when she gets a little melancholy. There is a small park w/ a statue of Simón Bolívar where you can buy cups of cracked corn for a few pesos. The kids feed the pigeons while we watch. By then the heat's eased up a little and I venture to hold her hand. At that hour there's this closeness I feel to her that I can't talk about. That I would lose if I talked about. It's like having an unopened letter in your breast pocket. That's what being married to someone for a long time feels like. I steal a glance when a sea breeze blows her dress against her knees.

I know what you're thinking, she says, huskily.

I have to tell her, No. No, you don't.

He really knew how to enjoy his food, my husband. In fact, he really knew how to enjoy the air too, and sailing, and negotiating with port captains—from first to last, he enjoyed the whole thing. He was a doer. He was a meeter of challenges. He was an appreciator of sausages. It was infectious. I remember how happy he looked, opening up the wax paper worshipfully, aromatic with oil and fennel. He'd eat his sausages pinkie-up, grunting, licking the grease off his wrist. It made me laugh.

This is why I cannot say I regret going. I don't regret watching my husband eat a sausage. I don't regret laughing.

I don't regret laughing in the Plaza de Bolívar.

March 29. LOG OF YACHT 'JULIET.' Club Nautico, Cartagena. Dinnertime. NOTES AND REMARKS: Sometimes it's the last thing you expect. Juliet got an email from her mother yesterday. The monster who hurt her is dead. The fucker had the good luck to die in his sleep after a short battle w/ cancer.

She's been doing so well. Will this set her back? I'm worried. We've got our big sail to Kingston coming up. Wondering now if we should put that off. Man, I hate this time of day.

I hate it for her sake. Too hot. Plus, in the late afternoon she gets sad. Sometimes the heat wrings it out of her. I'm angry, I guess. For her. And for me. I realize that now that he's dead, I'll never get a chance to punch his lights out. It was all kind of abstract for so many years, since we never saw Lucinda. That's going to be the hardest part, hearing from her mother again, after so little for so long. What a waste of time.

I say, Juliet tell me what I can do.

She says, Walk with me on the walls. You can tell me about pirates and empires and Napoleon. We can watch the kids run around.

Do you want a drink? I ask. Some firewater?

No, she says.

So we go to the walls. Everything is pinker this time of day.

What do you want me to do?

I don't want you to <u>do</u> anything, she says.

I'd cut off my hand to make you feel better, I say.

But that wouldn't make me feel better, she points out.

I know. I know! Then I will keep not doing anything, I say. Because doing nothing is the hardest thing for me to do.

Georgie and Sybil chase each other around us. Then they run ahead where a group of little kids are squatting over something.

Do you want to push back our departure? I ask.

No, she says. Absolutely not. He doesn't get to control me anymore.

I run my fingers over the words. His pen made ruts in the page. He pressed down hard when he was angry. I lean my head back, imagining the lightbulb in the closet as sunlight.

You would think, if you hadn't aired out a family secret by the time you were thirty, you would take it to your grave. But when I turned thirty, I became preoccupied with what had happened to me when I was ten. I became preoccupied with Gil.

My mother and I had lived with the events as an open secret. Once I left for college, the distant past didn't seem to matter. But sometimes the world around you won't let you forget. The ordinary landscape becomes a text that demands interpretation: I started seeing Japanese maples everywhere. Japanese maples were Gil's tree. They were often the pretext for our long drives, "to hunt for Japanese maples." They come in several colors, but it was the burgundy maples we hunted.

When I was thirty, the world was overrun with Japanese maples. Not only did I see them all over the countryside when Michael and I explored on the weekends, but in Cambridge itself, at innocent corners where I had previously noticed nothing. If Michael was driving, and we passed a Japanese maple, a feeling so ominous would come over me that I would have to roll down the window and hang out into the wind like a dog. Or, on the T, I'd see a young girl staring out the window with a certain tilt of the head and I would feel the unnameable panic. I couldn't quite remember—that is, I couldn't remember *in time* to prepare for the impact—why such ordinary sights were so heavy with meaning.

Maybe it was because I was thinking of becoming a mother myself. After three years apart, two of which I spent in England, as an au pair for a family in Stratford-on-Avon, Michael and I met up again at a Kenyon alumni get-together while we were both visiting New York City. He'd been in exile in Pittsburgh, terrified by the discovery that he literally *fit into* his dead father's clothes. The intervening years had been sexually austere for me. Michael jogged my memory. We canceled our flights and embarked on a sexual bender in a cramped New Jersey Hampton Inn. Five years, several cities, his MBA, and a couple long distances later, we tied the knot in a small wedding on the Kenyon campus. A neutral site, but drivable for both families. We relocated to Cambridge, where he got his first job in finance, and I enrolled at Boston College, the very gates of which made me feel holy, as if I were getting married to literature. The comfort of marriage, the unclenching of a safe life, backpacking on the weekends, reading in bed, eating figs in season . . . Well, you run out of excuses to avoid a thing.

With Michael's encouragement, I wrote my mother a letter. I told her that I had been thinking about the past, that I wanted to talk about Gil. When I did not hear back, I wrote her a longer, more explicit letter. I asked her to explain why she had never confronted Gil, or if she ever worried that he was a danger to other children. When I did not hear back from that letter, I got in the car and I drove from Cambridge all the way to Schenectady.

Ever since I was a kid, my mother had worked for the same clerk at Schenectady City Hall. From behind an oversize metal desk, she gave out marriage licenses, copies of birth or death certificates, and handicapped-parking permits. You have to remember that she was an eye-catching woman. Tall and straight-backed, with this hair, this wavy, ember-colored hair. In truth, she was a shy, withholding person, but her appearance made her seem much more confident than she was. I suppose she didn't mind people looking at her, because I think she felt somewhat invisible otherwise.

I thought she was important. Not least of all because she worked for The Government. Schenectady City Hall is a magnificently overdone building, with a full-height portico supported by four columns, marble everywhere, and intricate cornices, a clock tower. Inside, men and women rushed down either side of a splendid double staircase.

How different I must have looked when I walked up to that same desk as a thirty-year-old. Scarf tossed over my shoulder, flushed with anger.

You didn't write me back, I said.

We walked through the cold winter afternoon as I spoke—I don't remember what I said—a torrent of words to cover my real agenda. I wanted her to interrupt me. I wanted her to say, *Juliet, I failed you.* Because then I would have said, *Yes, you did, but all human beings fail one another. Love asks too much, expects too much; failure is written into the blueprint for love, but now that I am a grown woman, I understand that, and from now on, I will only ask you for things you can give.*

I was so eager to say these things. It only would have taken the smallest opening.

But my mother remained silent, hands stuffed into her coat. Our breath rose in columns to the sky. Suddenly she stopped walking. I turned to face her and receive her response. I was excited, smiling. Without even being aware of the suspense, I had waited a very, very long time to hear what she would say. In fact, what she would say in this moment had become the central unknown of my life.

Why are you doing this to me? my mother said. You know that Louise and Gil are my very best friends. And all this was so long ago. We all *loved* you.

She squinted into the winter sun. We were both tall, but she still had an inch on me.

Surely Gil would tell the story very differently, she said. You are a smart girl, Juliet. But you always exaggerate. You don't remember yourself the same way I do.

It was this final statement that sealed my defeat. Before I could stop them, the words had entered me, the anticipatory smile still on my face—the fact that, somehow, I had been complicit. I had seduced Gil. And worst of all, I could not remember doing so. I was nothing more than an amnesiac, an unreliable witness to my own life.

We walked back to City Hall in silence. My mother appeared exhausted, and I wondered if she was sick. I considered putting my arm through hers and helping her up that wide staircase, the one I had danced up and down as a girl, but something in me said, No, if you go any further, Juliet, you only have yourself to blame. You have reached the end of what's possible here.

We didn't see each other again for nearly a decade.

Estranged. A fitting word, and hard to say without a certain gothic inflection. Just as one should never go to bed angry, a woman should never give birth when she's estranged from her mother. Without a mother or a mother proxy nearby, the act of childbirth feels like an anti-climax. The most difficult physical feat, the bringing forth of new life, followed by days of excretions, not least of all tears of joy and sorrow, followed by years of preoccupation, all leading to what—*estrangement?*

I'm not trying to blame Lucinda; I was in trouble with or without her. I never believed that she had forgotten me, all those years of separation. In fact, I was sure that she thought of me often. And yet she could not find her way to me. She wasn't brave enough. From a safe distance, she sent letters, gifts. I didn't exactly rebuff her, but neither was I willing to re-enter a space in which we could not talk about Gil. When I didn't scrutinize the situation, it seemed reasonable—sometimes there was simply no solution to a problem that thorny. I kept waiting for the past to stop mattering. I believed that one day I would wake up and be a new Juliet—a Christ-like person who did not need an apology. I swear to you, if she had shown up at my door, I would have thrown my arms around her and wept.

They say that time is a healer. Well, some wounds fester. In which case, the clock works against you. I had been so desperate in Cambridge after Sybil was born, so alarmed, so *fugitive,* that my eventual recovery only made me angry: *Where had she been?* Did she not at least feel obliged to protect her granddaughter? Well, no. After all, long ago, she had not felt obliged to protect *me*.

After Georgie was born, she sent a little white linen suit, terribly cute and expensive-looking. It made me furious. *White linen?* It betrayed a total misapprehension of my domestic priorities. It was clear that my mother no longer knew who I was. Maybe because I had survived Gil, as well as my parents' divorce, and still did well in school, and wrote poetry, and had friends, and got into college, that I appeared immune to difficulty.

But isn't it the *responsibility* of human beings to be curious about one another? Aren't we required, as humans, to do that work? *Turn around,* I would call to my mother in my dreams. *Turn around, come closer, look at me.* And she *would* come closer, this dream Lucinda, through the dream-rain, the dream-light. I'd sit upright in the middle of the night with satisfaction on my tongue, as if I'd eaten a rose.

All this might explain the shock of receiving her email in Cartagena.

Dear Juliet, it began.

It will be surprising to get this letter out of the blue. I got your email address from your cousin JoAnne and I wanted to be in touch with some news. Gil Ingman has died. He died early in the morning on Tuesday and I thought you would want to know. He got a diagnosis of stomach cancer just after the New Year and died very quickly.

The letter went on to inform me that, as he was dying, Gil had unburdened himself of some secrets. Namely, the fact that he had "interfered" with me when I was little. And not just me, but a niece of Louise's, and another little girl from the neighborhood, whose family Gil had been paying for years to not report him, but eventually they did anyway, and Gil was under criminal investigation when he died. My mother assured me that Louise never knew, and that she was shattered by the news, that she was confined to bed and no longer wanted to live. But it was my mother herself, she was careful to say, who deserved the blame.

I did not listen to you back then. I told myself you were always such a dramatic kid (after all you are named after a Shakespeare character). Now I see that I never even considered believing you because I was a coward and I couldn't face the conflict that would result. I needed them too much.

And then she wrote:

I know it doesn't put a dent in the pain, but I am, I'm sorry.

Forgive me.

It's funny, because even though I'd been hobbled by the experience my whole life, and even though I suspected that it was at the root of my depressions after each child was born, I did—I forgave her. Instantly. I was dying to.

As for him, he was dead. I pitied him.

Dear Lucinda, I wrote.

It's so good to hear from you. Even though it's an email, I can "hear" your voice. I write to you from the deck of our 44-foot sailboat, the Juliet. *Michael, your grandkids, and I are currently anchored in sight of the mind-blowingly beautiful city of Cartagena, Colombia. It is cloudless and a cool 82 degrees . . .*

April 3. Bloody hell. Harry Borawski is here. We are due to set sail <u>tomorrow</u>.

The old guy is turning into quite the pain in the ass.

Calls me like 3 times in a row while I'm working on deck, then finally I answer.

Harry, old man! I say, very friendly.

Then he tells me a hard-to-follow story about how he was delayed in Miami, & somebody tricked him into taking a later plane, then he had to spend two nights in a cheap hotel, the gist being that it took him a long time to get to Cartagena but now he's here.

How's the boat, he crows.

Excellent, I say. I tell him about Arturo fixing the transmission.

Then he says, I was wondering. Would you and your wife need an extra hand aboard?

All sorts of alarm bells go off in my head. Can barely hear myself.

When you sail her back, you'll really need more crew, he says. Beating upwind for days. You can hardly imagine how tiring it is.

That's really nice of you, Harry, I say. But that's a ways away. As per our agreement, I'm not due back to Connecticut 'til <u>August</u>. (I remind him.) I get a whole year. There's places we want to see. Cuba, the DR.

Sure, but you've got to come up through the Bahamas long before August. Have you thought of that? Nobody but idiots are sailing through the Bahamas after July. That's a death wish.

Well, I have until June, then.

That's around the corner, he says.

It's only the beginning of April, Harry.

Most people leave the Caribbean in May, he says.

We can't leave too early either, I say. We'll get back up to the Intracoastal and it'll still be cold.

You're sailing into the wind. That makes the trip longer.

You're boxing me in, Harry.

I'm keeping you safe.

I thought you wanted me to feel the burden of carrying my own life, I say.

That shuts him up.

Let's talk about it over dinner, he says. Have you people checked out the Bazurto? We could meet there later and we can have a beer. You can tell me all about the boat. Dinner's on me.

Here's what I <u>should</u> have said: We are sailing to Jamaica tomorrow & we don't want you around. We don't want to see you & you are creeping me out. Screw off.

Instead, I kick my feet up on the cockpit pedestal.

Sure, I say. I can meet you in the Bazurto. Corner of Fish & Pork there's a bar. OK, Harry?

Great, he says, tentative now that I've made myself available. Righto. See you.

I hang up.

After a couple minutes of staring out at the anchorage, the boats all nosing around in the sunshine, everyone going about their day, I realize I'm angry. People won't leave you alone. There's always somebody trying to take the good things you've worked hard for. You escape one vampire only to jump into the arms of another.

My dad used to call it "the tyranny of the infirm." Those who play sick/weak/incapable, just to rope you into serving them at your own personal expense for <u>years</u> of your <u>life</u>.

Harry Borawski. I should push the old fucker into Cartagena Bay. That would shut him up. And I <u>know</u> he can't swim. He bragged about it. He was like, "Real sailors don't know how to swim, Mike." Implying I'm not a real sailor because I swim for fun, rather than saving it up for drowning. Plus, I hate when people call me Mike.

My dad was right. My dad was always right. Tyrants don't always look like tyrants. Sometimes they look like friendly old guys in baseball caps. Sometimes they look like your mom's friend's new boyfriend who wants to take you on drives in the country in his nice clean car and then sticks his fingers inside you and haunts you for the rest of your goddamned life.

I take out some of my anger by drilling eyebolts into 'Juliet.'

If it's not one thing then it's the other.

When will we be allowed to just <u>live</u>?

W/out being <u>undermined</u>.

My beautiful wife pops her head out of the companion-way.

Everything OK up here?

Her familiar grin makes me feel better.

Yeah, I say. Just doing a little rage drilling.

She laughs & rests her chin on crossed arms.

The galley is totally stocked, she says.

Super, I say.

We can fuel up in an hour. I just called the port captain.

Well done, I say.

I put the bit to my temple like it's a gun. Just to make her smile.

I can't go on, I say. I can't!

Don't do it! she says on cue. Think of the children!

I close the logbook. Fatigue overtakes me. Fatigue, and a grief so concentrated I swim in it. A grief that makes my arms heavy. A grief that makes my back slump. A grief that makes me close my eyes. I want to sleep like the unborn and the dead. I want to sleep so deeply that I see him again. I want to confront him. Who were you? I want to say. Why do you talk to me *now*? I want to shake his inert body.

But what's the use? Our losses will never be done with us. They have endless patience.

I toss the logbook to the back of the closet.

I put my chin on my knees, and for a long time, I just sit there.

I should push the old fucker into Cartagena Bay.

April 4. We sail today. It's early. I just have a couple minutes. But I want to write down a dream I had last night. Dad was in it.

In my dream, Therese & I are at our Aunt Joan's house. We're kids. We're sitting on the floor playing w/ a Lite-Brite. There's a big party in the other room. We can hear the adult talk & laughter. Therese is being very gentle w/ me. Which is unusual because she was v. bossy most of the time. We take turns plugging in the colored bulbs one by one. I'm filled w/ a feeling of gratitude & love for her. It's as if I am remembering in one moment all the times she took care of me in little ways. Reaching cereal boxes on high shelves for me. Jerking me back from intersections. Getting me soup when Mom was laid up in bed after Dad died.

I hear my father's voice from the other room. Not specific words, just the sound of it. In the dream, I know he's going to die. Even though I'm physically a child, I have this adult knowledge.

Emotion closes in on me. Should I tell Therese what I know?

Therese, I whisper. I have to tell you something.

But she says, All finished. Like she didn't hear what I said. Should we turn the lights on, Mikey?

Then she looks over my shoulder.

Who's that? she says.

I turn around.

In the doorway, there is a man. A stranger. He looks like just a normal Ohioan, parted hair, clean slacks, but I know who he is. He and I stare at each other.

My dad's in the other room, I tell the stranger. That way.

The stranger nods, and goes in. The party falls silent.

I wake up.

A pain in my neck wakes me. I have fallen asleep in the closet, my head kinked over on a stack of shoeboxes. Someone has spread a blanket over me. I blink hard and rub my eyes.

Good morning, whispers my mother.

She's sitting across from me. She wears her reading glasses, and the same clothes from yesterday. Sunlight falls across her face in the striped pattern of the closet louvers. Michael's logbook lies shut beside her.

What time is it, Mom? I say, using the word before I'm awake enough to stop it.

It's six, she says. The kids will be up soon.

How long have you been here? I ask.

She shrugs. Long enough.

I smile at her. Well? I say. What do you think?

It doesn't matter what I think, she says.

It does to me.

Well, you have to tell the police where Harry Borawski was. He was in Cartagena, looking for you.

Mom, I say, lowering my chin. But what do you *think* think?

I don't know, she says, taking off her glasses, and rubbing her eyes. He doesn't admit to doing anything. Just a threat.

But the picture?

She looks at me. We hear the tread of a child outside the closet.

He's gone, she says, eyes welling. He should be allowed to keep his secrets.

So, Sybil. How do you think your mommy is feeling these days?

Sad.

Do you worry about her?

All the time.

What does she say when you worry about her?

I don't tell her.

If you could tell her anything, what would you say?

I . . . I wish I could tell her about before. The life before. When we lived together. When we were babies. I would ask her, Do you remember when you were inside my heart and I was your baby *before*?

Oh, you mean other lives? You believe in reincarnation?

Yes. If something bad happens, don't worry, there's always the next life. I'm worried that in the next life I will live near a desert because I don't like sand in my eyes. Do you know how to make a distress call? You don't scream, Help! Help! You have to say, MAYDAY. You have to say it three times. MAYDAY MAYDAY MAYDAY.

Did you ever have to do that, Sybil? Did you ever have to make a distress call?

What?

Did you have to make a distress call when you were at sea on the boat?

No. I was only pretending. But I know the national anthem. Would you like to hear it?

Sure.

Never mind.

Sybil. Would you like to talk about your daddy today?

[. . .]

Do you feel like talking about him, Sybil?

Ugh.

It's your choice. You can talk or not. You choose.

Not.

That's absolutely fine. I have some new smelly mark-ers . . . We could draw, we could—

Can I tell you something?

Of course, Sybil.

He had a bad case of the stripes.

Who did?

My daddy.

VIII

~⫘~

S it, I told him. Rest.

It was our second day of sailing, and he'd been piloting for hours. He was worried about the current sweeping us too far west. He said it was a drain on the autohelm to fight the current, but when he sailed by hand, we went off course. He looked tired. I noticed this. He held himself differently from when we'd set out from Cartagena the day before.

Damned if you do, damned if you don't, he said.

Well, in that case, I said, let me have a turn at the helm.

He sat uneasily. But I didn't mind steering. Without a single landmark toward which to sail, I found that navigation took on a certain poetry. You sailed by faith toward the legend of where you were going. Back in the fall, when I learned to sail, I would nervously check the telltales, the masthead fly, but eventually I found that I was most attuned to wind direction with my eyes shut. That way, I could feel the angle of the wind on my face. Straight ahead, it would blow into both ears. I could hear and feel the wind much better than I could see it. Sometimes the wind gusted briefly from a different direction, and I'd have to wake up and look around, while the patient boat slid around at my nervous over-steering.

On the floor of the cockpit, the children peaceably snapped together Legos. Under way, they behaved like small animals, like ferrets. Fits of screaming energy and hijinks below were followed by indolent cuddling. They had become very close, right under our noses. They had a life within our family life, small in scale.

Sybil asked, Can I steer with Mommy?

Michael gave a wan smile. Ask me again.

Captain, she said, snapping her hand to her brow. Can I assist First Mate?

Of course you can, Peanut, I said, holding out one arm.

Mutineers, Michael muttered.

Standing between me and the wheel, Sybil's head came up to my ribs. She was growing so fast. Her ginger hair thrashed. I covered her hands with my hands. When a gust blew our nose leeward, slowly we turned the wheel together, like stirring a pot, correcting course.

Remember, never reach through the wheel, I said.

I know, she said.

After a moment, Michael picked up Georgie, put him on his lap, and embraced him. Drowsy from the motion, Georgie let himself be manhandled. Michael bent his head and put his cheek on the child's shoulder. I noticed the gesture; it was so vulnerable.

Eventually we came upon a chop. A confusion of waves.

The wheel strained in our hands.

She's really fighting now, I said.

Michael looked up. Good, he said. This is the edge of the current.

Finally, I said.

We had sailing for a day and a half.

Michael rose, taking Georgie by the hand. The four of us stood behind the wheel together.

Look, everybody, he said. Look, Doodle. You can see the actual line where the current ends.

On the other side of the confusion, the sea became smooth, a plane of navy-blue water.

We felt the boat wrench herself free, like a girl from a grip on her arm. She was no longer straining below the waterline, no longer in inner conflict with her own rudder. After that, she seemed to proceed with more dignity. Even though we sailed with the wind coming toward us, we went forward. That was the strange and simple genius of a sailboat, and why sailing hadn't changed in a thousand years—even a modest little sailboat could bend the wind.

Can you feel that? Michael said with a sigh. How much smoother this is?

I nodded.

It should be like this all the way to Kingston, he said.

The boat still had more pitch than I would have liked. And we occasionally got a faceful of seawater. The motion made it tiring to stand, even to sit. Better to just give in, I knew. We'd go to bed early.

I was thinking all this when Michael said, God. I'm feeling a little off.

I didn't even trouble to look at him. Hmn, I said. A little *off*?

Tired, he said. I guess all the excitement has finally worn me out. I think I might go below and take a nap. What do you say, Juliet?

It troubled me. Michael—nap?

It was four in the afternoon.

I looked in on him at five. On his back, legs spread, one arm flung over his eyes, he took up the whole berth. I said to myself, *Well, he hasn't napped in twenty years, so this will be a long one.* People were always commenting on his high energy level. He was so fit, but other than an occasional spasm of jogging, he never worked out, and people wanted to know how he did it. Alison used to say, What's his secret? What is the secret Michael Partlow Diet? OK, I said. You can't tell anybody. *It's eating entire bags of Funyuns in front of the TV.* Alison and I both struggled with our weight. Meaning, we lamented not being skinnier while doing nothing about it. We didn't really care. It was just a sport. We would have felt betrayed if one or the other of us had actually gone through with actual weight loss. Now, in bed, in the dusk, Michael's sleeping body still looked impressive, unstoppable. I closed the door to the aft berth.

I turned around to see both children staring at me openly.

They sensed it too. Daddy's *asleep*?

Let's all go up and watch the sunset, I suggested.

The seas that evening were tranquil, almost indolent. Long, slow swells gave the boat a cradle-like pitch. A blanket of stratus clouds had passed overhead and hung in the east. The sun, red as a poppy, planed down toward the horizon line, casting its fire-light across the sky. At times like that, the sky seemed cracked open, a geode. The children and I watched the show from under a blanket.

There's a rhyme, I told them. Red sky at morning, sailors take warning. Red sky at night, sailors' delight.

I was glad I had remembered that. It was a comfort.

He was still asleep at seven. The seas were calm enough that I'd been able to go below and make sandwiches. The wind was steady from the northeast. The sails were set to the portside quarter, and the boat was sailing herself. The children—maybe they felt that something important was transpiring too—were on their best behavior. No arguing. No loud sounds. Sybil was teaching her brother how to make a peanut butter and jelly sandwich on the saloon table. This would have been hard enough for him at anchor, but while under way he was hopeless. When he smeared some of it into his hair, she chuckled and said, Oh you little sugar bite.

We all were surprised when the aft berth door opened and Michael stood there, hair in disarray, looking miffed.

Juliet, he snapped, you've got to run the engine.

Before I could even respond, he disappeared back inside.

I thought it was anger I felt, but I now know it was adrenaline. I went to the door and was about to throw it open, but I didn't. I did what I should have done earlier. I went above and I started the engine. I did not have to look at the electrical panel: I knew the voltage would be low. The engine charged the house batteries, and everything ran on it. The cabin lights, the VHF, the GPS, the autohelm, the bilge plumps, everything.

We were sailing at a clip. I went back down to the children and watched them finish their sloppy sandwiches, the noise of the engine both deafening and reassuring. By bedtime, the batteries were fully charged. I cut the engine. The children watched me closely.

And Michael was still asleep.

Come now, scoundrels, I said in my best Francis Drake. Let's get ye to bed.

Why is it that the sea opens the mind? The motion of waves puts the sailor in a truth-telling trance. I sat in the cockpit in the bright darkness, wearing a hooded sweatshirt, my PFD, and my tether, and tried to trust the sea.

Michael was sick—this was clear. Likely something he'd eaten in Cartagena. We'd all had bouts, from queasy tummies to food poisoning. He would have to sleep it off. And I would stay above, beneath a sky that seemed unusually black. Unusually infinite.

The wind freshened, scooting low cloud scraps overhead, back toward where we had come. Hearing the luff of the sail, I remembered, as keenly as if I had just heard them, the percussion of moth wings against the screen door of our house on Morry Road in the summer. I remembered the Siamese cat who came to that door so often to look for me. The feel of her tail as she drew it suggestively through my fingers. I remembered a visit to a museum, a display of gemstones, and the actual physical strain of wanting to touch something that I was not allowed to touch, a pull in the chest not unlike that of a sheet tensioned on the winch.

I remembered some ordinary childhood things, and some things no childhood should contain.

Once the images scattered, there was just the sky.

Fatigue came like an undertow. It was getting hard to stay awake.

I wanted a cup of tea, so I went down and turned on the kettle and stood there watching it boil, the flame lighting the cabin sweetly, the pot tilting on the gimbals. But the memories had opened up a yawning loneliness, and I realized I was afraid. I pressed my hands over my mouth, overcome with the urge to cry. After a moment, the urge passed.

I'll wake him up at midnight, I said aloud to myself.

I went above, and again gave my mind over to the sea.

Michael, darling, I whispered. It's your watch.

He was still asleep, in the very same position. As if he had landed there from a great height. I touched his shoulder, then drew my hand away. His skin was burning hot. At my touch, he turned violently to his side, legs drawn up.

Michael, I pled.

I can't, he said.

You can't? But it's your watch. It's midnight.

No, he said, into the pillow. My *bones* hurt.

Have you taken anything? Ibuprofen? Michael?

What?

Have you taken anything for your fever? I asked again.

When he didn't respond, I went to the locker where we kept our medicines. Before we sailed, I had been responsible for stocking the boat with first-aid supplies. It had been therapeutic for me. I got to think of everything that might go wrong, and its solution. Much of the bottles were child doses of things, bubble-gum liquids, Pedialyte. I shook a couple of tablets out of the economy-size Tylenol bottle and went back to Michael.

Here.

He took the pills in his hand, then started to drift off again.

Michael. Wake *up.*

Forcing his eyes open, he looked at me in fury. He threw the pills down his throat, took a sip of water, winced, then let his head drop back to the pillow.

Let. Me. *Sleep.*

Michael, wait. What if I can't stay awake all night?

Set the kitchen timer, he said, his eyes still shut. Look around every twenty minutes.

Can I run the motor all night?

Of course you can, he said, irritably.

I mean, will we have enough fuel? If we had to run it all the way to Jamaica?

He sighed heavily, summoning a martyr's patience.

Probably, he said. But it might not be making us go any faster. You'll have to see.

I'll have to *see*? I asked. How?

I could literally hear his jaw clench.

People get *sick,* Juliet. I'm a *person.*

Of course. I'm not mad at you, Michael. But how sick are you, do you think?

From very far away, as if he were already asleep and speaking to someone in a dream, he said, We'll re-evaluate in the morning.

It was Sybil who woke me up at dawn. She bent down over me, her loose hair making a flower of her upside-down face. Her neat red cheeks, heavy and bed-warm. Her breath smelling of bubble-gum toothpaste.

Behind her, the sky was a faint hyacinth. She smiled down at me with an adoring expression. It was impossible not to see her as an angel.

You did it, Mommy, she said. You sailed all night!

But he was worse.

Sybil and I stood in the doorway of the darkened berth.

I think you should let Daddy sleep, Sybil said. He looks *really* tired.

He was curled in a ball, huddled against the bulkhead in the dim light. I walked over to his inert body.

Michael? I said.

No, he said, clear as day. Not yet. No questions.

You have to talk to me, I said. You have to *advise* me.

I'm freezing, he said, not looking at me.

You've got all the blankets we have on top of you.

I turned to where Sybil hung back in the doorway.

Be a quiet fairy, I said. Go get your blankets and bring them to Daddy.

While she was out of the room, I got three Tylenol from the bottle I'd left on the shelf. I shook him by the shoulder. He whined pitifully, as if he were a little boy.

Take these pills, goddammit, I said. I *order* you.

This got him to open one eye. A wan smile.

You're worse, I said.

My bones are breaking, he said. My eyes have sharp corners.

Talk to me, I said. What should we do?

Heeeere you go, chirped Sybil, returning with her blankets.

Good morning, Bosun, Michael managed.

Morning, Daddy!

But as she put one knee on the berth mattress, not even close to his body, he groaned.

Gently, I said.

She crawled around to my side of the berth and slowly drew her quilt up over her father's shoulders. Somehow the smiling face of Dora the Explorer was more than I could take. I raked my hands through my hair and looked away from them both.

We sat tensely, waiting for more instruction. Michael did not move.

I left the head out for air, Sybil informed me.

Smart thinking, I said.

We watched his form. His large, still body in the dawn light.

Then I went above to run the engine.

He wasn't going to have to tell me twice.

In the morning sun, the children and I ate our Colombian Corn Pops. Taking avid little bites in the fresh breeze. Banana slices. Orderly. The sails tight and clean. Everything as it should be. The children's spoons clinked in the shatterproof bowls.

All right, kids, I said. We are going to experiment.

Hoorah, said Sybil.

Go, bo, said George.

We are going to run the engine in gear, I said. This means the propeller will be pushing us along. Or, as Doodle calls it, the chopper.

'Opper, said George.

Sorry, the *'Opper,* I said. Sybil, darling, will you check the wash? I've put her in gear.

She leaned daintily out of the cockpit.

The 'Opper is working, First Mate Mommy.

Now we shall monitor our speed, crew. See what the 'Opper adds. Sybil, can you read the numbers there? That's the wind speed.

Ten. Now it says Nine. Still nine. Twelve.

Superb. And the boat speed, darling? There.

Five, she said.

Five knots, I said.

Five knots.

Lovely. Splendid. I gave them a shiny smile. Lovely sailing weather, wouldn't you say?

Sybil covered her laughter. You sound like Daddy, Mommy.

George frowned. Dada shleep, he said.

Sybil patted him on the head. Don't you worry. Daddy'll be OK.

Yes, I said, feeling a wave of fatigue. In fact, there's cause for celebration, crew. I tapped the GPS, clamped to the steering pedestal. We are, it looks to *me,* halfway to Jamaica.

Let me see, said Sybil.

We stared at the GPS screen, where the boat appeared as a tiny red arrow, following its linear course.

Oooh we *are.* Good *job,* Mommy.

Thank *you,* Sybil. Thank you for your help. I'm constantly amazed by you. You're such a good sailor. A natural.

She smiled, throwing a triumphal fish eye her brother's way. He gazed back, plump in his safety vest and fat baby legs, swinging his bare feet.

Now, I said, let's turn off the motor and compare.

We watched as the knot meter rose to 5.7. The difference of one knot at best. Only magical intervention would get us to Kingston as fast as I wanted to get there.

I could not speed time.

We'd just have to stay the course. We'd just have to keep sailing.

The fatigue came again, strong as an undertow.

Crew, I said. First Mate needs to lie down.

The children were stretched out on their bellies in Sybil's bunk. Gazing into the DVD player at the Scandinavian princesses to whom they both felt deeply connected, not just because of their pretty singing and their yo-yo eyes, but because the children had watched the movie so many times that they often chanted along with it. *Frozen* had become scriptural. Nothing would tear them away for the next two hours.

I'm going to take a nap, I told them. I'll be right here.

I lay down, right on the settee, flat on my back. I'd be close to the companionway. I could hear, God forbid, any child's attempt to go above. The cabin had so many portlights that either side of the boat had a generous view; the only point I couldn't see was straight ahead. I left the VHF on low. I knew I'd be able to pick the boat's name out of the chatter if I needed to. But the din of businesslike voices made it seem as if the problems of the sea were being taken care of, that there was some superstructure— an oversoul; I fell asleep instantly.

I think I know what I have, Michael said.

He was sitting across from me. At the nav station. Like a ghost captain.

I sat up too fast. Dizziness blinded me. I covered my face with my hands, my heart racing.

I have dengue fever, Michael said.

Wait, wait, I said. Start over.

He sat casually, cross-legged, leaning against the bulwark. He looked familiar and unfamiliar. His hair was dark with sweat. His eyes burned, strangely vacant.

One second, I said. Give me a second. OK?

I went to check on the children. They lay like two hanging

fish, staring into the screen. Hans had just condemned Anna to die from the cold. It would be another half hour before everyone in Arendelle would have their happy ending. Then, sliding past Michael, I went above. The sun was directly overhead. A rim of clouds hung in the west. But the weather was fine. I opened my mouth and let the wind fill it. I washed myself with wind.

I returned below and sat down across from him. OK, I said. Start over.

I have dengue fever, he said.

How do you know?

I remember learning about it in my Wilderness First Responders course. Look. He raised his T-shirt. The raw rash went from hip to opposite shoulder. A trail of livid red wounds, like a column of fire ants.

This is no good, I said.

What do you mean?

We have to get help.

We don't need help, he said.

I need help.

Who's going to help you, Juliet?

What do you mean? People get help. I raised my arms, gesturing at the portlights. Shit happens out here all the time.

Michael gave me a faraway look, tinged with disgust.

The Coast Guard, I said. Don't *look* at me like that.

He sighed heavily and did not respond. Without comment, he lay down on the settee and shut his eyes, as if our brief conversation had spent him, and he was gone again.

I went and got the SAT phone.

I'm going to call the Coast Guard, I announced.

Michael said nothing. Was he daring me?

In a fit of kindness, back when he was his normal self, he had put the number in the phone's emergency contacts. I held the phone to my ear and waited.

Coast Guard, a young man chirped on the other line.

Oh, well, *hello,* I said warmly, unsure of how to proceed. This is the yacht *Juliet.* I was wondering if I could talk to somebody.

What's your situation, *Juliet?*

I've got a sick crewmember. I'm just a little unsure of—of—

What are your coordinates, *Juliet?*

Coordinates, right. I looked around the cabin. I detected a grin on Michael's face, but he lay mutely. As if he were elsewhere.

I'm in Pain City, Juliet.

Do you have GPS? the young man asked.

Yes, I said. I ran up the companionway with the phone.

I gave him the coordinates.

Confirming fourteen degrees, forty-seven point five minutes North and seventy-five degrees, twenty-six point twenty-seven minutes West, he said.

Yes, I said. That's right.

Well, we have a vessel not far from you. About eighty miles southeast of you. Off the coast of Colombia.

You do? I cried. Christ, that's reassuring. That's great.

Is your crewmember in need of immediate evacuation?

No, I am not, Michael pronounced, from his prone position. Everything's fine. The boat is fine. He's just very sick.

Tell them I have dengue fever, Michael said. It's obvious.

He has dengue fever. He thinks.

Would you like to talk to a medic, *Juliet?*

Yes. Yes, I would, thank you.

We've got one aboard the *Magpie.* That's the vessel near you. We'll have to radio him. Hold the line.

Oh, this is all very good news, I said, turning to Michael. They're patching me over to a boat nearby.

This is Private Jones on the Coast Guard cutter *Magpie,* said a new voice. Do I have the yacht *Juliet* on the line?

Hi! I said. Yes, this is the yacht *Juliet.*

We're getting a medic for you, *Juliet.* In the meantime, I'm going to ask you more about your vessel. How many crew do you have aboard, Captain?

Oh, I said, laughing. I'm not the captain.

Are you in command of the vessel *Juliet*?

Yes.

Then I'm going to call you Captain, OK? So everyone's clear.

I opened my mouth. No words came. I was standing in the middle of the cabin, looking up at the perfect square of blue sky framed by the companionway.

Are you there, *Juliet*?

Yes. I'm here. Onboard it's just me, my husband, and our two children.

Are the children in distress?

No. They're just fine. They're watching *Frozen*.

What's your destination?

We were . . . We're headed for Jamaica. My husband's mother is meeting us there.

That's about three more days under sail, the young man noted. It's still two days if you turn around and head back downwind to Colombia. Have you considered a bailout location?

A bailout location?

Michael tugged on my shorts. He raised a finger.

What? I snapped. What is it?

I followed his gaze to the nav station.

Let me check the chart, I said. I don't even really know what's close.

A nautical mile is
A nautical mile is one minute of arc

Providencia is a possibility, said the young man. You could fall off to Providencia. You wouldn't have to fight the wind, but on the other hand, it's not much faster than where you're going. Also, as you said, you have someone waiting for you in Kingston. Hmm . . . The voice relaxed, and I could imagine him twirling a pencil. I closed my eyes and pretended he was right next to me.

What's your name again? I asked him.

Pardon me?

What's your actual name, please?

I'm Private Amani Jones, Captain.

My name's Juliet, I said. Like the boat.

That makes things easy to remember, Jones said. All right. We have Medic Grant Brown on another line. This is Medic Grant Brown from the Coast Guard cutter *Magpie*. Medic Grant Brown, this is the captain of the yacht *Juliet*. I'll stay on the line.

Hello, Captain.

Hi, Doctor.

For your information, Captain, I'm not a doctor, the new voice said. I'm in my final year in epidemiology at West Point. I've been down here a lot. I'm very familiar with dengue. Is that what we are suspecting here? You can speak to a doctor if you prefer. Most folks have a twenty-four-hour doctor on call associated with their traveler's—

I'd like to talk to you, please, I said. Please.

When did your crewmember start being symptomatic?

It's my—my husband started to complain yesterday afternoon.

Have you taken your husband's temperature?

Yes. It's a hundred and three. It was higher before, but it responded to Tylenol. I have to force him to take Tylenol.

Is he conscious?

Yes.

Is he lucid?

I looked at Michael. His hands hovered just over his thighs, séance-style. His lips moved privately.

That's a tough question, I said.

Has he mentioned pain in his eyes?

Yes.

Soreness?

Yes.

Any rash?

Yes. A big rash. Across his chest.

The medic sighed. There isn't any treatment for dengue, he

said. It's likely he'll get worse before he gets better. More delirious. Also, it's very painful. They used to call it breakbone disease. Ask anyone with dengue and they will tell you that it feels like their bones are broken. They all use the same phrase.

I said nothing.

But you should know that dengue is very common, the medic said. A mosquito-borne illness, endemic to the tropics. Only in rare cases is it fatal. Still. Your husband should get medical attention as soon as he gets ashore.

Ashore, I thought. Ashore sounded as magical a place as Arendelle.

Could we please go back a step? I asked. *When* should I worry? I mean, I'm worried already. But when would you *recommend* that I worry?

The real danger with dengue comes after the fever recedes, the medic said. If secondary symptoms present. This could indicate the possibility of hemorrhagic fever. Fairly quickly, the capillaries can fail, filling the lungs with—

Never mind, I said. Let's not talk about that, after all.

But hemorrhagic fever would only be evident once the fever recedes. You should be ashore by then.

I didn't mean to interrupt you, I said. Sorry.

Excuse me?

The music of closing credits strained from the quarter berth.

I've got to put my husband back to bed, I said.

That's a good place for him, the medic said. Try to get him to drink fluids. Treat him just as if he had a really bad flu.

Thank you so much for your help, I said.

No problem. It was Jones again. Don't forget, we're nearby, he said. You can always check in with further questions or updates. You can't see us, but we're here.

See? I said. You're amazing. I'm going to tell my husband. How well spent our tax dollars are. He's always complaining about taxes. When he gets better, he's going to have to admit that I was right.

Yes, ma'am, Captain, said Jones.

And the children charged in.

HOW YOU GO 'ROUND THE BOAT WITHOUT TOUCH-
ING THE FLOOR. Start on settee cushions. March 'round
table. This is easy part. Say to little brother, Keep up! Early
challenge getting into quarter berth. Can possibly ride door
clinging to doorknob. Come on, Doodle! Don't watch, he
can't do it. Thud. Tell him Junior Climbers are allowed to
use the floor at hard parts. Land on own bed. Two, three
steps, launch off bed rail and FLY to Doodle's bed. By the
way, NEVER grab a bungee for support. Two, three steps
across Doodle's bed, then monkey around to clothes closet.
Hands on underwear shelf. Feet on pants shelf. Thud.
Doodle grabbed a bungee. Super Black Diamond Difficult
shimmy around corner to nav station using ONLY wooden
trim as handhold and feet against squeaky wall. Ah, bench.
Rest. Pick Brother off the floor. Rest together. Whisper,
Don't touch ANYTHING on the nav table or Daddy's going
to break your butt. Step CAREFULLY around charts, laptop,
then it's a cinch along starboard settee, arriving at galley.
Don't forget to tell your brother he's doing good. Easy to
walk across countertop but must be done undercover as it
is a CHEEKY and BAD thing to do. Slippery near sink, so
tell Brother to exit course at end of settee and meet you over
at the door to the aft berth. Long handholds over galley
make this stretch of the course a cinch. Brother very excited.
Brother doesn't care that he looks like a jerking germ cell
compared to Sister. Who is very advanced. He thinks only
of the team. Then he does something dumb. Puts hand on
handle to aft berth and starts to open door. NO! you scream.
That's not part of the course, you tell him. That room is off
limits. Daddy's sick in there!
    The brother does not like loud, sudden screaming. He
babbles babystuff. Tears come like he's in big trouble. Must
distract Brother. LOOK! Jump—no, FLY—from galley coun-

tertop to companionway ladder. WOAH. Amazing. Now Brother is on ladder too, preparing for final leg of course through the head. Everything all right down there? asks the helmswoman, peering down. Give her thumbs-up.

Go over plan with Doodle. Loooooong step to shower shelf. Cross shower shelf to sink top. (DON'T pull on showerhead thingy.) Boing down to toilet seat from sink. Jump from there back into saloon.

END OF COURSE.

Hug Brother no matter what. Be kind. Snap off piece of chocolate from Sin Bin. Hand on shoulder. Tell him he won't always be such a spasm. Someday he'll be a sparkle, like his sister.

A nautical mile is
Slice the world in half. Pick up one half.
Divide the circle into 360 degrees
Divide each degree into 60 parts
A nautical mile is one minute of arc on the planet Earth.
I invented that. I also invented
I also invented Cartesian mathematics. The lightbulb.
The transistor radio
But that wasn't enough, no.
You wanted my soul
My submission
Well, I choose death.
America, you are going to have to let me go
Throw my stiffening body overboard.
Let my flesh be useful.
A nautical mile is
I also invented insurance
When London went up like matchsticks in the Great Fire of
What do I think of technological innovation, you ask?
Guess what. Technology doesn't give a fuck what I think
I finally invented the invention that would start

inventing without me
Democracy, damn it
I invented democracy too
I invented all these things
Can't you see I loved you
With everything I did?
I guess
It's time to wind this up
March off the gangplank while the mutineers
Death of the white man
I can't bear to
Honey?
Juliet, honey?
JULIET
Don't you feel that Juliet?
Smart as a whip and you can't feel
the rails in the water?
Juliet
JULIET DAMN IT
EASE THE SHEETS

I should have heard it earlier, the wind rising.

The falsetto in the rigging.

But weather came up so fast out there. Especially at night, when you couldn't see it coming. The clouds would just come marching down the horizon. This great orchestra of rain.

If I hadn't been single-handing the boat *and* putting the children to bed, I would have sensed the changing weather. I didn't even have time for Michael, all afternoon without a second to check and see if he was alive or dead. Until I heard him roaring from the aft berth, while I was tucking in the children:

Juliet damn it, ease the sheets!

Sybil and I exchanged a glance. Then we both felt the roll.

You have to understand how hard it is to move around a boat when it is under way. Even in fair weather, the motion presses the sailor down. Movement is resistance. So when I tried to cross the cabin, the tilted cabin of the yawing boat, I could only move with nightmarish slowness, swimming from handhold to handhold against the downward pressure. I wrenched open the wet locker and grabbed the first rain slicker I touched, kickstanding against the bulwark in order to use my hands to zip it. Holyshitholyshit. I secured my PDF and tether.

Sybil stood braced in the doorframe, the skirt of her nightgown swinging.

For the very first time, she looked scared.

You, I said. You will take care of your brother. You always do.

She nodded imperceptibly.

Can you put up the lee cloth by yourself?

She nodded.

Well, go on then, I said. Stay with him.

When she didn't move, I said, You can do it. You *know* you can.

She disappeared inside.

Once I had my gear on, I threw open the door to our berth. Michael lay pressed against the portside lockers, his head in his hands.

Do I let both sheets go?

God, no, he said, very calmly. Mainsheet.

I left his door to swing open. Knowing it would bang against the frame throughout the storm. Let him get up and at least fix that. Then I struggled up the companionway. I turned forward in the whipping wind.

There is something simply terrifying about the deck of a heeling boat. Michael wanted me to get the boat even so that I could work efficiently on deck, but I wanted to get the boat even in order to avoid the sight of her with her rails in the water, looking about to tip over. I fumbled for the mainsheet and threw it off the winch. A gust blew then, as hard as I'd ever felt on deck. Instinctively I raised both hands against the wind, as if I could block it. The boom swung out hard and the gust beat at the mainsail.

Stay calm, I told the boat. Hold tight.

I could see the storm cloud tumbling toward us, a mass of gray like a mountain of ashes. I clung to the helm with the mainsail muttering its way through the gust. The idea that I would ever go forward, that I would go forward to reef the mainsail, was ridiculous. I felt so outmatched that I barely noticed the boat was no longer at a terrifying heel. She now tilted leeward at a lesser angle.

That's good, I said aloud. That's great!

I waited for my mind to clear. The flywheel spun madly on top of the mast. It occurred to me that I had no idea how to reef a sail.

Christ, I said.

I went below.

Michael shook his head slowly, as if he'd been expecting me.

I don't know what I'm doing, I said.

Jib first, he said. Can't reef unless you furl the jib. It would flog the whole time. Don't let it flog. It will tear.

I crouched down in the narrow space beside his body. Why can't you help me? I begged.

Because I'm dying, he groaned.

Oh, come on, I said. You just *feel* like you are.

He looked at me with confusion. His eyes swam with tears.

Once, in Ashtabula . . . he said.

What?

Asht*abula,* he repeated, as if that word was what I had misunderstood.

I stood, threw open the door, and climbed back up the companionway. I gazed at the depowered mainsail. Couldn't I just leave her that way until the storm passed? But then what? What if there was more weather behind this? As if to answer me, the boom swung hard. I turned the boat into the wind and the boom came center. I started the engine, and we slowly began to motor upwind, toward the sky mountains, which were nearly upon us, as if we were two sides charging toward each other in a war. The jib began to luff nervously.

Be quiet! I told it. Wait your turn.

Two winches on either side of the cockpit. Things I'd only done with Michael. Easy enough with two people, but now what? My hands glowed pale in that strange storm light. I watched them as they looped the furling line around the lazy winch. Blinking hard against the wind, I took a couple wraps of jib sheet off the drum, and then let twenty feet of rope slip through my hands.

No! I cried, as the jib flogged in the wind.

I pulled hard on the furling line. The jib still thrashed over the water, making huge, cannon-like sounds as it flogged that could surely be heard below, that could have been heard for miles if there was a soul to hear it. I pulled madly at the loose line, an incompetent magician. The heat was crushing. My rain slicker trapped my body heat, but I could not stop to take it off, as it was under my life vest. My fear was hot. My fear of the nearness of the storm, my fear of the sea, my fear of the tower of smoke-colored clouds. I wanted to scream, but instead of screaming I grabbed the winch handle from its pocket, fit it down into the drum, and began grinding my sad little heart out.

Imperfectly, in inches, the jib came under control. I began again, easing out the line, carefully this time. In modest increments I eased, answering with the furling line, until the jib was rolled away. Then I sat back, surprised that I had done it. Step one.

The boat plugged along through the whistling wind.

All right, I said, nodding.

And then the rain came.

OK, I'm going to tell you a story. No interruptions. OK? Once there was a little sugar bite. His name was Sol. His mom and dad went to go pick him up at school. But he wasn't at school! He was at the airport. Oh, shoot. They went to the airport. But they first had to stop for an egg pie. Sol didn't know what to do. He got on a plane. Garatulations, said the people. You are heading to Palm Springs! Palm Springs? Sol was worried. But then they served dinner: washed burgers, crepes, and Valentine's Day candy. Then Sol was happy. He woke up in Palm Springs. Garatulations, now you can go on a hot-air balloon! they said. He thought, I can't do it. I miss my mommy and daddy and I don't know what to do. But suddenly, there was his sister. How did YOU get here? Sol asked her. She said, I got here by making the same mistake you did! Sol and his sister COULD do it. They COULD go in the hot-air balloon. TOGETHER. Also Sealie was there! The moral of the story is it's ALWAYS OK to ask for an extra hug.

Are you asleep yet?

It's raining so hard I can't even *breathe,* I told him, panting. I mean, I'm *breathing* rain. There's no *air* in between the rain.

Michael said nothing. He was still curled on his side, facing away. I dented the side of the mattress with my wet weight and my gear.

I'm just going to sit here for a moment, I said. I'm just going to take a little break.

He sighed, but again said not a word.

I'm getting your blankets wet—sorry, I said.

His feet were exposed at the end of the mattress. He looked too long for the bed. How had he ever been comfortable? Slowly, as if pedaling a bike, his feet churned, then rested.

The thing is, I said, it's not even a bad storm. Even *I* can tell that. The only problem is, we're at sea. If I were back at home, I'd just sit it out in the car. Listening to NPR. I wouldn't even really *notice.* I'd wait until it slowed down and just jog to the house . . .

His chest rose and fell. It was too early for more Tylenol.

I'm sorry for what I'm about to do, I said.

I reached down and squeezed his calf.

Ouuuuh, he groaned, animal. Noooooo.

OK, I said. I'm sorry, Michael. Just one thing, OK? Do I secure the boom topping lift first, or—

Yes, he said. The cleat is labeled.

Thank you.

And it's the *red* reefing line first.

Thank you, honey.

The boat pitched forcefully and I grabbed his shelving. I heard something go sliding off the countertop in the galley; I had not secured our dinner plates. I saw Michael's headlamp, which he kept on a shelf by his pillow. I stretched the band over my head and clicked it on. My husband lay inert like a body in a searchlight.

I went above.

The storm had changed, thickened. The sea and sky were battling. An even fight. The sky sent the wind to beat the sea, and the sea fought back, slapping the sky with waves. Neither would relent.

Michael had added eyebolts to the boat's deck in Cartagena— four fittings on either side of the deck, to which he could attach his tether if he needed to go forward in heavy weather, as he had in the storm outside of Narganá. I could attach to the first one without leaving the cockpit. I leaned over the cabin top, clipped in, and stayed there on my belly, hugging the slippery boat in the rain. Summoning courage, I hoisted myself onto my knees. From there I rose to a crouch, one foot braced against the handrail, the other, a winch, waiting for a break in the wind or rain. When none came, I scrambled forward anyway, trying to make a run for the mast, but my foot caught on the jib sheet, sending me tumbling down to the side deck. I cradled my head, preparing for the shock of seawater. But the plunge did not come. I'd been stopped by the stanchion, landing with my legs spread open on either side of the thin metal coil.

I hung there for a moment, speechless, my waterlogged shoes swinging over the sea. I was still holding my breath, as if air were implausible. I felt the presence of the drowned.

Terror energized me. I yanked at the tether, wrenching my body backward, extricating my legs from the stanchion, my sneakers gaining traction on the deck. From there, I could not leap away from the sea fast enough. I unclipped from the eyebolt and clipped to the next one forward, throwing my arms around the gently tilting mast. There I stayed for several long, consoling moments; nothing could have moved me.

I looked out into the storm. My headlamp illuminated the rain. I could see the boat and the slashes of white-lit rain like snow in headlights. But nothing beyond.

Act. Do. Remember. Boom topping lift. Cleat to the mast.

(Right there was his label. From when he was himself.) Still, looking up into the swarm of rain, I was sure it was impossible. All of it. The towering sail went so high up I could barely see the masthead. How would I shorten it? How would I pull it down in this weather? Again, I weighed the option of curling up on the floor of the cockpit and pretending this was not happening. The storm could not go on forever. Michael could not be sick *forever*. We would not drift forever and endlessly across this planet of water. That would not be—

Fair, what a useless word. A concept that is relevant only in the rare moments when there is no greater danger than unfairness.

I eased the halyard off the winch and groped through the reefing lines for the red one. And I pulled.

The sail inched down on the mast track.

I gave out a little more halyard.

I pulled the reefing line. Eased the halyard again.

Wind strafed the boat. The storm did not care about boats. The sail inched down the mast track. The wind beat the sea.

The sea said, DO NOT TOUCH ME.

The sky laughed wind. I'LL DO WHATEVER I WANT TO DO.

The sea said, I DO NOT GIVE YOU PERMISSION TO TOUCH ME.

I realized, in the battle between sea and sky, I would take the sea's side. I knew her anger.

And finally, I howled. At the top of my lungs.

The wind laughed. But the sea and I, we howled.

We're not meant to
We're not meant to own each other
the colonists of Nueva Granada
"Washed their hands" of Spain
It's a shame
Isn't it a shame, Dad
Shame on us

We came here to get away from kings
We're rogues and rebels and survivors and <u>that's</u>
what makes us great.
I'd rather live under robber barons than
I'd rather live under robber barons than Omnipotent
moral busybodies
Where is that man?
The one with the center part?
Do you know the man I'm talking about?
I have never been more interested to meet a person
Fascinating
I once saw him standing in the doorway of a dream
at a family gathering back in Ashtabula.
I was such a whiner as a kid.
Dad, I—
Dad—

I sat on the edge of the settee, head in hands. Half-dead. Spent. Midnight on *Juliet*. I still wore my vest and slicker. I had no strength left to take them off. Rain dripped from the coils of my sodden hair and onto the sole of the boat. A tap-tapping I could hear as the wind withdrew. I reached for the phone and dialed.

Amani? Private Jones? I said into the phone. Is this you?

Yes, Captain! Hello there.

How are you? I asked, cradling my forehead with my hand.

Um. Good. What's your status, *Juliet*?

Well, there was a squall, I said.

I see that. We're getting it here on the *Magpie*.

It's gone already. You'll probably barely feel it on your ship.

Couldn't have felt comfortable, Jones said.

Listen, I don't think I can do this anymore. I just—I need to be done. Can you come and get us, or—can someone come and help me?

OK, Captain. Are you requesting evacuation?

Yes. I don't know.

We can do that, if you feel you can no longer sail your boat.

How would that—how would that happen?

We would come to you. We would launch a dinghy to you. The easiest thing would be for everyone to board our craft.

Everyone? You can't just take Michael?

You—well, it's up to you, Captain. You have options. Option one is, you board our craft together. You and your entire crew. In this option, your vessel will be scuttled.

Scuttled?

Sunk. Deliberately sunk.

Why?

Why what?

Why does the boat have to be *sunk*? Why can't we just leave it?

You can't have a boat that size floating around the Caribbean. It's a danger to other boats.

My God. My *God*. I paced the length of the cabin, then paused. How do you *deliberately sink* a boat?

You would open all the through-hulls—

Me? *I* would sink my own boat?

Normally, folks just open all the through-hulls before disembarking. It doesn't take long for it to go down. Maybe a half an hour. But it gives you time to get off.

Don't you dare, Juliet.

It was Michael, standing unsteadily in the doorway of our berth.

I wheeled on him. *You* be *quiet*.

I turned away. I steadied my voice.

What's my other option? I asked Jones.

Well, we can take your sick passenger aboard our ship. You and your children proceed to Kingston. But the truth is, we'd need you to feel totally confident. That all of you would be safe. If we determined risk, we would not, we would not assume that risk. You don't sound—you sound a little—

I looked at Michael, biting my lip.

What? he said, narrowing his eyes. What are you *plotting*?

Are you there, Captain? said Jones.

How much would that cost? I asked. An evacuation?

Cost? Um. Nothing. We aren't any different from a fire department or police department. Your insurance would cover medical costs, most likely.

Michael staggered forward, holding on to the countertop.

Do. Not. Sink. This boat. I command you. I *order* you.

You can't order me, I said. I'm the captain.

I will never speak to you again in my life, he said.

One less thing to do, I hissed back.

Captain? asked Jones. Is everything all right over there?

I have to go, I told Jones. I have to think. I will call you back with my decision. Thank you so much for talking to me. I will call you back, I promise.

We're right here. Keep us posted.

I put the phone down. Michael and I stood facing each other in the darkness, only the safety lights glowing. He bent down so that he could look into my face.

Get rid of me, he said. I'm a corpse. Throw me overboard. Just don't sink the boat. *Please* don't sink the boat.

Why not? Is it because of money? Your debt to Harry? Your stupid Ponzi scheme?

It has nothing to do with that! he cried. Just don't sink the boat. I couldn't take knowing. Keep it for yourself! I don't care—I'll be dead.

I put my hands to my ears and groaned. I can't believe I'm having this debate with a man who is hallucinating.

I'm not hallucinating!

He's not hallucinating, says the well-dressed man sitting on the settee.

Holy crap, I say. It's *you.*

What did you say?

Nothing.

You're not in your right mind, Michael.

He turned away in frustration. I could see the rash on the back of his neck. When he faced me again, he looked *almost* like himself, the Michael I knew, but his face was swollen and pinched with pain.

You said you would not give up, he said. Do you remember? In the Plaza de Domingo? You said, *I don't want to give up.*

We both stood looking at each other.

On the countertop, the phone rang. Its screen illuminated both of our faces in the dark cabin.

Hello?

Captain? This is Jones on *Magpie.* The crew and I were just talking. There is one more thing, another option. We wanted to share it with you.

Please.

Speaker, whispered Michael, flapping his hands. Speaker.

I'm putting you on speaker, I said.

You could call a private boat in Kingston, Jones explained. A powerboat. You could hire this boat on your own. It would get to you quickly. A powerboat can cover a hundred miles in a fraction of the time a sailboat can. It could travel thirty or forty knots. Instead of your five or six.

Michael looked at me with encouragement, eyebrows raised.

You could even hire a Jamaican doctor to be on the boat, Jones continued. And your mother-in-law could come. *We* can't be responsible for any of those people, but that is not to say you can't do it on your own. You could, in effect, organize your own rescue.

How would I find this charter boat? I asked.

There are dozens of sportfishing outfits in Kingston. Very nice boats. With refrigeration, television. Comfortable. We're getting you some numbers. But you could also have your mother-in-law assist in chartering one, since she's ashore.

Would the powerboat take the children? I asked.

It's up to you. You're looking at better weather to Kingston. You don't have far to go. But you know how it is out here. . . . It's up to you.

I looked at Michael.

All this to save a boat? I asked him.

It's not "a boat," he said.

OK, stop trying to explain what you mean, I said.

We have some phone numbers for you, Jones said.

The night deepened, dark as a well, and time fell into it. I remember only the feeling of sheer, mindless effort, as if the boat were already in shards and the concerns of hunger or sleep were second to survival. I stayed on deck all night—there was no questioning this—but I was not "on watch" in the sense that I was scanning for another vessel. I was on watch for a hint of dawn light, for a basic narrative ending. Bits of sleep and stupor were interrupted every hour or so by the ringing of the SAT phone, as Michael's mother, Beth, updated me on the status of our powerboat rescue. I apologized for keeping her up all night, but she said she couldn't sleep anyway. Around three a.m. she called with the name of the sportfishing company. They would leave at first light. I remember the mechanically calm sound of my voice as I tried to reassure her; I must have sounded insane. But she was the clearheaded one, and she did not want assurance. I was surprised and relieved by this.

The motor droned on through the darkness. At some point I roused myself and unfurled the jib, trying to make up more distance. I went below to check on the children. They were sleeping in the same berth again that night, their bodies softly rocking against each other. I returned to the cockpit. There we were, inching across the ocean. The boat plugging along across calm seas. The sky was swabbed clean. In the storm's aftermath, the heavens sparkled.

I set the kitchen timer, and I nodded off. I slept knowing that rescue was coming. Once or twice, I blearily imagined that I saw the powerboat. But the white deck disintegrated into spindrift.

So when Michael touched me—when he squeezed my arm and drew my wet hair aside—he pulled me from a heavy sleep. I rolled into his arms. For a moment, I thought we were together in bed. Back home. If I opened my eyes, I was certain I would see the top-heavy crab apple out the bedroom window, sunlight streaming through it. For one brief week in May, this otherwise ordinary tree burst into blossom and rained white petals like tickertape.

Juliet.

He shook my arm.

Juli*et*.

I sat up and looked at him. His eyes looked different. Clearer. Clear and sad and returned. He wore a sweater, his hair a messy, grimy tuft. I dropped my face against his chest and smelled him. There. But he gently lifted me off, his face twisted.

Oof, he said.

What is it?

I'm tender there.

I'm so sorry.

It's OK, he said, taking my hand. I feel a little better.

You do?

I felt his forehead, cool and damp as a stone.

That's good, I said. That's *great*. Your fever is receding.

So you can call off the fishing-boat rescue, he said. We're OK now.

I took my hand back and sat up. It was dawn. To port, a pink incandescence. To starboard, the crown of the sun strained at the horizon line, one faint ray of light canting upward through loose clouds.

I'm sorry, I said. I'm not going to do that.

He laughed. Then he saw that I was serious.

We don't need to be rescued, he said, sharply.

Listen, I said, if you're feeling better, please sit here. Just keep watch while I go take a pee without having to worry. I need coffee. I need to brush my teeth. I need to change my shirt.

I moved quietly below in the galley. I lit the stove for coffee and drank a quart of water straight out of the jug. I looked in on the children. Still asleep, legs tangled.

You won't reconsider? Michael said, when I sat across from him with my coffee.

You could have secondary symptoms. That's what the medic said.

I don't want help. I don't want to use taxpayer money to rescue my sick ass. I hate this. I *hate* the sound of my own complaining.

I'm sorry you feel that way, I said.

Calling the Coast Guard was an admission of failure, he said.

Getting sick is not a failure, Michael.

It's a failure of my body, he said.

I stood up and walked to the other side of the cockpit.

A million years ago, it seemed, he had given me a little wooden boat with my name painted on it. He had said, *You don't need to know how to sail. All you need to know is which way to point the boat.* And I said no, no, no. But then I said yes. I had said *yes,* despite infinite misgivings.

I turned and stared at him, furious. What do you think you are, a god? You think you can't *die?*

I'm not scared of dying, Michael said. I'm *going* to die. I'm scared of weakness.

Well then maybe getting dengue fever is just the thing you need, I said, fighting back tears. You need to be taught a lesson. We *need* one another, Michael. It doesn't matter what you believe. We all *need* one another on this earth. Makers and takers, my ass. We are all makers and we are all takers. It's in the *design.*

I threw back the coffee and tried to find **something** to do with my shaking hands. But while I slept, Michael had coiled and tailed all the sheets. *Juliet's* deck was pristine. I rubbed my raw face. It was numb from exposure.

You'd think you would learn from the sea, I said. It's all a collaboration. The sea feeds the corals and the corals feed the fish and the fish eat the stuff that smothers the corals . . .

He stared out into the distance, looking miserable.

We all start out life being helped, I said. We're *fed* and *held.* That's the way we all *survive.* But to you, help is imprisonment. It's just another form of debt. What is this about, anyway, Mommy issues? I tried for a laugh, but it came out rusty. You can't stand feeling smothered. And the government—the government is like a smothering mother—

I *do* believe that, he said.

Ah, hell, I said, plopping down on the hard cockpit bench. You, you, you. What if your liberty comes at a terrible cost to others? People who rely on the help you happen not to want?

He said nothing, only held his tender sides.

What about children? *You* have children. You'd think we could all agree at least about needing to make this world safe enough for kids. Fine, at eighteen you get set loose into the great cockfight of life. But by what logic is it OK to let a *child* in a *rich* country like ours starve, or freeze, or be shot in school? Answer that.

I'm not happy about it, he said, rubbing his bleary eyes. It's just the way it *is*. You can't use the example of nature one way and not another. Nature is cruel. It'll sacrifice a thousand species if that's what it takes to keep life going. We're just a—a torch getting passed through time. Not one of us matters, not you or me or any group of people. You want it to be fair, but when you say that, you sound like Sybil. You're like a dreaming child.

Well, I sure am glad you aren't the pope, I said, laughing bitterly. Or a judge, or a teacher, or a cop, or anyone who actually has to be faced with living, breathing individuals in distress. I'm glad I didn't go to *you* when Gil Ingman stuck his hand down my pants.

He raised his hands and looked away.

Back on the old track, he said.

That's right. That's right. If it happened to me, then I get to fucking *talk* about it.

You talk like I had something to do with it, he said. Because I'm a man. From day one, you put us on separate sides.

We were both quiet then. The daylight was spreading. The morning was a straightforward blue. I put my face in my hands. I felt ancient.

When Michael spoke next, his voice was soft, almost mesmeric.

Here's what I love about the sea, he said. That this is the same sea as it was in the Pleistocene Age. It looked *exactly* the same to early man as it does to you and me right now. Then, thousands of years later, this view was the same view from the deck of a Spanish galleon. And if I could come back to this very spot in a thousand years, it would *still* look the same. There'd probably even be the same sounds, the same splashing against the hull. The same snapping sheets. As long as there's people, *somebody* will cross the ocean. I love that.

I raised my head, my hands full of tears.

Hey, he said. Why are you crying?

I'm so *mad* at you, I wept. Not just now, *all* the time. I don't even know if I love you anymore. But I don't want you to *die*.

Well, I still love you, Michael said simply. I always will. And I don't care if I die. So once again, we disagree.

> February 21. LOG OF YACHT 'JULIET.' Sometimes, on deck at night, I pretend I'm giving a talk about our life at sea— like to the Rotary Club or something, a big crowd of nicely dressed people having lunch. Weird, right? I lean down into the microphone. "Living at sea," I say, "we have learned that chasing down dreams and doing the 'impossible' is actually very possible. It's not just for other people. . . ." Folks in the imaginary audience nod their heads. "We have learned that we could be so much more than we thought."

We sat side by side, holding hands like old people. Waiting.

The afternoon had deepened into evening, a mood stone. I let the children eat dinner straight out of the Sin Bin. Chocolate bars. Ginger biscuits. Humid peppermints.

Mostly, I just feel wrung out, he said. Like I don't care. About any of it.

Please care, I said. We'd be lost without you. I'd be so fucking mad at you if you died.

He smiled. You'd be saved the cost of divorcing me.

I laughed. Who's being dramatic now? You want me to reassure you? OK, I'll reassure you. Despite the fact that you have dengue fever, *despite* the fact that I haven't slept in days, I'm *still* glad we took this journey. I'm glad we bought the boat.

Really? He turned his body toward me, wincing a little. It was the first time I'd seen him smile since he got sick. You mean that?

I do, I said.

He put a hand to his side. That's great, he said.

What's wrong?

Boat to starboard, Captain! cried Sybil, putting down her binoculars.

Unsure of whom she addressed, neither of us responded.

The powerboat approached, glinting white. Spume heaving to either side of the bow. We could see a figure in the bridge. Two figures on deck. Petulantly, Michael tucked his hands under opposite armpits. Sybil took a seat beside him in the cockpit and was nervously petting his arm.

I'm totally better, he said through gritted teeth. This is really unnecessary.

Well, they're here now, I said.

Such a production, he said.

Beth hadn't managed to find a doctor to come aboard. If we had waited for one, we would have lost the advantage of time. This way, they'd be back to shore before dawn. In my hand, the SAT phone rang.

Hello there, Mrs. Partlow! My name is Adolphis Charles and I've come to get your husband.

I see you, I said. I see you, Captain.

My heart clenched. We dropped into the trough of a wave. I covered my mouth with my hand.

Thank you for coming, I managed to say into the phone, my voice breaking.

No trouble at all! the man said, ignoring my tears. I see you got your fenders on. That's very good. We will circle you and come back around starboard side.

I understand.

I want to stay with Mommy, Sybil announced.

What? I asked her, drying my eyes. You do?

Michael shrugged. I agree she should stay, he said. I think we should *all* stay.

No, Daddy, you go to the doctor, Sybil said. I'll stay with Mommy.

One second please, Captain, I said into the phone. Then, to Sybil, You're *sure*?

I'm *sure*.

Captain Charles? I asked. Sorry. Could you please put Mrs. Partlow on the phone? The other Mrs. Partlow?

But of course.

I could hear the wind roar through the phone on the other end.

Hello?

Hello, Beth?

Hello, Juliet, honey. How are you?

Well, I'm doing all right. Better than I expected.

Everybody's so proud of you, Juliet.

They are? Well, it's too early for that. I know Michael will only be happy if I bring this boat to shore in perfect condition. I forced a chuckle. Hey, sorry this is kind of a shitty vacation so far, Beth. You deserve a refund.

Oh, well. Once this is over we can—

Yes—

It'll make a good story, won't it?

Listen, I said. Change of plans. Sybil wants to stay on the boat with me.

Beth didn't say anything at first.

Whatever you think is best, Juliet.

I think you'll have enough to handle with Georgie. He's the only one who distracts me from sailing. You know, you have to watch him like a hawk. Sybil is easy. She's helpful.

I think you know what you're doing at this point, Beth said.

Her confidence touched me. I swallowed the desire for more of it.

That's nice of you to say, Beth.

Beside me, George stared intently at the approaching boat, clutching his stuffed seal.

Oh, don't forget about Sealie, I said. Georgie can't sleep without his seal. The rest is in there, toothbrush, underwear, but I don't care if he doesn't brush his teeth or whatever. Keep him safe and just—just please take care of Michael.

Juliet, do you think it's— Do you think it's bad?

I could see my mother-in-law now, standing on deck, clinging to the wheelhouse, phone pressed to her ear. She wore cheerful white pants and a bright pink T-shirt, which the wind flattened against her chest. Beth, who had already lost so much.

My God, I hope not, I said. We all just have to stay positive, good or bad, stay positive and—

Wait. Juliet? Mr. Charles is saying—

Yes?

Juliet, he needs you to—

I see him, I said. Tell him I'm ready.

It took almost an hour. We had to get the two boats going at exactly the same speed, which was harder than you'd think. Michael sat indifferently in the cockpit, hands over his belly, his duffle bag at his feet.

When it was safe to pass George over, I hugged him with all my might.

See you in a flash, Doodle, I said. Mommy loves you everywhere.

I tilted him into the waiting arms of Adolphis Charles, a large man with a splendid gold tooth. Bravely, George clasped his arms around the man's neck. Once he was down on the deck of the powerboat, he went calmly to his grandmother, who was still clinging to the wheelhouse. The boat was sleek and modern, with a high tuna tower. Georgie looked impressed.

Bye, Doodle! cried Sybil. Hi, Grandma!

Hello, you brave girl! shouted Beth. I'm so proud of you!

Michael hugged Sybil, then stood looking mournfully at the powerboat.

I passed his duffle to Adolphis Charles.

OK, I said.

Michael looked at me for a long moment, the wind strafing his dirty hair and his thin shirt. I remember wishing that he would hurry up and step across. Because it was so hard to keep the boats together. But he smiled at me warmly.

You're turning into a really good sailor, he said.

It made me laugh. That this was his parting comment.

I did not know they were the last words he'd ever say to me.

IX

As soon as I hear the doorbell, I know exactly who it is.
It's like you have telepathy, I tell them. I was going to call
you today.

Sometimes I think I *do* have telepathy. Duran smiles.

Come in, I say.

She enters, followed by Ross, her silent footnote. He merely
nods.

We walk down the hall to the living room. Through the back
windows, the bushes are wet and vivid from a morning rain.
Lilacs glow in the dim afternoon.

Any good news? I inquire.

Duran shakes her ponytail. No good news, but no bad news
either. No Mr. Borawski, but no body either.

Ross pipes up. We like to say no news is no news.

But we now know that Mr. Borawski was in Cartagena, says
Duran.

That's what I was going to tell you, I chirp.

How did you know that?

I read it in my husband's journal.

OK, says Duran. Well, here's how *we* know that.

This is the sort-of-bad news, says Ross. We learned this from
the record of your satellite phone.

I look from face to face. Had I given it to someone, maybe during those first chaotic days in Kingston? I barely remembered.

We traced a couple of unknown numbers of calls received

before your April fourth departure from Cartagena. Several were from a hotel called the Mariposa. We rang them up, and, lo and behold, Harry Borawski stayed there.

Is he still there?

He checked in April third. That's where we lose the thread. He never checked out.

OK, I say.

So. I just want to make sure I have your answer right. You said you never met Mr. Borawski in Cartagena. You never saw him. So it wasn't you who received calls from his hotel, right?

That's right.

And you shared the phone with your husband?

That's right.

So, *he* must have been the one talking to Mr. Borawski?

Yes, he *did* talk to Harry. That's in the journal too. That's the other thing I was going to tell you.

This journal sounds very informative, says Ross.

I don't like his tone. But he's not incorrect, of course.

This is all great news, says Duran. Because that's why we came here.

Suddenly the obvious occurs to me: They are going to take the logbook.

Duran says, So we were getting cold—I mean it's hard to investigate a missing-person case on another continent. And then we were talking to a colleague of ours who sails. He told us that most captains keep a record of everything that happens on a boat. Repairs. Business transactions. Itinerary. Visitors. That kind of record might help us pinpoint exactly where Mr. Borawski *is*.

Because the man's time is running out, says Ross. Statistically.

Do you think you could help us, Mrs. Partlow?

You mean you want Michael's logbook?

Yes! Duran says, clasping her hands, as if I've already agreed.

I look down into my lap. How had I not anticipated this moment? I, whose few talents include the ability to plan for disaster—how? They will read the entries. They will see the drawing of Harry. They will accuse my husband of murder. And why wouldn't they?

I myself wonder. Michael left that gap of darkness. Missing time. Room for doubt. *I should push the old fucker into Cartagena Bay.*

If I had been *smart*—if I were *loyal*—if I were a *good wife*—

Mrs. Partlow?

Just then—it's the oddest thing—I imagine myself flying through the house, fast as a passing shadow, no footsteps, even. Flying upstairs, unseen, into the closet. I am a bird flying through the house.

I look up at Duran.

I've been reading it for the past several weeks, I begin. I can only read a page or two at a time. I read a little, and it's like I can hear his voice in my head. And I have to stop. Because it's *him*. It's very personal. Over the course of our trip, the logbook turned into more of a diary. Michael hardly slept. He didn't need a lot of sleep. He was a little manic. This was really useful for us at sea, because you need to be vigilant all the time, even at anchor, because your anchor can drag, from the current, what have you . . .

Uh-huh, says Duran, looking at me closely.

So Michael was awake a lot. When we lived here, on land, he'd do his work at night. Or build things in the basement. When we lived on the boat, he would tinker with boat things. There was always something to fix. Batteries to clean, electronics to take apart, knots to practice. Or he'd write in his logbook. I'm just trying to explain why there's so much writing in it.

I have the flying sensation again. Just then, in my peripheral vision, I see my mother on the landing at the top of the stairs. She pauses, then moves silently onward, into the bedroom. It takes all my effort not to turn my head.

He filled pages and pages, I continue. I know he didn't mean it this way, but it's like he left me a letter. A very long letter.

What kind of letter, says Duran quietly, as if trying not to wake me.

Ross looks back and forth between us, confused.

That's what I'm trying to decide, I say. Sometimes, I think it's a goodbye letter. Like he knew he wasn't going to make it back. Other times, I think it's a love letter. But not a simple kind of love.

Like I said, it's very personal. Intimate. It would be very, very difficult for me to share it with others.

Yesss, Duran exhales, having found the point of resistance. I can understand how you'd feel that way. It's his last remaining document. The last words he wrote.

Yes, I say.

We don't want to *take* it from you, she says. We only want to borrow it. We will not read it word for word, I promise. We will only examine the entries that pertain to our search. And when we are done, I will *personally* hand-deliver it back to you. We're trying to save a person's life.

My mother's tread is very light for such a sizable woman. She has made it down the stairs without drawing notice. Suddenly, she stands in the threshold of the hallway with her jacket on.

Hello, she says to the officers.

Hello, they say, surprised.

Ross looks suddenly nervous. Too much movement. I stand up.

Are you two going somewhere? he asks.

Juliet, my mother says, I just wanted to know if I should go get Sybil at the bus stop? So you can keep talking a little longer?

I stare at her for the briefest moment. She wants me to understand.

Great, I say. Thank you, Mom.

She turns around. We watch her pass through the hallway. The front door closes softly.

Well, I say. We don't have long before my daughter comes home. So, if you don't mind . . .

They react slowly. They stand. Duran smiles.

But the logbook, she says, very conciliatory.

There's very personal information in there about *me,* I say. About my childhood, and events from my—

We need to leave with the book, ma'am, says Ross. This is a very active phase of our search.

Duran cuts her eyes his way.

OK, I say. OK. I'll go get it.

I'll come with you, Duran exclaims, upbeat.

We walk together. I feel extremely close to her—I mean proximate, not intimate. I feel her moving close behind me on the stairs. At my heels. So close I could catch her with my heel. We get to the top of the landing and turn left down the short hall. We enter the bedroom.

I love the neutral colors, she says. Very Scandinavian.

I open the closet doors and step in.

It's like living in a birch tree, she says.

You have to remember, I say from inside the closet, Michael got sick very suddenly. It was a matter of hours. Hours. He was normal Michael. Then he was dying. He began to hemorrhage on the boat ride back to Kingston. He had severe dengue fever. From a mosquito. He passed away in the hospital. I wasn't there.

I hand her the logbook. She takes it with a sympathetic expression, and pauses a moment with her hand on the cover. I watch closely as she pages through it. She makes a point of turning the pages delicately. I can't imagine what her partner is doing downstairs. I just hope he's not gone to the bus stop. My mother won't be there. Sybil's bus doesn't come for another forty-five minutes. Which way has my mother gone, and can Ross see her? Is he tracking her, right this very moment? Is he following her?

Duran pages on, licking her thumb. I realize I am holding my breath.

She raises her eyebrows and whistles.

Holy smokes, he had a lot to say, your husband did.

Yes. He was a very thoughtful person.

Seems like he wrote even more than he sailed, she says with a chuckle.

I watch her sift through the empty pages at the end of the logbook.

He *does* write about Harry, I say. You'll see. I think it's true that they had—Michael and Harry—a complicated relationship.

Who doesn't, right? Duran shakes her head.

She finds the last entry.

The ink drawing is gone.

The entry about pushing him into the water is gone.

My mother didn't even leave a telltale shred of perforation.

And I smile—I can't help it. Duran does not see.

You know what? I say. Maybe it will be good for me to take a break from reading that. It's difficult to relive.

She looks at me, an inch away. I'm sure it is, she says.

I want to focus on what I still have, I say. I want to try to join the world again.

As I say this, I realize that whether or not I mean it, it's true.

Yesss. You've got your little ones—

Who need me more than ever.

Think of what your husband would want you to do. I doubt he'd want you to sit around missing out on the rest of your life.

I look out the back window. A thin finger of smoke in the woods.

Ah, of course—Michael's fire pit. My mother has gone to the fire pit.

I snap back to attention. I turn to Duran.

What would *Michael* want me to do? I respond. I know exactly what he would want me to do. He would want me to be sailing. He'd want me to take the kids and get back on the boat. He'd say everything else was a waste of time.

I feel safe in her room. I always have. Especially at bedtime, when the room is dark except for the constellation of stars from her nightlight, and her hair is perfumed from the bath. She wants to talk then. She wants to tell me anything so that she doesn't have to go to sleep. I also remember longing for the absconding parent at bedtime. Every night before he left the room, my father used to sing me "You Are My Sunshine" in a warbling, off-key voice. Then there was just the yawning doorway, a rectangular void, rimmed with light.

Sybie, I say, I want to ask you about something I'm puzzling over. It's about the night before we left for our trip. The—our last trip. The crossing to Jamaica. You and Daddy went to the Bazurto to grab some final supplies. And you were supposed to come back with some *arepas* for me and Doodle, but you forgot?

Oh, yes.

Do you remember what you did? You and Daddy? I mean, did you meet anyone there, or did anything weird happen?

Well, Daddy got bit by a sick mosquito.

Yes, I say. I know.

He bought coffee.

Daddy loved his coffee.

Coffee, yuck.

And did you run into anyone there?

I watch her eyes search the past. Her gaze roams across the stars, a scrutinizing expression that reminds me so much of Michael that I physically brace against the grief. I'm consumed with shame. It was her last night out with her father. Let her keep it.

You know what? I say. Never mind. It doesn't matter.

I'm driving again. Driving is getting easier. No ontological crises at the stoplights. You just push the pedal, the car goes. You push the pedal, streets unfurl. The firehouse. The library. Bagels. Flowers. Accountants. The café we used to go to for hot chocolates. Up on the left, the Church Basement School. That wasn't its real name. It had a very cutesy name—appropriate for a nursery, but grating. Every time I see it, I feel lost and perplexed. This is why I've sent George to a different preschool, a brand-new, shiny one unaffiliated with any religious institution.

Today I meet with Dr. Goldman alone. I agreed willingly. In fact, I was glad to have the appointment on the horizon. It wasn't just something to *do*. I wanted to be near her, to sit there on her small chairs in the sunlight and be safe. The realization embarrasses me, but in front of whom?

I fly down the highway, swishing past towering evergreens on either side of the sound barrier. Today is a clear day. The sky blinding and etched with cirrus clouds. Dr. Goldman's office is the farthest I've gone from Milbury since our return. I feel sequestered in Milbury. Mapped. I have Main Street memorized. The firehouse. The library. Bagels . . . The Lollipop School! *That* was its name. Much more cheerful. And it *was,* it was cheerful for a basement. And it wasn't *in* the church. It was in an annex off the back of the church. Turns out, my only reservation about the school was its name. The name seemed to impugn administrative judgment. Lollipops? Who were the lollipops, in that conceit? The children? Ugh. Or were they *fed* lollipops (also not good)? Or had the owners just liked the spirit of the singsongy word? I never understood.

Somehow this question oppresses me now as I walk the flight of stairs to Dr. Goldman's office. I take a seat in her waiting room, and do not even attempt to peruse the magazines.

When Dr. Goldman opens the door to her waiting room, I feel on the verge of tears. I feel *peeled,* exposed. I feel terrified.

How are you doing? she asks me.

It's very—it's been a rough several days, I confess.

Take your time.

We had a—I bark laughter—you won't believe it. It's not funny. I'm not laughing because it's funny. Sorry.

She waits.

We had a visit from the police a couple of days ago. They think maybe my husband did something bad. They think he hurt somebody. Absurd—that's the word I'm looking for.

My God, Dr. Goldman says. How *stress*ful.

But the worst part is when I wonder if they're right. I mean, *could* he have? *Did* he? Michael could be, at times, pitiless. I'm sorry, I say, blotting tears. I can't believe I'm saying this. I did not think things could get worse. You'd think, your husband internally bleeds to death and leaves you to raise two children alone. That's enough, right? Next person!

Dr. Goldman nods. I'm so very sorry, she says.

Thank you.

She scoots the tissue box closer to me, on the arm of my easy chair. She pauses while I swab my face dry.

I'm curious, she says. Was Sybil aware of the visit from the police? Did they come while she was present?

No, I say. Thankfully, she and her brother were both at school. My mother was with me. My mother has been very—the words catch, and I cannot speak. My mother has been very—

Oh, Dr. Goldman says. I'm so sorry, Mrs. Partlow.

I don't know what I'd do without her, I whisper.

I'm sure it must be hard to imagine easier times, she says.

I look up. It's impossible, I say. And please call me Juliet.

She takes a long breath. Well, let's talk about good developments, Juliet. Your thoughtful little girl. Sybil is responding very well to our meetings—

She *loves* coming here, I say.

Dr. Goldman smiles and goes on. Sybil is a thoughtful, creative, good-natured child with a great sense of humor, a survival skill that is not to be underestimated—

She's a clown, I say.

Dr. Goldman sighs and crosses her legs. Research shows that most kids really do bounce back after trauma, she begins. Even after terrible things. Children are resilient. They largely grow back into shape. I feel really good about Sybil. She's strong. And it helps her prognosis that the loss of her father wasn't something she had to witness firsthand. It seems that you and your husband did your best to stay calm during the crises, which is truly commendable.

Again, Dr. Goldman breathes deeply. But research also shows that kids don't heal as well if there are other, secondary losses. Those losses can feel more profound than the first, catalyzing loss. A common example is, one parent dies, and the other one emotionally collapses. And say, as a result, the child has to go live with relatives, or change schools. The trauma doesn't abate in a clear way. The child starts thinking it's all one series of losses. Life, that is.

I nod, suddenly quiet.

That said, even some of *those* kids flourish. Dr. Goldman leans back, meditatively. It can be a kind of secret weapon, early trauma. It can potentially strengthen you. It can teach you—and I don't know your life philosophy, or your religious beliefs, Juliet—

but early loss can also be empowering. To possess the knowledge of the impermanence and uncertainty of life. It's a very radical perspective that most don't reach until old age, if at all.

I've never thought about it that way, I say. As empowering.

It makes sense, doesn't it?

Yes, it does.

A kind of secret weapon. Why had no one suggested this to me before?

It's unfortunate about this new development with the police, Dr. Goldman says, puzzled. You are already under extreme stress. I wouldn't be surprised if your stress level were the same as a soldier in battle. Self-care will be so important in this next phase. Even if it means leaving the kids with your mom or a trusted babysitter for a little. So that you can be present to your kids when you're with them. Have you talked with your therapist about modes of stress reduction?

I don't have a therapist, I say.

She raises her eyebrows.

I've always thought of poetry as my therapy.

She doesn't say anything for a moment.

I would think of this as a five-alarm fire, says Dr. Goldman. Use your poetry. But throw everything else possible at this. Therapy, exercise, prayer, medication. I'll send you home with a couple of names. Therapists I know and like.

Thank you, I say.

She goes to her desk, scratches out a list.

When I look at her again, she has her arms crossed on her desk and is intently looking my way.

From the bottom of my heart, I'm sorry, she says.

Why? I say with a laugh. *You* didn't kill my husband.

She chuckles. I have worn her down.

Sorry, I say. It's a knee-jerk reaction. Sometimes I think I *try* to be hostile. Michael said it himself, in his journal. I'm hard to love.

Well, maybe he was too, Dr. Goldman says. Everyone is hard to love, if you do it for long enough.

I stare back at her.

Sybil loves you, she says. So just let her. Try not to reject it, even when you feel unworthy. There's nothing "to do" but let her love you.

Dear God. I am not a cheeky girl. Cheeky girls get mush at Christmas. But I DO remember the Bazurto. Because I wanted a Happy Girl and Daddy SAID he was going to buy it for me (a Happy Girl is just a Barbie but without the word "Barbie" on it) but we had somewhere to be. Then we saw a man and I knew right away he was Father Time. White hair fat belly. He was sitting at a table and he was crying. Daddy said to me, SYBIL, if you stay right here and don't move a muscle then I will let you stay up as late as you want.

I did EXACTLY what he said. I waited for lots of minutes. A lady gave me watermelon on a stick. I could see Daddy talking to Father Time. Daddy had coffee, but Father Time had glasses of firewater. Crying, crying. Daddy waved and Arturo and another man came over. Everybody shook hands. The men went away with Father Time but Daddy came back to me. I felt bad for the old man. I'd cry too if I was in charge of time.

That night I stayed up 'til 10:75!! Me and Daddy sat on deck and watched the stars and ate dinner donuts and everybody ashore was dancing. Daddy always let me have or do the thing I wasn't supposed to have or do.

But I don't cheat, and I don't tattle.

Dear God, what I really don't understand is how old are you when you start to like coffee? And when it rains, do ALL dogs get wet? Let me know. Love, Sybil.

Everywhere I look in this house, things are filled with Michael. Objects are waiting to be animated by his touch. I really can't reason my way into knowing he's gone. *Denial* isn't the right word. I might use the word *refusal*. I *know* he's gone, I just refuse to cooperate with that fact. His tools *refuse* to belong to anyone else.

His suit *refuses* to forget his shape. I *refuse* to use the past tense. Once, in those first days home, deep in the closet, I stuffed the woolen sleeve of his favorite suit into my mouth, just to mute the awful song of grief.

Just take baby steps, my mother tells me. Tiny steps. Why not clear out his closet first?

The closet? I think. The closet is the *last* place I will clear out. In fact, I may never touch it.

He kept some interesting crap in there. In the back of the closet, in shoeboxes I'm compelled to explore since I no longer have the journal to read, I discover many things. A baby's tiny white sheath, which must have been his baptismal gown. Items of his father's: a report card from the 1960s, an ancient baseball, Reagan memorabilia. The pennant from Kenyon that had hung on the wall in Michael's senior dorm room. He also kept the play-bill from the night we met—an awful production of *Equus,* after which he somehow swindled me out of my phone number. Soon after, we went to bed together. For a week, we stayed in bed like we were chained to it. We skipped all our classes. We joked that we were going to graduate *summa cum loudly.*

After graduation, Michael was supposed to head back to Pittsburgh for the summer, but he moved in with me instead, in a corner room in the Morgan Apartments, with a perfect view of the striped slate roof of the Church of the Holy Spirit. I was a summer intern for the *Kenyon Review.* (He also kept a copy of the *Kenyon Review,* my name in tiny font way below the masthead.) All day long I read unsolicited poems about longing and rain. Meanwhile Michael was having an econ major's equivalent of Rumspringa—sleeping in, splashing around in the Kokosing, writing me dirty notes that he tucked in my clogs.

We always planned that it would end. In the fall, he'd move to Pittsbugh, where his mom and his sister Therese still lived, a couple streets away from each other, and he'd save up money for grad school. I was on to England—Stratford-on-Avon. I'd been hired to take care of a young couple's nine-year-old kid. I would live in their basement and become a brilliant poet due to my proximity to Shakespeare's birthplace.

As planned, in September, we said goodbye, standing in the Cleveland airport. We kept it light. We joked around. We said, Let's not hug goodbye, let's not make this harder. So instead we gave each other a shove.

Fuck you, I said.

Get out of my sight, he said. Buzz off.

I was smiling violently so that I wouldn't cry.

I watched his backpack until I couldn't tell him apart from the crowd.

But in England, after I realized what I had done, I felt the loss of him like a death. I wondered how I was going to stand the feelings, how I was going to survive them. Because only then did I realize how badly I had wanted love. I had wanted love, and for such a short time, I'd had it. I had fallen in love, and then I had done absolutely nothing to secure it. I did not think I could keep it, because I did not think I deserved it in the first place. Inside me was still a little kid in a car, her own wishes irrelevant, a hostage to fortune.

I tried to do right by the poor, somewhat friendless boy I babysat in Stratford. But I cried so much in his presence that after a while, he didn't even flinch when I would blubber into a Kleenex on the bus. He'd sit there while we rode clear across Warwickshire until I could pull myself together. Then we'd calmly disembark, the wallflower and his demented American companion. I cried in the library, in the grocer, watching him coast back and forth on the sidewalk in front of his house on his scooter. I cried when anyone was rude to me, and even more so when they were kind.

In my room, I wrote murderously bad poetry and chugged from bottles of warm white wine and was occasionally very concerned about my mental health. I got Sundays off, but Sundays were the worst.

There was this Sunday in Stratford, overlooking the River Avon, my raincoat flapping in the cold rain, when I felt my aloneness so keenly that I realized that I had no chance against it. All I could do was give in.

But what would giving in look like? I could tip right over into the river, falling asleep in the current. That seemed to be the most straightforward approach to resolving the paradoxes of the heart.

And just then, as if it were a real person, I felt my massive loneliness beside me, and I greeted it—my lifelong twin—and made friends with it, and for however long I stood there next to it on the bridge, I understood what love was.

Juliet?

My mother is knocking rapidly on the closet door.

I push open the doors. She stands there looking surprised. I haven't hung out in the closet for a couple of days. Maybe she thought I'd quit.

Do you have an appointment? I joke.

But my mother doesn't laugh. She looks pale.

She's back, my mother says. The policewoman.

She is? Did she—

I have no idea, my mother says. She wants to see you.

We walk down the hall in silence. At the landing, I see that Duran is already standing at the back windows of the living room, looking outside. We descend the stairs. She turns and smiles prettily. This can't be the expression of a person about to come and deliver terrible news.

Birds, she says. There are so many *birds* in your backyard. That's the difference between a place like this and the city. And there's so many different *kinds*. It's like a national park back there.

They—they like the brook, I say. The water attracts them.

Beautiful, she says. She looks back outside. A world of birds, she says.

I step closer to her. That purple bush, I say, pointing, the rhododendron. It always blossoms this week. I can set my watch by it. Just for a couple of days. Then all the blossoms fall off in an hour.

Poetry, Duran says, lost in thought.

My mother clears her throat. I look at her. Her eyes are wide, urgent.

Where's your partner? I ask Duran.

Who knows, she says. Somewhere sucking on a lemon.

Then she laughs robustly.

I'm not sure if it's wise for me to laugh along.

Hey, she says, businesslike. I have something for you.

She takes Michael's logbook out from under her arm and hands it to me.

We found Harry Borawski, she says.

Alive? my mother says. Then, to soften it, Thank God.

Yeah, Duran says with a chuckle. We got a call from a partner on the police force that an old crazy gringo was found wandering the streets of Mompox. That's a little tourist town not far from Cartagena. You can only get there by boat. He got there somehow, stayed on for a while, then became disoriented, didn't know how to get back. When they found him, he didn't know where he was, didn't know where his belongings were. But he seemed happy. You know, I've always thought that senility would be a relief. If you don't know what you're doing, you don't worry about the consequences. You just hop on the damned boat. Better that than a tiny room in assisted living.

Duran pauses. My mother and I stand side by side, gaping.

I know—it's a surprise, right? she asks.

Yes, I say.

I didn't imagine such a happy ending for the man myself, she says.

Yes, I say. I didn't know *what* to think.

I want to thank you for sharing your husband's book, Mrs. Partlow. I can't imagine how hard it was to part with. And I'm sorry. It's just my job. Anyway, it's back with you now. And I hope you get to do what you said. To thrive. To live your life. Despite this loss.

Thank you, I say.

Take solace in your kids, she says. Take solace in your birds.

I'll try, I say.

You are a beautiful family in these photographs, she says.

She gives me a wink. The wink startles me. For a cop in a backwater city like ours, this woman is much more than she seems.

Her wink says, *Don't feel bad about thinking he did it. Any one of us is capable.*

Her wink says, *But for next time, destroying evidence is a federal crime.*

She walks to the door and turns around one last time.

I smile back at her.

What does this one look like, this smile?

Because it feels genuine.

He did *what?* the boy said.

He'd take me for long drives. I don't know—fondle me? What should I call it?

Abuse! He abused you.

It's crazy—the guy still comes to our house for Christmas. I avoid him.

The boy and I were walking through another winter night. Did we ever sleep? The lamps made soft circles in the snow all around campus. Our footfalls loud and creaky. *Why,* after years of never telling a soul about Gil, did the vault doors swing open, the information instantly declassified, for this boy alone, this small-town Ohio boy, a boy who couldn't even pronounce "Albert Camus" right? I looked at him quickly, my heart pounding.

But can you believe I never tried to get help? I said, anticipating his objections. I should have told someone. I *could* have told. We stopped at a million different tourist traps, all staffed with kindly countryfolk. I could have told any one of them! I could have screamed.

He stopped in his tracks.

How can you *say* that? he asked. You didn't tell anyone because that might have been *dangerous.*

I looked at him warily.

But to be so *obedient,* I said. Not to run or to scream. God. I hate that little fucking Girl Scout.

Spacious darkness. I tried not to search his face for that imagined look of disgust. In that high Ohio cold, the snap of a snow-burdened branch in the woods sounded near.

Well, scream now, then, he said. Scream, if you want. I don't mind.

Michael, I said, laughing. That's ridiculous.

Why? He shrugged.

The cold air carried the sound cleanly outward like a call to prayer. I screamed until I was dizzy. I sat, spent. Right there on the snow. The silence of the night sky afterward sounded shocked.

He did not tell me to get up. Neither did he leave my side.

I don't even think he had a coat on.

As with all college boys, he never got cold.

Bus stop. Children emerge, mid-story, and scatter, alone or paired with a parent. I wave to the others and lead Sybil up the street toward our house.

When we step inside the doorway, I kneel down and wrap her up in my arms. It's one of those full-body hugs. I'm on my knees, my cheek to her chest. Indifferent, vaguely bored, she drapes her arms over my shoulders and lets her backpack fall to the floor.

I love you, Sybil, I say.

I love you too, Mommy, she says. Can I have a snack?

I laugh into her shirt. Yes, I say.

Can I have two snacks?

Yes, I say.

Can I eat them in my room?

Sure.

Can I eat them in my room while playing with my Barbies?

I carry up the basket of clean laundry. She carries a bowl of grapes and a bowl of salty corn puffs. I begin to fold the laundry, as she thoughtfully arranges her Barbies in a circle. A panopticon of Barbies. You're home! they cry. But of *course,* she says, straightening them when they fall over. The gathering perfected, Sybil lies down on her belly and eats the puffs loudly, one by one, getting crumbs everywhere.

Dr. Goldman thinks you're the cat's meow, I say. She really enjoys talking with you.

Uh-huh, Sybil says.

Do you like talking with *her*? Does it feel good to do it?

Uh-huh.

OK, good. I'll tell her we'll keep coming for a while.

OK, Mommy. Do you want to play Barbies?

I think about the dinner to make. The laundry to fold. I hear my mother's car pull up, Georgie on board.

I sit on the floor, heavy-bodied.

Yes, I say.

Which Barbie do you want to be?

She holds up a brown one and a white one, both naked. I reach for the brown one. She shoves the white one in my lap.

You be her, she tells me.

Her brown Barbie jumps along the mattress on her stiff legs. Hello!

Hello, I say. I am wondering if you have seen my clothes.

Your clothes are all dirty, sorry.

Then I will clean them.

There is no soap, sorry.

Whatever will I wear to the ball?

Sybil's Barbie sighs. You can't *go* to the ball, she says. You have a wicked stepmother. Sorry.

Wow, I say. Barbie life is hard.

It's not me making it up, Sybil says. It's for true. Well—she tilts her head and rolls her eyes skyward. It's not *true* true. My bones are making it up.

She chuckles. Then she stands and takes down Rainbow's terrarium. She lifts the hermit crab out by its painted shell and sets it on the carpet.

Oh, no! There's a monster! An ancient vegetarian monster! RUN!

The Barbies scream and hop across the carpet on their stiff leg-objects.

Rainbow was a gift from Sybil's school. All the families in her first grade class pitched in to get a terrarium as a sympathy present. The kids helped to fill it with sand and pebbles and of course Rainbow. Every once in a while, one of these classmates comes over and they and Sybil paint the shell a new color. Now, the crab taps its way delicately across the wooly terrain, moving at a steady pace. It appears to be giving chase. My Barbie trips and falls.

Go on without me! my Barbie screams.

No WAY! screams her friend, who hops back to her fallen sister. What hurts?

My arm is broken and both legs and my ears are broken! And my appendix.

Here's a Band-Aid. Get up! The monster is COMING!

What's going on in here? my mother asks from the doorway. She's holding Georgie, who has most of the fingers of one hand in his mouth.

Barbies, I say. It's not for the faint of heart.

I play, says Georgie.

Hi, Doodle, I say, opening my arms.

He gets down and runs into them, looking jealously at the Barbie party.

I play Barbie too, he suggests.

Sybil, can Georgie play?

She sighs heavily and blows out through her cheeks. A gesture I recognize as mine.

He can *watch,* she concedes.

He sits on the rug with us, cross-legged and attentive.

Thinking better of it, Sybil gives George a Barbie. George's Barbie is the broken one, with no hands and chopped-off hair. He looks at it.

You get what you get and you don't get upset, she tells him.

My mother and I exchange a grin.

Rainbow moves anciently across the carpet.

I want to go back home. I want to go back to the boat.

You do? Do you ever tell your mommy that, Sybil?

I tell God.

You talk to God? Is God a good listener?

Yes. There used to be other gods, you know.

Oh. Like Roman and Greek gods?

Yes. Do you know what happened to the other gods?

What happened to the other gods?

Jesus killed them. *That's* the mystery of Easter.

I love hearing your ideas about things, Sybil. You are *so* creative. What a wonderful thing, it will keep your life interesting.

Thanks.

[. . .]

So, Sybil. When you think of your daddy these days, what do you think about?

Oh, lots of things.

Like what?

Plonking and hammering. And jokes. If you pulled his finger, his tongue came out.

Where do you think he is now? Do you wonder about that? Some kids do, when they lose a daddy or mommy.

Well . . . nobody really knows for sure.

True. But what about you? What's your guess?

Well, his *body* is in the dirt. His *name* is on a stone. But the rest of him . . .

The rest of him is where?

[. . .]

I think he is waiting until I am old enough to have a baby. Why?

Because then *he* will be that baby.

[. . .]

Where is your daddy waiting? Where's he waiting until he can come back and be your baby?

He's walking in a field. A field with grass. He's in a field where good things are true.

[. . .]

What would you say to your daddy, if you could say anything to him right now, and he could hear you?

I miss you, Captain. I loveded you. I wish I could have known you when you were a baby. That's all.

X

〜⚜〜

Tears or sweat—so many stories end in salt water. I had thought my grief would be unique, keeping me apart from others. But in some ways, I have only become more typical.

when I was a child things being hurt made me sorry
for them but it seemed the way men and women did

Some days are hard. Today, the light feels tentative. It retreats behind the houses in the late morning. It's September again. The trees are still lush. The only sign of autumn is the cooling sunlight, which retains no warmth. I decide to dry the bed sheets outside while I still can. I hang them over the rail of the deck. Then I sit on the back steps and try to stand it, the impossible length of the day. A wind rises. I can hear it blow through the woods behind the house.

Other days have been OK, almost pleasant. Those days, I've listened to music, smoked a stale cigarette or two through the attic skylights. Those days, I have reached out, and lo and behold, a friend arrived, a good friend like Alison, holding an uncut pineapple or box wine. Those days, I have gotten a handle on something new. How to use a drill. How to redeem gas points. How to behave in a socially acceptable way at the bus stop. How to pad a résumé. I know, small victories. But these are what make those days good days.

But today is agony. It inches along.

I wonder, Is the slowness due to grief, or waiting? I am waiting for news.

I clean the fingerprints off the storm door. I empty the deck planters into the compost pile. When despair looms, I transcribe another poem. It doesn't matter which poem. Any poem will do. I take out a fresh sheet of paper. I flatten the book against the kitchen table. The scratching of the pencil calms me. The way the sharp tip of the pencil rounds down until it disappears. I copy all the lines in my own hand.

> *when I was a child things being hurt made me sorry*
> *for them but it seemed the way men and women did*
> *and we had not made the world*

> *coming into it crying*
> *(I wanted so not to hurt you)*
> *and going out of it like a sudden pouring of salt*

My phone rings. It's the marina.

She's at the bridge, they tell me.

Already? I laugh. She's early.

Well, you know how it goes.

It doesn't matter—I've been ready for hours.

I grab our things and run out to the car, calling the school on the way.

Maybe I was wrong—maybe today is a good day masquerading as a bad day.

Today, I feel alive.

When I arrive, Sybil is already waiting in the front office. She's in Mrs. Peretti's second grade class this year. Mrs. Peretti's a lucky draw. Kind, big-chested—a hugger. Still, Sybil finds it hard to sit through class. Reports from even the lenient Mrs. Peretti are so-so to poor. She has "difficulty focusing." There is "room for progress in relating to others." Even though the year just started, Sybil keeps asking how many days are left.

Now, she sits on the edge of a chair, staring straight ahead. Her backpack takes up the whole depth of the chair, so that she's leaning forward on the toe box of her sneakers. She's taken out her braids again; her hair is loose and crimped.

Hello, Mrs. Partlow, the secretary says, beaming. Sybil tells me there's something *special* planned—

But Sybil has already run past me, toward the front doors.

Sorry, I say, cringing. Sorry. Nice to see you!

We dive into the waiting car. Buckle our belts.

We should have left earlier, she says. Now we might not see them come in.

It's all right, I say. It doesn't matter.

It matters to me, she says.

It matters to me too, but I can't say so. If it had been up to me, I would have kept her home all day. But I can't keep her home just to keep me company. Just to wait together.

They must have made unexpected progress yesterday, I say.

We drive in a complex silence. For a little girl, she has a great deal of gravitas. Her stubbornness has mellowed into a kind of burgeoning authority. When she was little, she used to say, *Me do it! Me do it!* waving a tube of toothpaste over the prone brush, a long slug of toothpaste swinging from the nozzle. OK, OK, yes, *you* can do it, I'd say. Let's not squeeze the tube so hard. Just a tiny smidge. Yes, you can hold the brush. OK, let's hold it together. Open up. OK, wider. Good job. Now *spit*.

and it doesn't matter, it doesn't mean what we think it does
for we two will never lie there
we shall not be there when death reaches out his sparkling hands

Michael, I remember how you told me, one night in Salar, *I've lived my whole life with a land mind. Thinking land thoughts. But I want to think sea thoughts. I want to have a sea mind.*

I understand you now.

If we had lived with sea minds, maybe we could have had a sea marriage. And we could have loved each other differently. That is, beyond deserving.

> We are 102 nautical miles ENE of Panama City, catching prevailing winds into the sovereign territory of San Blas. The shape of the coast is still visible behind us, but ahead is just water. Nothing but water. That's when I realize there's only one ocean. One big mother ocean. Yes, there are bays & seas & straits. But those are just words. Artificial divisions. Once you're out here, you see there's just one unbroken country of water.
>
> You would never feel this way on land.
>
> (Not in our country.)
>
> What a feeling. Generations of sailors have failed to describe it, so what are <u>my</u> chances? Me, Michael Partlow. Michael Partlow, who can't tell you the title of a single poem. Just ask my wife, her head is full of them.

A stroke of good luck: There's a problem at the bridge, and all boats have been held up. I pull in to the marina parking lot just as the captain, Merle, texts me an ETA of twenty minutes. Sybil shoots out of the car before I can pass on the information. She's already down the footpath and onto the main dock, her feet thundering over the boards. It's useless to call her back.

The dockmaster, Olin, comes out of his office, shirt sleeves rolled up, squinting uphill as I pull on my sweater. There's another, younger man with him. They walk toward me.

Good afternoon, Olin calls. It's the big day.

I laugh. Can you tell we're excited?

Olin offers his substantial hand my way. He's a good-looking older man. *Older?* He's probably not much older than I am. I like him.

This is Miles, he says, gesturing at his companion. He's my dockhand. My unofficial photographer. And my nephew.

I shake Miles's hand. The kid blushes. He's got a camera around his neck.

Miles wanted to meet you, Olin says. He's read about you. We all followed your story closely. I hope you don't mind me saying so.

No, I say. I don't.

I look out to the open water. With a glance, I know she's not out there. Only a powerboat, two unfamiliar yachts, and the crisscrossing sails of some student keelboats. It's funny how every boat has its own gait. I could tell hers in an instant.

We're thrilled to have *Juliet* here, Olin says. She's a special boat to us.

Thank you, I say.

You should know that any of us would be happy to help you crew, he says. If you want to sail her around the Sound. Anytime. When you're ready.

The sailing community is a tight one. It's partly pride—sailors are a clan of the sea, invisible to land dwellers. But their bond is also practical. For such brave souls, they have to spend a great deal of time clinging to their VHF radios, to get the news only other sailors know. Some of them dutifully keep the emergency channel open at all times. A steady stream of nautical gossip comes through in this manner. As soon as they're at port, they hop on one of the online cruising forums and word spreads. I guess that's how everyone knew about *Juliet* before I even brought her in to Kingston. I can almost hear Michael chuckling. *Nosey know-it-alls. Can't wait to tell you what you did wrong.*

We walk to the end of the main dock, where Sybil already waits, hair blown back. Overhead, the September sky is cobalt. Clouds cross at a clip. Flags on the bridge snap in the wind.

We're just going to tie *Juliet* up on the face dock for now, Olin tells me. We'll fuel her up for you, unload the crew. You'll have her all to yourself in no time. The captain will most likely give you a list of stuff to fix. Anything that broke on the sail up from

Kingston. My advice? Read it later. Olin smiles handsomely. I know of what I speak, he says.

Uh, Mrs. Partlow? stammers Miles. I'd like to get a picture of you with your boat. If it's OK. I don't want to—

I look at the kid. He's got clean, kinky hair, an air of newness. I smile. It's OK, really.

Mommy! Sybil cries.

She points. It's *Juliet. Juliet* is coming.

She slides out from under the drawbridge. Bowsprit first, with her trademark carvings, her jib unfurled to show the brick-red trim on the luff, the red of her hull glimpsed just above the waterline, her mainsail at a comfortable trim. Behind her skips *Oily Residue.*

I hear Miles snap away.

Beautiful, says Olin.

They left the sails up for us, I say.

Merle does a great job, he says.

I look down at my daughter, who clutches my arm.

Sybil? I say, but she is transfixed.

In the near distance, we see the jib being furled. But the mainsail stays up. She turns patiently to shore.

My gosh, I marvel. They're going to bring her in under sail.

I kneel down beside Sybil and say, Now, if it were me, I'd just motor in. But your daddy would approve **of them** sailing her to the dock. He'd be impressed.

We can see two figures now, two crew members. One is dropping the fenders. Another is at the helm. Sybil waves. The figure on deck waves back enthusiastically. It's a young man with floppy hair in a red sweatshirt. He looks like a college student working for pot money. He shouts to someone below.

When the captain comes above, into the bright sun, I'm caught off guard. She's got coppery hair in a buoyant mass of ringlets, and a large, brilliant smile. In jeans and a white polo, she's leggy like a volleyball player, or some recent Olympic qualifier. She takes off her reflective sunglasses and waves them.

That's *Merle*? I say.

Olin chuckles. Not what you expected?

I look down at Sybil. Her mouth has fallen open. She stares at the woman like she's just seen God. A face of ecstatic recognition.

I want to *talk* to her, she declares.

Oh, Lord, I think. Here we go.

Dear Friend,

Time has passed, but I'm still thinking. Do you ever think in fragments that belong to the same whole, and while you can grasp each fragment, never the totality? You live your days, you try to get a better angle on the whole, but it never quite shows itself. Then one day, you realize that the act of trying to get a better angle on the whole *is* life; it is your perpetual motive, and you'd be lost if you succeeded?

Love,
Juliet

P.S. If not, you can ignore the following with a clean conscience.

Notes Toward a Whole

in other words, some things I cannot forget

by Juliet Partlow

FROM "MAN AND WIFE" (1963)
by Anne Sexton

that pair who came to the suburbs
by mistake,
forsaking Boston where they bumped
their small heads against a blind wall,
having worn out the fruit stalls in the North End,
the amethyst windows of Louisburg Square,
the seats on the Common
And the traffic that kept stamping
and stamping.

Now there is green rain for everyone
as common as eyewash.
Now they are together
like strangers in a two-seater outhouse,
eating and squatting together.
They have teeth and knees
but they do not speak.
A soldier is forced to stay with a soldier
because they share the same dirt
and the same blows.

Church Basement School Day #14

Stay-at-home mom. That's a good word for it. It's like a command: Stay at home, Mom!

Good thing we're not called *left*-at-home moms.

I'd be happy to be left at home. I'm a leave-me-the-hell-alone-at-home mom.

They should redo the movie *Home Alone*. But instead of forgetting the kid, they should forget the mom.

Yeah! That's a great idea. The dad and the kids arrive in Paris, and they're like, "Why don't we have any clothes or maps or books or plans or reservations or food or anything? Wait. Did we forget *Mom*?"

Hilarious!

What does any of it matter? The planet is dying. We are literally drowning in melted ice caps.

Are you serious? Is she serious?

That's Juliet. She just moved here from Boston.

Oh.

We can see the influence of the Narcissus myth upon Freud; in *On Metapsychology*, Freud names a "primary and normal narcissism" that is an early and necessary stage of the ego, one that must be completed in order to later be transcended. In other words, self-love is the basis for the love of the "other" that must necessarily replace it when the subject takes his or her proper place in relation to parents, children, or the wider world.

But what of the people who remain narcissistically focused well into adulthood? And should we count among them every confessional poet? (Every poet?) The "others" in Sexton's life were in agreement about her self-absorption. Arguably, there is no more selfish act than the withdrawal of one's presence from the world. Her suicide in 1974 left two young children motherless.

But what of the love between narcissist-poet and her audience? Does the presence of the implied reader of the confessional poem ameliorate the intensity of the poem's focus on the self? Asked another way: Why did so many readers love Sexton's work so deeply if she was "merely" a narcissist?

Perhaps the reader is drawn to the narcissistic text because she *herself* has struggled with her narcissism in the journey toward loving an other. Sometimes she wants to leave her narcissism behind, sometimes she wants to embrace it and leave loving behind. This would suggest a social value of narcissists among us; their service is to celebrate the mirror stage to which we all secretly long to return, but which we have renounced in the exchange for human society, and thereby survival.

Partlow, Juliet. *Same Dirt, Confession and Narcissism in Suburbia: The Poetics of Anne Sexton.* Fairleigh Dickinson University Press (forthcoming), p. 24.

Church Basement School Day #23

Six months. Six months, that's it. I throw out all my spices after six months.

Jesus, not me. Maybe after six *years*. But I'm a fascist with the tea drawer. At one point, I had it perfectly organized. All the boxes fit together. Like a jigsaw.

I don't know. I'm no longer romantic. I don't feel romantic feelings.

Me neither. Love, ick. Like, no thank you.

But I *want* to feel them. Don't you?

Sure. I don't know. Yes. But we had our time, you know?

It's hard to get all the boxes to fit in one drawer.
I use a shelf. Use a shelf.

> I still believe in soul mates, though. But my definition
> has changed. There *is* someone who is meant for you. But
> you know who this person is? It's the person who loads the
> dishwasher in the same way you would.
> Oh my God, that's *awful*!
> Isn't it?
> What do you think, Juliet?
> Yeah. Why so quiet, Juliet?

"Julie" from Connecticut:
I really love my new Brookstone Nap throw blanket in Stone. At first, I wasn't sure I liked the pattern. It's kind of a cross between pebbles and the skin of cartoon dinosaurs. My Nap has an almost pelt-like appearance. Like somebody killed an acrylic cheetah. Sometimes when it's draped over a chair back and I'm walking by, I unconsciously "pet" my Nap. I can't be the only person who does this. I agree with others that the Nap is "softer than soft" and "huggable," but these descriptors don't really do justice to its nearly liquid quality. I feel like I could *pour* my Nap. In terms of texture, it's genre-defying. As for Carmen, who writes of her Nap, "I have never been so disappointed in my entire life!" I'd like to know what her secret is. Would that my roster of disappointments even registered a blanket. She speaks of some kind of fusion that took place when drying her Nap in a dryer. Well, I would never put my Nap in a dryer. Not only because it runs contra to the clearly stated cleaning instructions, but also because my Nap feels a little bit *alive*. Would I put a living thing in the dryer? No. How much do I love my Nap? To the depth and breadth and height my soul can reach. THANK YOU FOR MAKING MY LIFE BETTER, BROOKSTONE!
YES, I would recommend this product to a friend.

Church Basement School Day # 55

I don't know. It's like I go to the grocery store on a loop. All this getting and consuming. It's eternal. Why eat it, if you're only going to crap it out a couple of hours later? It's cruel. It's unending. You know what I mean?

Yeah, sure. I guess so.

I mean, we spend so much time shoving things in our mouths, forgetting that all we're doing is giving our colons something to excrete. Why do we *enjoy* ourselves so much when we eat—why all the smelling and exclaiming, the ordering, the *paying*—why all the pleasure, when eating is something we *have* to do? Do we forget that we are about to do precisely the same thing in about three hours? It's like we've never tasted food before. I just don't understand why we aren't more embarrassed. I literally walk around *embarrassed* to be human.

That's so bleak, Juliet. Maybe you're overthinking it?

Rain? Were they predicting rain?

It's really coming down.

Someone share with Juliet. She's got the baby.

I don't think she notices.

You want my umbrella, Juliet? Juliet?

And *loy*alty. We are so sure that we mean what we say. But we can't make promises. The person who makes a promise in one moment vanishes in the next. Because of course selfhood is constantly shifting. No one can keep a promise because no one can remain the same *person* for long enough. To keep a promise would require a psychotically consistent self. Which is impossible.

Juliet. Are you OK?

What do you mean?

Is everything OK with you and Michael? Are you . . . are you trying to tell me something?

I'm not *trying* to tell you something, Alison. I *am* telling you something. I'm telling you why I'm embarrassed to be human.

OK, OK. I'm sorry.

> Why don't they ever open these doors early? I mean, it's *pouring* out here.

> Let us in early, people!

> This is a *church*! Have mercy!

> Yeah, people. Make an exception. Let us stand in the freaking *vestibule*.

No. *I'm* sorry, Alison. It must be terrible. To have to listen to me when I'm—when I'm—I've been a little depressed. I think I—

Oh, Juliet. Oh, poor Juliet. Please don't cry.

FROM "THE DOUBLE IMAGE" (1960)
by Anne Sexton

I.

I am thirty this November.
You are still small, in your fourth year.
We stand watching the yellow leaves go queer,
flapping in the winter rain,
falling flat and washed. And I remember
mostly the three autumns you did not live here.
They said I'd never get you back again.
I tell you what you'll never really know:
all the medical hypothesis
that explained my brain will never be as true as these
struck leaves letting go.

Harry Borawski December 10, 8:12 p.m.

Michael,

Hola from the Connecticut River Valley. How is she sailin'?

> Harry

"Man marks the earth with ruin—his control stops with the shore." —Byron

Harry Borawski December 23, 9:33 p.m.

Michael.

Harry again. How is the boat? I am itching to know. Didn't you leave from Bocas last month? I'm an old man—it could be I've lost count of the days. We are having a cold winter here. These big ice floes come downriver with birds standing on them.

Merry Christmas.

Harry

"Man marks the earth with ruin—his control stops with the shore." —Byron

Harry Borawski January 3, 10:39 p.m.

Michael.

I'm worried now. But I have checked the nets and so far no reports of a yacht sunk in the gulf of San Blas with all hands lost. Write back—it will just take a minute.

Harry

"Man marks the earth with ruin—his control stops with the shore." —Byron

Harry Borawski January 4, 12:27 a.m.

Did I ever tell you my dad was in the army? For three years when I was a kid I lived in a tiny seaside town in the Philippines called Olongapo where my dad was stationed. My dad, my mom, and my three sisters, and I lived in family housing about fifty paces from the sea. I haven't thought about it in years. They were great times, with hordes of us kids running around the city and the seaside, nobody giving a crap. White kids and Filipino kids. Nobody cared. By the time I was ten I could speak Tagalog but as you might imagine, there wasn't much Tagalog spoken in Bridgeport Connecticut in the '60s. So it all faded. I grew up and I wasn't good at any sport and I didn't really fit in and wasn't strong academically so I was perfect for Vietnam. I signed right up. For a millisecond, even my dad was proud of me.

What I didn't realize until I got back from 'Nam was that I didn't sign up out of patriotism or even loyalty to my dad, I just wanted to get back to Olongapo. Dumb shit! But there it was, right there across the South China Sea. And if you shut your eyes you could smell it. The grasses made the same sound in the wind. Too bad I was busy crawling through tunnels and shitting in bushes. I might have even enjoyed myself. That's how poor white kids traveled back then. It was our version of study abroad. I've always thought maybe I'd go retire down there. I've heard of vets doing it. It's like they were born and died in 'Nam and they're just ghosts anywhere else. The Filipino kids used to make me eat peppers so that I would turn red. Get the little round-eye to turn red. I didn't know that ten years later I'd be shooting people who looked just like them in the face.

Every winter I still can't believe I'm still here dealing with rock salt and bronchitis and liberal fascism but I never leave. Glad you'll be back before too long. I miss having you around. I'd like to tell you stories I've never told anyone.

Harry

"Man marks the earth with ruin—his control stops with the shore."—Byron

Harry Borawski March 7, 2:05 a.m.

There's real urgency now because I can't stay here anymore. Yesterday I saw a boat coming up the mouth of the river and guess what. It was called the *Tagalog.* And then, some things I ordered online arrived and by the time I got home the package was gone. I tracked the package and it said it had arrived. I called FedEx and I said it wasn't there and they said yes, it was. It was scanned and delivered. Well. I couldn't sleep that night. I would really appreciate if you wouldn't tell anybody what happened next. The package showed up. It had been opened and re-taped poorly. Well I think you and I both know what's going on. Anybody who has an opinion that doesn't fit the Statist agenda is being surveilled. I am one of many. You and I saw this coming. I might not write for a while. I think it's much safer to speak face-to-face. As they say, it always gets deeper before it gets shallower.

Harry

"Man marks the earth with ruin—his control stops with the shore." —Byron

The "confessional school" of poetry was first
delineated by M. L. Rosenthal in his 1959 review
of Robert Lowell's *Life Studies*. According to
Rosenthal, the author's "private humiliations,
sufferings, and psychological problems" are
central to the confessional poem. The label
"confessional" stuck, but in retrospect it seems
to have emphasized the wrong thing, treating the
poems as rising from shame, not self-knowledge.

For Sexton, the poem was a wholly appropriate
vehicle for exploring the ways in which, as Diane
Middlebrook writes, "family life gave permanent,
empowering, and also deforming structure to
individual experience." The confessional poet did not
restrict this tension to her own experience. Sexton
took on the subject of motherhood and daughterhood
with equal ardency. The poem "The Double Image" asks
the reader to consider the wages of intimacy upon the
child herself: "I needed you. I didn't want a boy/only
a girl. A small milky mouse/of a girl, already loved,
already loud in the house/of herself. We named you
Joy."

Why does the speaker want a girl? At the conclusion
of the poem, she admits to her "worst guilt."

I, who was never quite sure
about being a girl, needed another
life, another image to remind me.
And this was my worst guilt, you could not cure
nor soothe it. I made you to find me.

As the child empowers and deforms her mother, the
mother empowers and deforms her child. She names
her Joy, but immediately finds the name circumspect,
not only because this name is selected by a woman
suffering from severe depression, but also because
the very naming of a child is the first distortion,

avoided only if the child were to voluntarily name herself. After all, the child cannot be given a name for her adult self, who cannot yet be intuited, but rather she is named for the "small milky mouse" as which she first appears. Yes, Sexton is "ashamed," but largely as an object lesson for any parent. The speaker of "The Double Image" owns an uncomfortable reality few parents would care to admit—that we "make" our children to find ourselves, or at least, to find the children we wish we'd been; or, failing that, to invoke the myth of childhood itself.

Partlow, Juliet. *Same Dirt, Confession and Narcissism in Suburbia: The Poetics of Anne Sexton.* Fairleigh Dickinson University Press (forthcoming), pp. 88-89.

Harry Borawski February 19, 5:19 p.m.

Dear Michael,

I know I haven't written in a long time. Almost a year? No hard feelings or anything. I have a nice room down here in Mompox now and more importantly I have a lady friend. Today she took me all the way to Cartagena just so I could find some public internet so I could write you an email. I have been very lost. I keep seeing people who are dead that appear Lazarus-style. They sometimes take the shape of a little kid on the street. Once I saw my father as an old lady on the chicken bus.

I'm living like a beggar but I don't regret my losses. Best decision ever to come down here. I guess decision is a strong word. You literally sent me down the river to this remote place non compos trying to banish me. But the truth is you saved my life. I'd even packed the pills I was going to take. Seppuku in a suitcase. You couldn't have known. But thank you anyway.

In my mind's eye I see you and your nice family sailing your boat around the Sound. Say hello to America. Say hello to George Washington. Write when you have a second.

Harry

"Man marks the earth with ruin—his control stops with the shore." —Byron

UNPUBLISHED INTERVIEW WITH THE PARTLOWS
FOR KENYON COLLEGE ALUMNI BULLETIN

KCAB caught up with the Partlow family this April in Cartagena, Colombia. Michael Partlow '00 and Juliet Partlow '00 have two children, Sybil and George. They have been sailing on their 44-foot sailboat, the Juliet, *since September of last year.*

KENYON COLLEGE ALUMNI BULLETIN: So. Sybil. First of all, how old are you?

SYBIL PARTLOW: I'm seven.

KCAB: And how old is your brother?

SP: Almost three. But he can hardly talk.

JULIET PARTLOW: Sybil . . .

KCAB: What do you like best about living on a boat?

SP: Flying. I fly from the mast.

JP: We got the idea from another sailing family. What you do is, you attach this long extra line to the masthead. She swings on it like Tarzan. It's amazing.

KCAB: Fun! And what do you miss about living on land, Sybil? Anything?

SP: Bathtubs.

[*Laughter.*]

KCAB: What do *you* miss, Mom?

JP: Storage space. Kids want to keep everything. You know how kids are. Conch shells, sea stars, old bottles, anything. All the cool stuff we find ashore. But at some point, there's nowhere left. Under your pillow?

MICHAEL PARTLOW: Currently Sybil is collecting crabs' eyes.

SP: They look like marbles. Want to see?

JP: I also miss our house, of course. The luxury of separate places. So that two kids can be doing two separate activities at the same time. We do try to give Sybil some schoolwork, to keep her at grade level. But then Georgie wants to . . .

SP: Copy me.

[*Laughter.*]

KCAB: What about you, Michael? What are some of the challenges for you?

MP: I learned how to sail on a lake. There are no coral heads in a lake. When I sailed as a kid, I didn't care what happened to the boat, per se.

JP: You cared what happened . . .

MP: Yeah, of course, I *cared.* I just didn't care like this. Now, this boat I'm sailing is my *home.* With my family in it! I had to learn how to sail my home, if you will.

KCAB: You became more cautious?

MP: Yeah. I'm more likely to be like, to Juliet, Should we put in a reef?

KCAB: So he consults you.

JP: Well. I'm more like the wall he bounces things off of.

MP: You're not my *wall.* [*Laughter.*] We've had a couple of blowouts. That's really hard. Over time, I think we've learned to communicate better. We do OK. Given the stressors.

JP: We do. It's interesting how we really rely on each other at sea. I was a total novice. You have to understand. I had *no* sailing experience. I'm a poet. Can you think of anything more useless at sea than a poet?

KCAB: A poet! That's great. Are you published?

JP: Actually, I didn't mean to call myself that. Could you not print that?

KCAB: But a lot of sailors *do* write about the sea.

JP: I'm neither a poet nor a sailor. Really.

MP: Juliet was getting her Ph.D. in American literature. She was writing a brilliant dissertation. And then things changed, you know. Kids came along . . .

JP: As I like to say, I got the Ph. but not the D.

[*Laughter.*]

KCAB: Well, it's never too late.

JP: Sometimes it is. Sometimes it really is too late.

KCAB: Never say never.

JP: I'm going to say it—never.

MP: So, do you want to see the boat? Want to look around?

JP: Want to see the head?

SP: Want to see my crabs' eyes?

[*Child crying.*]

MP: What's wrong, Doodle?

KCAB: Is he OK?

JP: He's OK. He's got a little rash. Nothing alarming. We sort of . . . we've gotten all sorts of tropical rashes and stuff. Par for the course.

KCAB: OK. You sure? Well, I wanted to ask more about the joys and sorrows. Sorrows seem to be . . . not enough space. No baths. You said you argue sometimes. What do you argue about?

MP/JP: Politics.

[*Laughter.*]

KCAB: Out here in the middle of *paradise*?

JP: You asked!

MP: And we also argue about whether or not to use the GPS.

JP: He's a purist. He thinks it's cheating.

MP: Oh, here's another challenge. Getting diarrhea in foreign ports.

KCAB: Yeah! I bet you have some pretty visceral stories . . .

MP: Worry. You worry. Anchors dragging.

SP: Bad weather.

KCAB: How do you get through bad weather, Sybil?

SP: I tell stories. To my brother. Belowdecks.

KCAB: That's cool. You make up stories to stop worrying about the weather?

SP: And sometimes Mommy gives me peppermints from the Sin Bin.

[*Laughter.*]

KCAB: So some of these adversities . . . these inconveniences . . . make you closer?

MP: Yeah.

JP: Yeah. Yeah, they do.

[*Silence.*]

MP: Though I think we could skip feeling closer to the head. [*Laughter.*] Man, sometimes you just want a hot shower! A bathroom all your own. With one of those huge showerheads that like *dump water* down on you. That dump *gallons* of water on you.

JP: Ahh, yes! Like the hotel we just stayed at here in Cartagena. And I wouldn't mind eating on a delicate piece of china.

KCAB: So if it weren't for the lack of conveniences—bathtubs and big showerheads, and storage—would you want to stay aboard forever?

JP: Oh, that's a no-brainer for Michael.

MP: I—I like to think so. But. I'm just a human being. Maybe I'd just get restless and want to change things up again. Maybe, despite having everything, I would just want more.

JP: Wow.

MP: What? Was that silly?

JP: No. I love you. I love that you just said that. You still surprise me, Michael Partlow. Uh, please don't print that either.

[*Laughter.*]

GEORGE PARTLOW: Doodle say!

MP: What is it, Doodle?

JP: I think he wants to say something. Doodle, do you want to say something?

KCAB: Talk into the phone, George.

GP: See 'nake up!

[*Laughter.*]

SP: He saw a snake. That's what he wants to tell you.

KCAB: Ah, you can understand your brother.

MP: She's the only one who can!

GP: 'Nake fall da boat. 'Nake fall DOWN.

SP: The snake fell off a branch and almost into our dinghy.

KCAB: Wow. Were you scared?

SP: No.

GP: My!

JP: No, no, George, don't touch that phone. It's not ours.

MP: Sorry!

JP: George, give the phone to Mommy.

GP: My! My!

[*Crying.*]

MP: He's just in a mood. We'd better . . .

KCAB: Yeah. Absolutely. I have plenty of useful stuff. Thank you so much for talking to me. I think folks will be interested to hear what you're doing.

MP: Thank you for being interested.

JP: Yes, thank you, really.

KCAB: A lot of people *talk* about doing stuff like this . . . I myself have planned to hike the Appalachian Trail for years.

MP: You *should*.

KCAB: But I never take the plunge.

JP: Never say never!

[*Laughter.*]

MP: No, I'm serious. You should. You kind of *have* to.

GP: My! I hold!

MP: Stop it, George. That's not yours.

JP: Sorry about Doodle. He's probably just . . .

MP: He's just tired.

KCAB: Absolutely. Let me just turn off this

Acknowledgments

I would like to thank Jordan Pavlin for her unwavering support and her masterly editorial judgment. Thanks to Sonny Mehta, Nicholas Thomson, Maria Massey, Paul Bogaards, Nicholas Latimer, Emily Murphy, Ann Kingman, and Abby Endler at Knopf. Thanks to Kim Witherspoon for her advice and advocacy, as well as Lyndsey Blessing and Maria Whelan at Inkwell. I honor the memory of Wendy Weil and my father, Frederick Gaige. Their love and support lasts undimmed all these years, such was the original quantity.

Many people in the boating community have offered their wisdom, whether in person or via their blogs. Thanks to Behan and Jamie of *Totem,* and Behan's indispensable book *Voyaging with Kids.* I'm indebted to the work of Nancy Schwalbe Zydler and Tom Zydler, who charted the islands of Guna Yala in *The Panama Guide.* I thank the estate of Anne Sexton, and the estate of Kenneth Patchen.

Friends, this is a song for you, especially the mothers and mother-artists—Susie Pourfar, Youna Kwak, with special gratitude to Sarah Moore for sending me the article that sparked this book. I thank my community here in Connecticut: Kelly Proulx, Paul Wutinski, Artie Hill, Darrell Hill, Catherine Blinder, Michael Robinson, Michelle Troy, Rand Cooper, Molly Cooper, Kristina Newman-Scott, Ethan Rutherford, Amy Bloom, Stephanie Weiner, Mark Weiner, Andy Curran, and Jen Curran. Thanks to J. M. Holmes, Cary Goldstein, and my colleagues and students at Yale and at Amherst College.

This book could not have been written without the support of the John Simon Guggenheim Memorial Foundation. I have also been the beneficiary of life-changing support from the MacDowell Colony.

ACKNOWLEDGMENTS

I am grateful to my sister, Karina Gaige, lifelong friend, and our incredible mother, Austra Gaige, as well as to Norman Cohen, Sarma Ozols, Ted Watt, Bob Groff, Linda Frankenthaler, David Groff, Lisa Groff, Kerry Halloran, Laura Watt, Clark Thompson, and adopted family Keith Flaherty and Mira Kautzky.

Thank you to my writing brother, Adam Haslett.

To my children—Atis and Freya. Atis, we witnessed Guna Yala together, and I will never forget. Thank you, Freya, for the fabulous stories. I'm sorry to steal them, they were too good. Thank you both for allowing me to roam, and for being curious about my travels when I returned. As you grow, I will try and do the same for you.

Most deeply, thank you, Tim, shipmate.

Lastly, I must thank Ben Zartman and his family—wife Danielle and children Antigone, Emily, and Damaris. Your strength, good nature, and unconventionality are the gold standard neither I nor the Partlows ever quite attain, but I knew it was possible when you took me out on the *Ganymede*. Ben, you were my co-creator on this story, helping me to plot where my own knowledge and imagination failed. Thank you, thank you.

A NOTE ABOUT THE AUTHOR

Amity Gaige is the author of three novels, *O My Darling, The Folded World,* and *Schroder,* which was short-listed for the Folio Prize in 2014. To date, *Schroder* has been published in eighteen countries. It was named one of the Best Books of 2013 by *The New York Times Book Review, The Huffington Post, The Washington Post, The Wall Street Journal, Kirkus Reviews, Cosmopolitan,* and *Publishers Weekly,* among others. Gaige is the winner of a Fulbright Fellowship, fellowships at the MacDowell and Yaddo colonies, and a 2016 Guggenheim Fellowship. She lives in Connecticut with her family and teaches at Yale. Find her at amitygaige.com.

A NOTE ON THE TYPE

This book was set in Monotype Dante, a typeface designed by Giovanni Mardersteig (1892–1977). Conceived as a private type for the Officina Bodoni in Verona, Italy, Dante was originally cut for hand composition by Charles Malin, the famous Parisian punch cutter, between 1946 and 1952. Its first use was in an edition of Boccaccio's *Trattatello in laude di Dante* that appeared in 1954. The Monotype Corporation's version of Dante followed in 1957. Although modeled on the Aldine type used for Pietro Cardinal Bembo's treatise *De Aetna* in 1495, Dante is a thoroughly modern interpretation of the venerable face.

Composed by Digital Composition,
Berryville, Virginia

Printed and bound by Berryville Graphics,
Berryville, Virginia

Designed by Cassandra J. Pappas

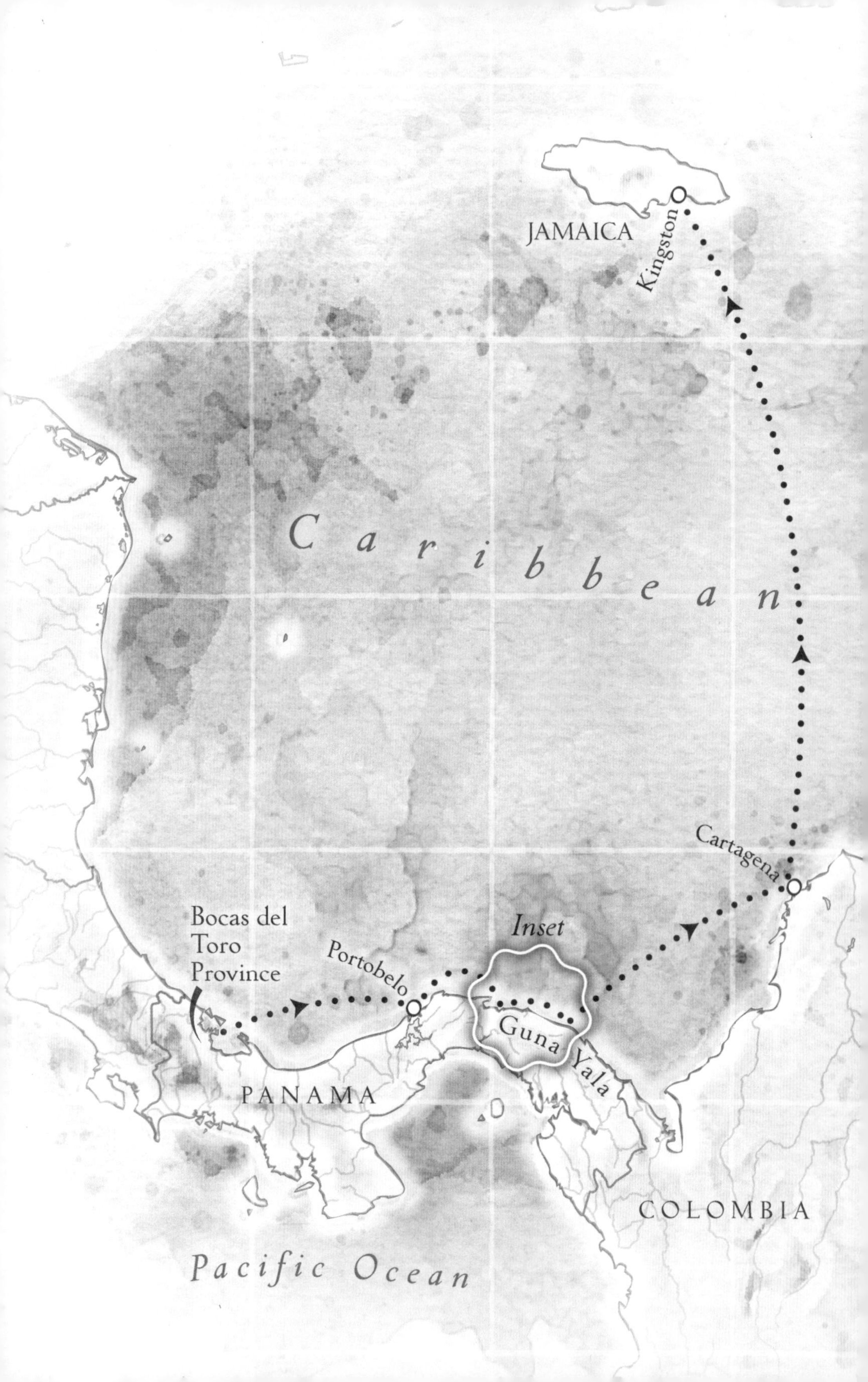
JAMAICA
Kingston
Caribbean
Cartagena
Bocas del Toro Province
Portobelo
Inset
Guna Yala
PANAMA
COLOMBIA
Pacific Ocean